THE
WHITE DESERT

COURTNEY RYLEY COOPER

1ˢᵗ WORLD
LIBRARY
Literary Society

The White Desert

Courtney Ryley Cooper

© 1st World Library, 2008
PO Box 2211
Fairfield, IA 52556
www.1stworldlibrary.com
First Edition

LCCN: 2007935371

Softcover ISBN: 978-1-4218-9322-8
Hardcover ISBN: 978-1-4218-9422-5
eBook ISBN: 978-1-4218-9222-1

Purchase *"The White Desert"*
as a traditional bound book at:
www.1stWorldLibrary.com/purchase.asp?ISBN=978-1-4218-9322-8

1st World Library is a literary, educational organization
dedicated to:

- Creating a free internet library of downloadable ebooks

- Hosting writing competitions and offering book publishing
  scholarships.

Interested in more 1st World Library books? contact:
literacy@1stworldlibrary.com
Check us out at: www.1stworldlibrary.com

1ˢᵗ World Library Literary Society

Giving Back to the World

"If you want to work on the core problem, it's early school literacy."

- James Barksdale, former CEO of Netscape

"No skill is more crucial to the future of a child, or to a democratic and prosperous society, than literacy."

- Los Angeles Times

"Literacy... means far more than learning how to read and write... The aim is to transmit... knowledge and promote social participation."

- UNESCO

"Literacy is not a luxury, it is a right and a responsibility. If our world is to meet the challenges of the twenty-first century we must harness the energy and creativity of all our citizens."

- President Bill Clinton

"Parents should be encouraged to read to their children, and teachers should be equipped with all available techniques for teaching literacy, so the varying needs and capacities of individual kids can be taken into account."

- Hugh Mackay

To a Certain Little Gray Lady
who seems to like everything
I write, the main reason being
the fact that she is

MY MOTHER

CHAPTER I

It was early afternoon. Near by, the smaller hills shimmered in the radiant warmth of late spring, the brownness of their foliage and boulders merging gradually upward to the green of the spruces and pines of the higher mountains, which in turn gave way before the somber blacks and whites of the main range, where yet the snow lingered from the clutch of winter, where the streams ran brown with the down-flow of the continental divide, where every cluster of mountain foliage sheltered a mound of white, in jealous conflict with the sun. The mountains are tenacious of their vicious traits; they cling to the snow and cold and ice long after the seasons have denoted a time of warmth and summer's splendor; the columbine often blooms beside a ten-foot drift.

But down in the hollow which shielded the scrambling little town of Dominion, the air was warm and lazy with the friendliness of May. Far off, along the course of the tumbling stream, turbulently striving to care for far more than its share of the melt-water of the hills, a jaybird called raucously as though in an effort to drown the sweeter, softer notes of a robin nesting in the new-green of a quaking aspen. At the hitching post before the one tiny store, an old horse nodded and blinked,—as did the sprawled figure beside the ramshackle motor-filling station, just opened after the snow-bound months of winter. Then five minutes of absolute peace ensued, except for the buzzing of an investigative bottle-fly before the figure shuffled, stretched, and raising his head, looked down the road. From the distance had come the whirring sound of a motor, the forerunner of a possible customer. In the hills, an automobile speaks before it is seen.

Long moments of throbbing echoes; then the car appeared, a mile or so down the canon, twisting along the rocky walls which rose sheer from the road, threading the innumerable bridges which spanned the little stream, at last to break forth into the open country and roar on toward Dominion. The drowsy gasoline tender rose. A moment more and a long, sleek, yellow racer had come to a stop beside the gas tank, chortled with greater reverberation than ever as the throttle was thrown open, then wheezed into silence with the cutting off of the ignition. A young man rose from his almost flat position in the low-slung driver's seat and crawling over the side, stretched himself, meanwhile staring upward toward the glaring white of Mount Taluchen, the highest peak of the continental backbone, frowning in the coldness of snows that never departed. The villager moved closer.

"Gas?"

"Yep." The young man stretched again. "Fill up the tank—and better give me half a gallon of oil."

Then he turned away once more, to stare again at the great, tumbled stretches of granite, the long spaces of green-black pines, showing in the distance like so many upright fronds of some strange, mossy fern; at the blank spaces, where cold stone and shifting shale had made jagged marks of bareness in the masses of evergreen, then on to the last gnarled bulwarks of foliage, struggling bravely, almost desperately, to hold on to life where life was impossible, the dividing line, as sharp as a knife-thrust, between the region where trees may grow and snows may hide beneath their protecting boughs and the desolate, barren, rocky, forbidding waste of "timber line."

Young he was, almost boyish; yet counterbalancing this was a seriousness of expression that almost approached somberness as he stood waiting until his machine should be made ready for the continuance of his journey. The eyes were dark and lustrous with something that closely approached sorrow, the lips had a tightness about them which gave evidence of the pressure of suffering, all forming an expression which seemed to come upon him unaware, a hidden thing ever waiting for the chance to rise uppermost and assume command. But in a flash it was gone, and boyish again, he had turned, laughing, to survey the gas tender.

"Did you speak?" he asked, the dark eyes twinkling. The villager was in front of the machine, staring at the plate of the radiator and scratching his head.

"I was just sayin' I never seed that kind o' car before. Barry Houston, huh? Must be a new make. I—"

"Camouflage," laughed the young man again. "That's my name."

"Oh, is it?" and the villager chuckled with him. "It shore had me guessin' fer a minute. You've got th' plate right where th' name o' a car is plastered usually, and it plum fooled me. That's your name, huh? Live hereabouts—?"

The owner of the name did not answer. The thought suddenly had come to him that once out of the village, that plate must be removed and tossed to the bottom of the nearest stream. His mission, for a time at least, would require secrecy. But the villager had repeated his question:

"Don't belong around here?"

"I? No, I'm—" then he hesitated.

"Thought maybe you did. Seein' you've got a Colorado license on."

Houston parried, with a smile.

"Well, this isn't all of Colorado, you know."

"Guess that's right. Only it seems in th' summer thet it's most o' it, th' way th' machines pile through, goin' over th' Pass. Where you headed for?"

"The same place."

"Over Hazard?" The villager squinted. "Over Hazard Pass? Ain't daft, are you?"

"I hope not. Why?"

"Ever made it before?"

"No."

"And you're tacklin' it for the first time at this season o' th' year?"

"Yes. Why not? It's May, isn't it?"

The villager moved closer, as though to gain a better sight of Barry Houston's features. He surveyed him carefully, from the tight-drawn reversed cap with the motor goggles resting above the young, smooth forehead, to the quiet elegance of the outing clothing and well-shod feet. He spat, reflectively, and drew the back of a hand across tobacco-stained lips.

"And you say you live in Colorado."

"I didn't say—"

"Well, it don't make no difference whether you did or not. I know—you don't. Nobody thet lives out here'd try to make Hazard Pass for th' first time in th' middle o' May."

"I don't see—"

"Look up there." The old man pointed to the splotches of white, thousands of feet above, the swirling clouds which drifted from the icy breast of Mount Taluchen, the mists and fogs which caressed the precipices and rolled through the valleys created by the lesser peaks. "It may be spring down here, boy, but it's January up there. They's only been two cars over Hazard since November and they come through last week. Both of 'em was old stagers; they've been crossin' th' range for th' last ten year. Both of 'em came through here lookin' like icicles 'an swearing t' beat four o' a kind. They's mountains an' mountains, kid. Them up there's th' professional kind."

A slight, puzzled frown crossed the face of Barry Houston.

"But how am I going to get to the other side of the range? I'm going to Tabernacle."

"They's a train runs from Denver, over Crestline. Look up there—jest to the right of Mount Taluchen. See that there little puff o' smoke? That's it."

"But that'd mean—."

"For you t' turn around, go back to Denver, leave that there chariot o' your'n in some garage and take the train to-morrow mornin'. It'd get you t' Tabernacle some time in the afternoon."

"When would I get there—if I could make the Pass all right?"

"In about five hours. It's only fourteen mile from th' top. But—"

"And you say two other cars have gone through?"

"Yep. But they knowed every crook an' turn!"

For a long moment, the young man made no reply. His eyes were again on the hills and gleaming with a sudden fascination. From far above, they seemed to call to him, to taunt him with their imperiousness, to challenge him and the low-slung high-powered car to the combat of gravitation and the elements. The bleak walls of granite appeared to glower at him, as though daring him to attempt their conquest; the smooth stretches of pines were alluring things, promising peace and quiet and contentment,—will-o-the-wisps, which spoke only their beauty, and which said nothing of the long stretches of gravelly mire and puddles, resultant from the slowly melting snows. The swirling clouds, the mists, the drifting fogs all appeared to await him, like the gathered hosts of some mighty army, suddenly peaceful until the call of combat. A thrill shot through Barry Houston. His life had been that of the smooth spaces, of the easy ascent of well-paved grades, of streets and comforts and of luxuries. The very raggedness of the thing before him lured him and drew him on. He turned, he smiled, with a quiet, determined expression of anticipation, yet of grimness.

"They've got me," came quietly. "I'm—I'm going to make the try!"

The villager grunted. His lips parted as though to issue a final warning. Then, with a disgruntled shake of the head, he turned away.

"Ain't no use arguin' with you Easterners," came at last. "You come out here an' take one look at these here hills an' think you can beat Ole Lady Nature when she's sittin' pat with a royal flush. But go on—I ain't tryin' t' stop you. 'Twouldn't be nothin' but a waste o' breath. You've got this here conquerin' spirit in your blood—won't be satisfied till you get it out. You're all th' same—I've seen fellows with flivvers loaded down till th' springs was flat, look up at them hills an' figure t' get over an' back in time for supper. So go on—only jis' remember this: once you get outside of Dominion an' start up th' grade, there ain't no way stations, an' there ain't no telephones, ner diner service, ner somebody t' bring y' th' evenin' paper. You're buckin' a brace game when y' go against Hazard Pass at a time when she ain't in a mood f'r comp'ny. She holds all th' cards, jis' remember that—an' a few thet ain't in th' deck. But jis' th' same," he backed away as Barry stepped into the racer and pressed a foot on the starter, "I'm wishin' you luck. You'll need it."

"Thanks!" Houston laughed with a new exhilaration, a new spirit of desire. "It can't do any more than kill me."

"Nope." The villager was shouting now above the exhaust of the powerful engine, "But it shore can take a delight in doin' that! S' long!"

"So long!" The gears meshed. A stream of smoke from the new oil spat out for a second. Then, roaring and chortling with the beginning of battle, the machine swept away toward the slight turn that indicated the scraggly end of the little town of Dominion, and the beginning of the first grade.

The exhilaration still was upon Barry Houston. He whistled and sang, turning now and then to view the bright greenness of the new-leafed aspens, to watch the circling sallies of the jaybirds, or to stare ahead to where the blues and greens and purples of the foliage and rocks merged in the distance. The grade was yet easy and there was no evidence of strain upon the engine; the tiny rivulets which ran along the slight ruts at each side of the road betokened nothing to him save the slight possibility of chains, should a muddy stretch of straightaway road appear later on. But as yet, that had not occurred, and Barry was living for the moment.

The road began to twist slightly, with short raises and shorter level stretches winding among the aspens and spruces, with sudden, jagged turns about heavy, frowning boulders whose jutting noses seemed to scrape the fenders of the car, only to miss them by the barest part of an inch. Suddenly Barry found himself bending forward, eyes still on the road in spite of his half-turned head, ears straining to catch the slightest variation of the motor. It seemed to be straining,—yet the long, suddenly straight stretch of road ahead of him seemed perfectly level; downhill if anything. More and more labored became the engine. Barry stopped, and lifting the hood, examined the carbureter. With the motor idling, it seemed perfect. Once more he started,—only to stop again and anxiously survey the ignition, test the spark plugs and again inquire into the activities of the carbureter. At last, reassured, he walked to the front of the machine, and with the screwdriver pried the name plate from its position on the radiator and tossed it into the tumbling, yellow stream beside the road. Then he turned back to the machine,—only to stop suddenly and blink with surprise. The road was not level! The illusion which comes to one at the first effort to conquer a mountain grade had faded now. A few feet away was a deserted cabin, built upon a level plot of ground and giving to Barry a chance for comparison, and he could see that his motor had not been at fault. Now the road, to his suddenly comprehending eyes, rose before him in a long, steady sweep of difficult grades, upward, steadily upward, with never a varying downfall, with never a rest for the motor which must climb it. And this was just the beginning! For Barry could see beyond.

Far in the distance he could make it out, a twisting, turning, almost writhing thing, cutting into the side of the mountain, a jagged scar, searing its way up the range in flights that seemed at times to run almost perpendicular and which faded, only to reappear again, like the trail of some gigantic cut-worm, mark above mark, as it circled the smaller hills, cut into the higher ones, was lost at the edge of some great beetling rock, only to reappear once more, hundreds of feet overhead. The eyes of Barry Houston grew suddenly serious. He reached into the toolbox, and bringing forth the jack, affixed the chains, forgetting his usually cheery whistle, forgetting even to take notice when an investigative jay scrambled out upon a dead aspen branch and chattered at him. The true meaning of the villager's words had come at last. The mountains were frowning now, instead of beckoning, glowering instead of promising, threatening instead of luring. One by one he locked the chains into place, and tossing the jack once more into the tool-box, resumed his place at the wheel.

"A six per cent. grade if it's an inch!" he murmured. "And this is only the beginning. Wonder what I'm stepping into?"

The answer came almost before the machine had warmed into action. Once more the engine labored; nor was it until Barry had answered its gasping plea by a shift to second gear that it strengthened again. The grade was growing heavier; once Barry turned his head and stared with the knowledge that far beneath him a few tiny buildings dotted what seemed to be a space of ground as level as a floor. Dominion! And he had barely passed outside its environs!

He settled more firmly in his seat and gripped hard at the steering wheel. The turns had become shorter; more, Barry found himself righting the machine with sudden jerks as the car rounded the short curves where the front wheels seemed to hang momentarily above oblivion, as the chasms stretched away to seemingly bottomless depths beneath. Gradually, the severity of the grade had increased to ten, to twelve and in short pitches to even eighteen and twenty per cent! For a time the machine sang along in second, bucking the raises with almost human persistence, finally, however, to gasp and break in the smooth monotony of the exhaust, to miss, to strain and struggle vainly, then to thunder on once more, as Houston pressed the gears into low and began to watch the motormeter with anxious eyes. The mercury was rising; another half-hour and the swish of steam told of a boiling radiator.

A stop, while the red, hissing water splattered from the radiator cock, and the lifted hood gave the machine a chance to cool before replenishment came from the murky, discolored stream of melted snow water which churned beneath a sapling bridge. Panting and light-headed from the altitude, Barry leaned against the machine for a moment, then suddenly straightened to draw his coat tighter about him and to raise the collar about his neck. The wind, whistling down from above, was cold: something touched his face and melted there,—snow!

The engine was cool now. Barry leaped to the wheel and once more began his struggle upward, a new seriousness

Courtney Ryley Cooper

upon him, a new grimness apparent in the tightness of his lips. The tiny rivulets of the road had given place to gushing streams; here and there a patch of snow appeared in the highway; farther above, Barry could see that the white was unbroken, save for the half-erased marks of the two cars which had made the journey before him. The motor, like some refreshed animal, roared with a new power and new energy, vibrant, confident, but the spirit was not echoed by the man at the wheel. He was in the midst of a fight that was new to him, a struggle against one of the mightiest things that Nature can know, the backbone of the Rocky Mountains,—a backbone which leered above him in threatening, vicious coldness, which nowhere held surcease; it must be a battle to the end!

Up—up—up—the grades growing steadily heavier, the shifting clouds enveloping him and causing him to stop at intervals and wait in shivering impatience until they should clear and allow him once more to continue the struggle. Grayness and sunshine flitted about him; one moment his head was bowed against the sweep of a snow flurry, driving straight against him from the higher peaks, the next the brilliance of mountain sunshine radiated about him, cheering him, exhilarating him, only to give way to the dimness of damp, drifting mists, which closed in upon him like some great, gray garment of distress and held him in its gloomy clutch until the grade should carry him above it and into the sun or snow again.

Higher! The machine was roaring like a desperate, cornered thing now; its crawling pace slackening with the steeper inclines, gaining with the lesser raises, then settling once more to the lagging pace as steepness followed steepness, or the abruptness of the curve caused the great, slow-moving vehicle to lose the momentum gained after hundreds of feet of struggle. Again the engine boiled, and Barry stood beside it in shivering gratitude for its warmth. The hills about him were white now; the pines had lost their greenness to become black silhouettes against the blank, colorless background Barry Houston had left May and warmth and springtime behind, to give way to the clutch of winter and the white desert of altitude.

But withal it was beautiful. Cold, harassed by dangers that he never before knew could exist, disheartened by the even more precipitous trail which lay ahead, fighting a battle for which he was unfitted by experience, Houston could not help but feel repaid for it all as he flattened his back against the hot radiator and, comforted by the warmth, looked about him. The world was his—his to look upon, to dissect, to survey with the all-seeing eyes of tremendous heights, to view in the perspective of the eagle and the hawk, to look down upon from the pinnacles and see, even as a god might see it. Far below lay a tiny, discolored ribbon,—the road which he had traversed, but now only a scratch upon the expanse of the great country which tumbled away beneath him. Hills had become hummocks, towering pines but blades of grass, streams only a variegated line in the vast display of Nature's artistry. And above—

Barry Houston looked upon it with dazzled eyes. The sun had broken forth again, to stream upon the great, rounded head of Mount Taluchen, and there to turn the serried snows to a mass of shell-pink pearl, to smooth away the glaring whiteness and paint instead a down-like coverlet of beauty. Here and there the great granite precipices stood forth in old rose and royal purple; farther the shadows melted into mantles, not of black, but of softest lavender; mound upon mound of color swung before him as he glanced from peak to peak,—the colors that only an artist knows, tintings instead of solid grounds, suggestions rather than actualities. Even the gnarled pines of timber line, where the world of vegetation was sliced off short to give way to the barrenness of the white desert, seemed softened and freed from their appearance of constant suffering in the pursuit of life. A lake gleamed, set, it seemed, at an upright angle upon the very side of a mountain; an ice gorge glistened with the scintillation of a million jewels, a cloud rolled through a great crevice like the billowing of some soft-colored crepe and then—

Barry crouched and shivered, then turned with sudden activity. It all had faded, faded in the blast of a shrilling wind, bringing upon its breast the cutting assault of sleet and the softer, yet no less vicious swirl of snow. Quickly the radiator was drained and refilled. Once more, huddled in the driver's seat, Barry Houston gripped the wheel and felt the crunching of the chain-clad wheels in the snow of the roadway. The mountains had lured again, only that they might clutch him in a tighter embrace of danger than ever. Now the snow was whirling about him in almost blinding swiftness; the small windshield counted for nothing; it was only by leaning far outside the car that he could see to drive and then there were moments that seemed to presage the end.

Chasms lurked at the corners, the car skidded and lurched from one side of the narrow roadway to the other; once the embankment crumbled for an instant as a rear wheel raced for a foothold and gained it just in time. Thundering below, Barry could hear the descent of the dirt and small boulders as they struck against protruding rocks and echoed forth to a constantly growing sound that seemed to travel for miles that it might return with the strength of thunder. Then for a moment the sun came again and he stared toward it with set, anxious eyes. It no longer was dazzling; it was large and yellow and free from glare. He swerved his gaze swiftly to the dashboard clock, then back to the sun again. Four o'clock! Yet the great yellow ball was hovering on the brim of Mount Taluchen; dusk was coming. A frightened glance showed him the black shadows of the valleys, the deeper tones of coloring, the vagueness of the distance which comes with the end of day.

Anxiously he studied his speedometer as the road stretched out for a space of a few hundred feet for safety. Five miles—only five miles in a space of time that on level country could have accounted for a hundred. Five miles and the route book told plainly that there were four more to go before the summit was reached. Anxiously—with a sudden hope—he watched the instrument, with the thought that perhaps it had broken, but the slow progress of the mile-tenths took away that possibility. He veered his gaze along the dashboard, suddenly to center it upon the oil gauge. His jaw sagged. He pressed harder upon the accelerator in a vain effort. But the gauge showed no indication that the change of speed had been felt.

"The oil pump!" came with a half gasp. "It's broken—I'll have to—"

The sentence was not finished. A sudden, clattering roar had come from beneath the hood, a clanking jangle which told him that his eyes had sought the oil gauge too late,—the shattering, agonizing cacophony of a broken connecting rod, the inevitable result of a missing oil supply and its consequent burnt bearing. Hopelessly, dejectedly Barry shut off the engine and pulled to one side of the road,—through sheer force of habit. In his heart he knew that there could be no remedy for the clattering remonstrance of the broken rod, that the road was his without question, that it was beyond hope to look for aid up here where all the world was pines and precipices and driven snow, that he must go on, fighting against heavier odds than ever. And as he realized the inevitable, his dull, tired eyes saw from the distance another, a greater enemy creeping toward him over the hills and ice gorges, through the valleys and along the sheer walls of granite. The last, ruddy rim of a dying sun was just disappearing over Mount Taluchen.

CHAPTER II

Hazard Pass had held true to its name. There were yet nearly four miles to go before the summit of nearly twelve thousand feet elevation could be reached and the downward trip of fourteen miles to the nearest settlement made. And that meant—

Houston steadied himself and sought to figure just what it did mean. The sun was gone now, leaving grayness and blackness behind, accentuated by the single strip of gleaming scarlet which flashed across the sky above the brim of Mount Taluchen, the last vestige of daylight. The wind was growing shriller and sharper, as though it had waited only for the sinking of the sun to loose the ferocity which too long had been imprisoned. Darkness came, suddenly, seeming to sweep up from the valleys toward the peaks, and with it more snow. Barry accepted the inevitable. He must go on— and that as swiftly as his crippled machine, the darkness and the twisting, snow-laden, treacherous road would permit.

Once more at the wheel, he snapped on the lights and huddled low, to avail himself of every possible bit of warmth from the clanking, discordant engine. Slowly the journey began, the machine laboring and thundering with its added handicap of a broken rod and the consequent lost power of one cylinder. Literally inch by inch it dragged itself up the

Courtney Ryley Cooper

heavier grades, puffing and gasping and clanking, the rattling rod threatening at every moment to tear out its very vitals. The heavy smell of burnt oil drifted back to the nostrils of Barry Houston; but there was nothing that he could do but grip the steering wheel a bit tighter with his numbed hands,—and go on.

Slowly, ever so slowly, the indicator of the speedometer measured off a mile in dragging decimals. The engine boiled and Barry stopped, once more to huddle against the radiator, and to avail himself of its warmth, but not to renew the water. No stream was near; besides, the cold blast of the wind, shrilling through the open hood, accomplished the purpose more easily. Again a sally and again a stop. And Barry was thankful, as, huddled and shivering in his light clothing, he once more sought the radiator. Vaguely there came to him the thought that he might spend the night somewhere on the Pass and go on with the flush of morning. But the thought vanished as quickly as it came; there was no shelter, no blankets, nothing but the meager warmth of what fire he might be able to gather, and that would fade the minute he nodded. Already the temperature had sunk far beneath the freezing point; the crackling of the ice in the gulleys of the road fairly shouted the fact as he edged back once more from the radiator to his seat.

An hour—and three more after that—with the consequent stops and pauses, the slow turns, the dragging process up the steeper inclines of the road. A last final, clattering journey, and Barry leaped from the seat with something akin to enthusiasm.

Through the swirling snow which sifted past the glare of his headlights, he could discern a sign which told him he had reached the summit, that he now stood at the literal top of the world.

But it was a silent world, a black world, in which the hills about him were shapeless, dim hulks, where the wind whined, where the snow swept against his face and drifted down the open space of his collar; a world of coldness, of malice, of icy venom, where everything was a threatening thing, and never a cheering aspect except the fact that the grades had been accomplished, and that from now on he could progress with the knowledge that his engine at least need labor no longer. But the dangers! Barry knew that they had only begun. The descent would be as steep as the climb he had just made. The progress must be slower, if anything, and with the compression working as a brake. But it was at least progress, and once more he started.

The engine clanked less now, the air seemed a bit warmer with the down grade, and Barry, in spite of his fatigue, in spite of the disappointment of a disabled car, felt at least the joy of having conquered the thing which had sought to hold him back, the happiness of having fought against obstacles, of having beaten them, and of knowing that he now was on the down trail. The grade lessened for a few hundred feet, and the machine slowed. Houston pressed on the clutch pedal, allowing the car to coast slowly until the hill became steeper again. Then he sought once more to shift into gear,— and stopped short!

Those few moments of coasting had been enough. Over-heated, distended, the bearings had cooled too suddenly about the crank shaft and frozen there with a tightness that neither the grinding pull of the starter nor the heavy tug of the down grade could loosen. Once more Barry Houston felt his heart sink in the realization of a newer, a greater foreboding than ever. A frozen crank shaft meant that from now on the gears would be useless. Fourteen miles of down grade faced him. If he were to make them, it must be done with the aid of brakes alone. That was dangerous!

He cupped his hands and called,—in the vain hope that the stories of Hazard Pass and its loneliness might not be true, after all. But the only answer was the churning of the bank-full stream a hundred yards away, the thunder of the wind through the pines below, and the eerie echo of his own voice coming back to him through the snows. Laboriously he left the machine and climbed back to the summit, there to seek out the little tent house he had seen far at one side and which he instinctively knew to be the rest room and refreshment stand of the summer season. But he found it, as he had feared he would find it, a deserted, cold, napping thing, without a human, without a single comfort, or the possibility of fire or warmth through the night. Summer, for Hazard Pass, at least, still was a full month away. For a moment he shivered within it, staring about its bleak interior by the aid of a flickering match. Then he went outside again. It was only a shell, only a hope that could not be realized. It would be less of a hardship to make the fight to reach the bottom of the Pass than to attempt to spend the night in this flimsy contraption. In travel there would be at least action, and Barry clambered down the hill to his machine.

Again he started, the brake bands squeaking and protesting, the machine sloughing dangerously as now and again its sheer weight forced it forward at dangerous speeds until lesser levels could be reached and the hold of the brake bands accomplish their purpose again. Down and down, the miles slipping away with far greater speed than even Barry realized, until at last—

He grasped desperately for the emergency brake and gripped tight upon it, steering with one hand. For five minutes there had come the strong odor of burning rubber; the strain had been too great, the foot-brake linings were gone; everything depended upon the emergency now! And almost with the first strain—

Careening, the car seemed to leap beneath him, a maddened, crazed thing, tired of the hills, tired of the turmoil and strain of hours of fighting, racing with all the speed that gravity could thrust upon it for the bottom of the Pass. The brakes were gone, the emergency had not even lasted through the first hill. Barry Houston was now a prisoner of speed,—cramped in the seat of a runaway car, clutching tight at the wheel, leaning, white, tense-faced, out into the snow, as he struggled to negotiate the turns, to hold the great piece of runaway machinery to the crusted road and check its speed from time to time in the snowbanks.

A mile more—halted at intervals by the very thing which an hour or so before Barry Houston had come almost to hate, the tight-packed banks of snow—then came a new emergency. One chance was left, and Barry took it,—the "burring" of the gears in lieu of a brake. The snow was fading now, the air was warmer; a mile or so more and he would be safe from that threat which had driven him down from the mountain peaks,—the possibility of death from exposure, had he, in his light clothing, attempted to spend the night in the open. If the burred gears could only hold the car for a mile or so more—

But a sudden, snapping crackle ended his hope. The gears had meshed, and meshing, had broken. Again a wild, careening thing, with no snow banks to break the rush, the car was speeding down the steepest of the grades like a human thing determined upon self-destruction.

A skidding curve, then a straightaway, while Barry clung to the wheel with fingers that were white with the tightness of their grip. A second turn, while a wheel hung over the edge, a third and—

The awful, suspended agony of space. A cry. A crash and a

dull, twisting moment of deadened Suffering. After that—blackness. Fifty feet below the road lay a broken, crushed piece of mechanism, its wheels still spinning, the odor of gasoline heavy about it from the broken tank, one light still gleaming, like a blazing eye, one light that centered upon the huddled, crumpled figure of a man who groaned once and strove vaguely, dizzily, to rise, only to sink at last into unconsciousness. Barry Houston had lost his fight.

How long he remained there, Barry did not know. He remembered only the falling, dizzy moment, the second or so of horrible, racking suspense, when, breathless, unable to move, he watched the twisting rebound of the machine from which he had been thrown and sought to evade it as it settled, metal crunching against metal, for the last time. After that had come agonized hours in which he knew neither wakefulness nor the quiet of total unconsciousness. Then—

Vaguely, as from far away, he heard a voice,—the sort of a voice that spelled softness and gentleness. Something touched his forehead and stroked it, with the caress that only a woman's hand can give. He moved slightly, with the knowledge that he lay no longer upon the rocky roughness of a mountain side, but upon the softness of a bed. A pillow was beneath his head. Warm blankets covered him. The hand again lingered on his forehead and was drawn away. A moment more and slowly, wearily, Barry Houston opened his eyes.

It was the room of a mountain cabin, with its skiis and snowshoes; with its rough chinkings in the interstices of the logs which formed the mainstay of the house, with its four-paned windows, with its uncouthness, yet with its comfort. Barry noticed none of this. His eyes had centered upon the form of a girl standing beside the little window, where evidently she had gone from his bedside.

Fair-haired she was, though Barry did not notice it. Small of build and slight, yet vibrant with the health and vigor that is typical of those who live in the open places. And there was a piquant something about her too; just enough of an upturned little nose to denote the fact that there was spirit and independence in her being; dark blue eyes that snapped even as darker eyes snapped, as she stood, half turned, looking out the window, watching with evident eagerness the approach of some one Barry could not see. The lips carried a half-smile of anticipation. Barry felt the instinctive urge to call to her, to raise himself—

He winced with a sudden pain, a sharp, yet aching throb of agony which involuntarily closed his eyes and clenched tight his teeth until it should pass. When he looked again, she was gone, and the opening of a door in the next room told him where. Almost wondering, he turned his eyes then toward the blankets and sought to move an arm,—only again to desist in pain. He tried the other, and it responded. The covers were lowered, and Barry's eyes stared down upon a bandaged, splinted left arm. Broken.

He grunted with surprise, then somewhat doggedly began an inspection of the rest of his human machine. Gingerly he wiggled one toe beneath the blankets. It seemed to be in working order. He tried the others, with the same result. Then followed his legs—and the glorious knowledge that they still were intact. His one free hand reached for his head and felt it. It was there, plus a few bandages, which however, from their size, gave Barry little concern. The inventory completed, he turned his head at the sound of a voice— hers—calling from the doorway to some one without.

"He's getting along fine, Ba'tiste." Barry liked the tone and the enthusiastic manner of speaking. "His fever's gone down. I should think—"

Courtney Ryley Cooper

"Ah, *oui*!" had come the answer in booming bass. "And has he, what you say, come to?"

"Not yet. But I think he ought to, soon."

"*Oui*! Heem no ver' bad. He be all right tomorrow."

"That's good. It frightened me, for him to be unconscious so long. It's been five or six hours now, hasn't it?"

"Lemme see. I fin' heem six o'clock. Now—eet is the noon. Six hour."

"That's long enough. Besides, I think he's sleeping now. Come inside and see—"

"Wait, *m' enfant*. M'sieu Thayer he come in the minute. He say he think he know heem."

The eyes of Barry Houston suddenly lost their curiosity. Thayer? That could mean only one Thayer! Barry had taken particular pains to keep from him the information that he was anywhere except the East. For it had been Fred Thayer who had caused Barry to travel across country in his yellow speedster, Thayer who had formed the reason for the displacement of that name plate at the beginning of Hazard Pass, Thayer who—

"Know him? Is he a friend?"

"*Oui*. So Thayer say. He say he think eet is the M'sieu Houston, who own the mill."

"Probably coming out to look over things, then?"

"*Oui*. Thayer, he say the young man write heem about

coming. That is how he know when I tell heem about picking heem up from the machine. He say he know M'sieu Houston is coming by the automobile."

In the other room, Barry Houston blinked rapidly and frowned. He had written Thayer nothing of the sort. He had—Suddenly he stared toward the ceiling in swift-centered thought. Some one else must have sent the information, some one who wanted Thayer to know that Barry was on the way, so that there would be no surprise in his coming, some one who realized that his mission was that of investigation!

The names of two persons flashed across his mind, one to be dismissed immediately, the other—

"I'll fire Jenkins the minute I get back!" came vindictively. "I'll—."

He choked his words. A query had come from the next room.

"Was that heem talking?"

"No, I don't think so. He groans every once in a while. Wait—I'll look."

The injured man closed his eyes quickly, as he heard the girl approach the door, not to open them until she had departed. Barry was thinking and thinking hard. A moment later—

"How's the patient?" It was a new voice, one which Barry Houston remembered from years agone, when he, a wide-eyed boy in his father's care, first had viewed the intricacies of a mountain sawmill, had wandered about the bunk houses, and ridden the great, skidding bobsleds with the lumberjacks in the spruce forests, on a never-forgotten trip of inspection. It was Thayer, the same Thayer that he once had looked upon with all the enthusiasm and pride of boyhood, but whom he now viewed with suspicion and distrust. Thayer had brought him out here, without realizing it. Yet Thayer had known that he was on the way. And Thayer must be combatted—but how? The voice went on, "Gained consciousness yet?"

"No." The girl had answered. "That is—"

"Of course, then, he hasn't been able to talk. Pretty sure it's Houston, though. Went over and took a look at the machine. Colorado license on it, but the plates look pretty new, and there are fresh marks on the license holders where others have been taken off recently. Evidently just bought a Colorado tag, figuring that he'd be out here for some time. How'd you find him?"

The bass voice of the man referred to as Ba'tiste gave the answer, and Barry listened with interest. Evidently he had struggled to his feet at some time during the night—though he could not remember it—and striven to find his way down the mountain side in the darkness, for the story of Ba'tiste told Barry that he had found him just at dawn, a full five hundred yards from the machine.

"I see heem move," the big voice was saying, "jus' as I go to look at my trap. Then Golemar come beside me and raise his hair along his neck and growl—r-r-r-r-r-u-u-f-f-f—like that. I look again—it is jus' at the dawn. I cannot see clearly. I raise my gun to shoot, and Golemar, he growl again. Then I think eet strange that the bear or whatever he is do not move. I say to Golemar, 'We will closer go, *ne c'est pas?*' A step or two—then three—but he do not move—then pretty soon I look again, close. Eet is a man, I pick heem up, like this— and I bring heem home. *Ne c'est pas*, Medaine?"

Her name was Medaine then. Not bad, Barry thought. It rather matched her hair and the tilt of her nose and the tone of her laugh as she answered:

"I would say you carried him more like a sack of meal, Ba'tiste. I'm glad I happened along when I did; you might have thrown him over your shoulder!"

A booming laugh answered her and the sound of a light scuffle, as though the man were striving to catch the girl in his big embrace. But the cold voice of Thayer cut in:

"And he hasn't regained consciousness?"

"Not yet. That is, I think he's recovered his senses, all right, and fallen immediately into a heavy sleep."

"Guess I'll go in and stay with him until he wakes up. He's my boss, you know—since the old man died. We've got a lot of important things to discuss. So if you don't mind—"

"Certainly not." It was the girl again. "We'll go in with you."

"No, thanks. I want to see him alone."

Within the bedroom, Barry Houston gritted his teeth. Then, with a sudden resolve, he rested his head again on the pillow and closed his eyes as the sound of steps approached. Closer they came to the bed, and closer. Barry could feel that the man was bending over him, studying him. There came a murmur, almost whispered:

"Wonder what the damn fool came out here about? Wonder if he's wise?"

CHAPTER III

It was with an effort that Houston gave no indication that he had heard. Before, there had been only suspicions, one flimsy clue leading to another, a building-block process, which, in its culmination, had determined Barry to take a trip into the West to see for himself. He had believed that it would be a long process, the finding of a certain telegram and the possibilities which might ensue if this bit of evidence should turn out to be the thing he had suspected. He had not, however, hoped to have from the lips of the man himself a confession that conditions were not right at the lumber mill of which Barry Houston now formed the executive head; to receive the certain statement that somewhere, somehow, something was wrong, something which was working against the best interests of himself and the stern necessities of the future. But now—

Thayer had turned away and evidently sought a chair at the other side of the room. Barry remained perfectly still. Five minutes passed. Ten. There came no sound from the chair; instinctively the man on the bed knew that Thayer was watching him, waiting for the first flicker of an eyelid, the first evidence of returning consciousness. Five minutes more and Barry rewarded the vigil. He drew his breath in a shivering sigh. He turned and groaned,—quite naturally with the pain from his splintered arm. His eyes opened slowly, and he stared about him, as though in non-understanding wonderment, finally to center upon the window ahead and retain his gaze there, oblivious of the sudden tensity of the thin-faced Thayer. Barry Houston was playing for time, playing a game of identities. In the same room was a man he felt sure to be an enemy, a man who had in his care everything Barry Houston possessed in the world, every hope, every dream, every chance for the wiping out of a thing that had formed a black blot in the life of the young man for two grim years, and a man who, Barry Houston now felt certain, had not held true to his trust. Still steadily staring, he pretended not to notice the tall, angular form of Fred Thayer as that person crossed the brightness of the window and turned toward the bed. And when at last he did look up into the narrow, sunken face, it was with eyes which carried in them no light of friendship, nor even the faintest air of recognition. Thayer put forth a gnarled, frost-twisted hand.

"Hello, kid," he announced, his thin lips twisting into a cynical smile that in days gone by had passed as an affectation. Barry looked blankly at him.

"Hello."

"How'd you get hurt?"

"I don't know."

"Old Man Renaud here says you fell over the side of Two Mile Hill. He picked you up about six o'clock this morning. Don't you remember?"

"Remember what?" The blank look still remained. Thayer moved closer to the bed and bending, stared at him.

"Why, the accident. I'm Thayer, you know—Thayer, your manager at the Empire Lake mill."

"Have I a manager?"

The thin man drew back at this and stood for a moment staring down at Houston. Then he laughed and rubbed his gnarled hands.

"I hope you've got a manager. You—you haven't fired me, have you?"

Barry turned his head wearily, as though the conversation were ended.

"I don't know what you are talking about."

"You—don't—say, you're Barry Houston, aren't you?"

"I? Am I?"

"Well, then, who are you?"

The man on the bed smiled.

"I'd like to have you tell me. I don't know myself."

"Don't you know your name?"

"Have I one?"

Thayer, wondering now, drew a hand across his forehead and stood for a moment in disconcerted silence. Again he started to frame a question, only to desist. Then, hesitatingly, he turned and walked to the door.

"Ba'tiste."

"Ah, *oui!*"

"Come in here, will you? I'm up against a funny proposition. Mr. Houston doesn't seem to be able to remember who he is."

"Ah!" Then came the sound of heavy steps, and Barry glanced toward the door, to see framed there the gigantic form of a grinning, bearded man, his long arms hanging with the looseness of tremendous strength, his gray eyes gleaming with twinkling interest, his whole being and build that of a great, good-humored, eccentric giant. His beard was splotched with gray, as was the hair which hung in short, unbarbered strands about his ears. But the hint of age was nullified by the cocky angle of the blue-knit cap upon his head, the blazing red of his double-breasted pearl-buttoned shirt, the flexible freedom of his muscles as he strode within. Beside him trotted a great gray cross-breed dog, which betokened collie and timber wolf, and which progressed step by step at his master's knee. Close to the bed they came, the great form bending, the twinkling, sharp eyes boring into those of Houston, until the younger man gave up the contest and turned his head,—to look once more upon the form of the girl, waiting wonderingly in the doorway. Then the voice came, rumbling, yet pleasant:

"He no remember, eh?"

"No. I know him all right. It's Barry Houston—I've been expecting him to drop in most any day. Of course, I haven't seen him since he was a kid out here with his father—but that doesn't make any difference. The family resemblance is there—he's got his father's eyes and mouth and nose, and his voice. But I can't get him to remember it. He can't recall anything about his fall, or his name or business. I guess the accident—"

"Eet is the—" Ba'tiste was waving one hand vaguely, then placing a finger to his forehead, in a vain struggle for a word. "Eet is the—what-you-say—"

"Amnesia." The answer had come quietly from the girl. Ba'tiste turned excitedly.

"Ah, *oui*! Eet is the amnesia. Many time I have seen it—" he waved a hand—"across the way, *ne c'est pas*? Eet is when the mind he will no work—what you say—he will not stick on the job. See—" he gesticulated now with both hands— "eet is like a wall. I see eet with the shell shock. Eet is all the same. The wall is knock down—eet will not hold together. Blooey—" he waved his hands—"the man he no longer remember!"

This time the stare in Barry Houston's eyes was genuine. To hear a girl of the mountains name a particular form of mental ailment, and then to further listen to that ailment described in its symptoms by a grinning, bearded giant of the woods was a bit past the comprehension of the injured man. He had half expected the girl to say "them" and "that there", though the trimness of her dress, the smoothness of her small, well-shod feet, the air of refinement which spoke even before her lips had uttered a word should have told him differently. As for the giant, Ba'tiste, with his outlandish clothing, his corduroy trousers and high-laced, hob-nailed boots, his fawning, half-breed dog, his blazing shirt and kippy little knit cap, the surprise was all the greater. But that surprise, it seemed, did not extend to the other listener. Thayer had bobbed his head as though in deference to an authority. When he spoke, Barry thought that he discerned a tone of enthusiasm, of hope:

"Do they ever get over it?"

"Sometime, yes. Sometime—no. Eet all depend."

"Then there isn't any time limit on a thing like this."

"No. Sometime a year—sometime a week—sometime never. It all depend. Sometime he get a shock—something happen quick, sudden—blooey—he come back, he say 'where am I', and he be back again, same like he was before!" Ba'tiste gesticulated vigorously. Thayer moved toward the door.

"Then I guess there's nothing more for me to do, except to drop in every few days and see how he's getting along. You'll take good care of him?"

"Ah, *oui*."

"Good. Want to walk a piece down the road—with me, Medaine?"

"Of course. It's too bad, isn't it—"

Then they faded through the doorway, and Barry could hear no more. But he found himself looking after them, wondering about many things,—about the girl and her interest in Fred Thayer, and whether she too might be a part of the machinery which he felt had been set up against him; about the big, grinning Ba'tiste, who still remained in the room; who now was fumbling about with the bedclothes at the foot of the bed and—

"Ouch! Don't—don't do that!"

Barry suddenly had ceased his thoughts to jerk his feet far up under the covers, laughing and choking and striving to talk at the same time. At the foot of the bed, Ba'tiste, his eyes twinkling more than ever, had calmly rolled back the covering and just as calmly tickled the injured man's feet. More, one long arm had outstretched again, as the giant once more reached for the sole of a foot, to tickle it, then to stand back and boom with laughter as Barry involuntarily sought to jerk the point of attack out of the way. For a fourth time he repeated the performance, followed by a fourth outburst of mirth at the recoil from the injured man. Barry frowned.

"Pardon me," he said rather caustically. "But I don't get the joke."

"Ho, ho!" and Ba'tiste turned to talk to the shaggy dog at his side. "*L'enfant* feels it! *L'enfant* feels it!"

"Feel it," grunted Houston. "Of course I feel it! I'm ticklish."

"You hear, Golemar?" Ba'tiste, contorted with merriment, pointed vaguely in the direction of the bed, "M'sieu l' Nobody, heem is ticklish!"

"Of course I'm ticklish. Who isn't, on the bottom of his feet?"

The statement only brought a new outburst from the giant. It nettled Houston; further, it caused him pain to be jerking constantly about the bed in an effort to evade the tickling touch of the trapper's big fingers. Once more Ba'tiste leaned forward and wiggled his fingers as if in preparation for a new assault, and once more Barry withdrew his pedal extremities to a place of safety.

"Please don't," he begged. "I—I don't know what kind of a game you're playing—and I'm perfectly willing to join in on it when I feel better—but now it hurts my arm to be bouncing around this way. Maybe this afternoon—if you've got to play these fool games—I'll feel better—"

The thunder of the other man's laugh cut him off. Ba'tiste was now, it seemed, in a perfect orgy of merriment. As though weakened by his laughter, he reeled to the wall and leaned there, his big arms hanging loosely, the tears rolling down his cheeks and disappearing in the gray beard, his face reddened, his whole form shaking with series after series of chuckles.

"You hear heem?" he gasped at the wolf-dog. "M'sieu l' Nobody, he will play with us this afternoon! M'sieu l' Ticklefoot! That is heem, my Golemar, M'sieu l' Ticklefoot! Oh, ho—M'sieu l' Ticklefoot!"

"What in thunder is the big idea?" Barry Houston had lost his reserve now. "I want to be a good fellow—but for the love of Mike let me in on the joke. I can't get it. I don't see anything funny in lying here with a broken arm and having my feet tickled. Of course, I'm grateful to you for picking me up and all that sort of thing, but—"

Choking back the laughter, Ba'tiste returned to the foot of the bed and stood wiping the tears from his eyes.

"Pardon, *mon ami*," came seriously at last. "Old Ba'teese must have his joke. Listen, Ba'teese tell you something. You see people here today, *oui*, yes? You see, the petite Medaine? Ah, *oui*!" He clustered his fingers to his lips and blew a kiss toward the ceiling. "She is the, what-you-say, fine li'l keed. She is the—*bon bebe*! You no nev' see her before?"

Barry shook his head. Ba'tiste went on.

"You see M'sieu Thayer? *Oui*? You know heem?"

"No."

"You sure?"

"Never saw him before."

"So?" Batiste grinned and wagged a finger, "Ba'teese he like the truth, yes, *oui*. Ba'teese he don't get the truth, he tickle M'sieu's feet."

"Now listen! Please—"

"No—no!" The giant waved a hand in dismissal of threat. "Old Ba'teese, he still joke. Ba'teese say he tell you something. Eet is this. You see those people? All right. *Bon*—good. You don' know one. You know the other. Yes? *Oui*? Ba'teese not know why you do it. Ba'teese not care. Ba'teese is right—in here." He patted his heart with a big hand. "But you—you not tell the truth. I know. I tickle your feet."

"You're crazy!"

"So, mebbe. Ba'teese have his trouble. Sometime Ba'teese wish he go crazy—like you say."

The face suddenly aged. The twinkling light left the eyes. The big hands knitted, and the man was silent for a long moment. Then, "But Ba'-teese he know—see?" He pointed to his head, then twisting, ran his finger down his spine. "When eet is the—what-you-say, amnesia—the nerve eet no work in the foot. I could tickle, tickle, tickle, and you would not know. But with you—blooey—right away, you feel. So, for some reason, you are, what-you-say?—shamming. But you are Ba'teese' gues'. You sleep in Ba'teese' bed. You eat Ba'teese' food. So long as that, you are Ba'teese' friend. Ba'teese—" he looked with quiet, fatherly eyes toward the young man on the bed—"shall ask no question—and Ba'teese shall tell no tales!"

CHAPTER IV

The simple statement of the gigantic trapper swept the confidence from Houston and left him at a disadvantage. His decision had been a hasty one,—a thing to gain time, a scheme by which he had felt he could, at the proper time, take Thayer off his guard and cause him to come into the open with his plans, whatever they might be. Fate had played a strange game with Barry Houston. It had taken a care-free, happy-go-lucky youth and turned him into a suspicious, distrustful person with a constantly morbid strain which struggled everlastingly for supremacy over his usually cheery grin and his naturally optimistic outlook upon life. For Fate had allowed Houston to live the youth of his life in ease and brightness and lack of worry, only that it might descend upon him with the greatest cloud that man can know. And two years of memories, two years of bitterness, two years of ugly recollections had made its mark. In all his dealings with Thayer, conducted though they might have been at a distance, Barry Houston could not place his finger upon one tangible thing that would reveal his crookedness. But he had suspected; had come to investigate, and to learn, even before he was ready to receive the information, that his suspicions had been, in some wise at least, correct. To follow those suspicions to their stopping place Barry had feigned amnesia. And it had lasted just long enough for this grinning man who stood at the foot of the bed to tickle his feet!

Courtney Ryley Cooper

And how should that grotesque giant with his blazing red shirt and queer little cap know of such things as amnesia and the tracing of a deadened nerve? How should he,—then Barry suddenly tensed. Had it been a ruse? Was this man a friend, a companion—even an accomplice of the thin-faced, frost-gnarled Thayer—and had his simple statement been an effort to take Barry off his guard? If so, it had not succeeded, for Barry had made no admissions. But it all affected him curiously; it nettled him and puzzled him. For a long time he was silent, merely staring at the grinning features of Ba'tiste. At last:

"I should think you would wait until you could consult a doctor before you'd say a thing like that."

"So? It has been done."

"And he told you—"

"Nothing. He does not need to even speak to Ba'teese." A great chuckle shook the big frame "Ba'teese know as soon as *l' M'sieu Doctaire*."

"On good terms, aren't you? When's he coming again?"

"*Parbleu!*" The big man snapped his fingers. "Peuff! Like that. Ba'teese call heem, and he is here."

Houston blinked. Then, in spite of his aching head, and the pain of the swollen, splint-laced arm he sat up in bed.

"What kind of—"

"Old Ba'teese, he mus' joke," came quickly and seriously from the other man. "Ba'teese—he is heem."

"A doctor?"

Slowly the big man nodded. Barry went on "I—I—didn't know. I thought you were just a trapper. I wondered—"

"So! That is all—jus' a trapper."

Quietly, slowly, the big man turned away from the bed and stood looking out the window, the wolf-dog edging close to him as though in companionship and some strange form of sympathy. There was silence for a long time, then the voice of Ba'tiste came again, but now it was soft and low, addressed, it seemed, not to the man on the bed, but to vacancy.

"So! Ba'teese, he is only a trapper now. Ba'teese, he had swear he never again stand beside a sick bed. But you—" and he turned swiftly, a broken smile playing about his lips—"you, *mon ami*, you, when I foun' you this morning, with your head twisted under your arm, with the blood on your face, and the dust and dirt upon you—then you—you look like my Pierre! And I pick you up—so!" He fashioned his arms as though he were holding a baby, "and I look at you and I say—'Pierre! Pierre!' But you do not answer—just like he did not answer. Then I start back with you, and the way was rough. I take you under one arm—so. It was steep. I must have one arm free. Then I meet Medaine, and she laugh at me for the way I carry you. And I was glad. Eet made Ba'teese forget."

"What?" Barry said it with the curiosity of a boy. The older man stared hard at the crazy design of the covers.

"My Pierre," came at last. "And my Julienne. Ba'teese, he is all alone now. Are you all alone?" The question came quickly. Barry answered before he thought.

"Yes."

"Then you know—you know how eet feel. You know how Ba'teese think when he look out the window. See?" He pointed, and Barry raised himself slightly that he might follow the direction of the gesture. Faintly, through the glass, he could see something white, rearing itself in the shadows of the heavy pines which fringed the cabin,—a cross. And it stood as the guardian of a mound of earth where pine boughs had been placed in smooth precision, while a small vase, half implanted in the earth, told of flowers in the summer season. Ba'tiste stared at his palms. "Julienne," came at last. "My wife." Then, with a sudden impulse, he swerved about the bed and sat down beside the sick man. "Ba'teese—" he smiled plaintively—"like to talk about Pierre—and Julienne. Even though eet hurt."

Barry could think only in terms of triteness.

"Have they been gone long?"

The big man counted on his fingers.

"One—two—t'ree year. Before that—*bon!*" He kissed his fingers airily. "Old Ba'teese, he break the way—long time ago. He come down from Montreal, with his Julienne and his Pierre—in his arm, so. He like to feel big and strong—to help other people. So, down here where there were few he came, and built his cabin, with his Pierre and his Julienne. And, so happy! Then, by'm'by, Jacques Robinette come too, with his petite Medaine—"

"That's the girl who was here?"

"Ah, *oui*. I am *l' M'sieu Doctaire*. I look after the sick for ten—twenty—thirty mile. Jacques he have more head. He buy land." A great sweep of the arm seemed to indicate all outdoors. "Ev'where—the pine and spruce, it was Jacques! By'm'by, he go on and leave Medaine alone. Then she go 'way to school, but ev' summer she come back and live in the big house. And Ba'teese glad—because he believe some day she love Pierre and Pierre love her and—"

Another silence. At last:

"And then war came. My Pierre, he is but eighteen. But he go. Ba'teese want him to go. Julienne, she say nothing—she cry at night. But she want him to go too. Medaine, she tell funny stories about her age and she go too. It was lonely. Ba'teese was big. Ba'teese was strong. And Julienne say to him, 'You too—you go. You may save a life.' And Ba'teese went."

"To France?"

Ba'tiste bowed his head.

"Long time Ba'teese look for his Pierre. Long time he look for Medaine. But no. Then—" his face suddenly contorted "—one night—in the cathedral at St. Menehould, I find heem. But Pierre not know his *pere*. He not answer Ba'teese when he call 'Pierre! Pierre!' Here, and here, and here—" the big man pointed to his breast and face and arms—"was the shrapnel. He sigh in my arms—then he is gone. Ba'teese ask that night for duty on the line. He swear never again to be *l' M'sieu Doctaire*. All his life he help—help—help—but when the time come, he cannot help his own. And by'm'by, Ba'teese come home—and find that."

He pointed out into the shadows beneath the pines.

"She had died?"

Courtney Ryley Cooper

"Died!" The man's face had gone suddenly purple. His eyes were glaring, his hands upraised and clutched. "No! Murder! Murder, mon ami! Murder! Lost Wing—he Medaine's Indian —he find her—so! In a heap on the floor—and a bullet through her brain. And the money we save, the ten thousan' dollar—eet is gone! Murder!"

A shudder went over the young man on the bed. His face blanched. His lips lost their color. For a moment, as the big French-Canadian bent over him, he stared with glazed, unseeing eyes, at last to turn dully at the sharp, questioning voice of the trapper:

"Murder—you know murder?"

There was a long moment of silence. Then, as though with an effort which took his every atom of strength, Houston shook himself, as if to throw some hateful, vicious thing from him, and turned, with a parrying question:

"Did you ever find who did it?"

"No. But sometime—Ba'teese not forget. Ba'teese always wait. Ba'teese always look for certain things—that were in the deed-box. There was jewelry—Ba'teese remember. Sometime—" Then he switched again. "Why you look so funny? Huh? Why you get pale—?"

"Please—" Barry Houston put forth a hand. "Please—" Then he straightened. "Ba'tiste, I'm in your hands. You can help me, or you can harm me. You know I was shamming when I acted as though I had lost my identity. Now—now you know there's something else. Will you—"

He ceased suddenly and sank back. From without there had come the sound of steps. A moment later, the door opened, and shadows of a man and a girl showed on the floor. Thayer and Medaine had returned. Soon they were in the room, the girl once more standing in the doorway, regarding Barry with a quizzical, half-wondering gaze, the man coming forward and placing one gnarled hand on the Canadian's shoulder, staring over his head down into the eyes of the injured man on the bed.

"I couldn't go back to the mill without making one more try," he explained. "Has he shown any signs yet?"

Barry watched Ba'teese closely. But the old man's face was a blank.

"Signs? Of what?"

"Coming to—remembering who he is."

"Oh." Ba'tiste shrugged his shoulders. "I have give eet up."

"Then—"

"So far Ba'teese is concern'," and he looked down on the bed with a glance which told Barry far more than words, "he is already name. He is M'sieu Nobody. I can get no more."

Thayer scratched his head. He turned.

"Anyway, I'm going to make one more attempt at it. See what you can do, Medaine."

The girl came forward then, half smiling, and seated herself beside the bed. She took Barry's hand in hers, then with a laugh turned to Thayer.

"What shall I do? Make love to him?"

"Why not?" It was old Ba'tiste edging forward, the twinkle once more in his eyes. "Bon—good! Make love to him."

"Do you suppose it would help?" The girl was truly serious now.

"Why not?"

"I don't think—" Thayer had edged forward, nervously. Ba'tiste pushed him gently.

"Peuff! And when did M'sieu Thayer become *l' M'sieu Doctaire*? Ba'teese say ask him if he like you."

Medaine laughed.

"Do you like me?"

Brown eyes met blue eyes. A smile passed between them. It was with an effort that Houston remembered that he was only playing a part.

"I certainly do!"

"Ask him, 'Do you like me better than anybody you ever—'"

"What sense is there to all this?"

"Blooey! And why should you ask? Why should you stand with a frown on your face? Peuff! It is ugly enough already!" To Barry, it was quite evident that there was some purpose behind the actions of Old Ba'tiste, and certainly more than mere pleasantry in his words. "You ask Medaine to help Ba'teese, and then *facher vous*! Enough. Ask him, Medaine."

"But—" the girl was laughing now, her eyes beaming, a

slight flush apparent in her cheeks—"maybe he doesn't want me to—"

"Oh, but I do!" There was something in the tone of Barry Houston which made the color deepen. "I—I like it."

"That's enough!" Thayer, black-featured, his gnarled hands clenched into ugly knots, came abruptly forward. "I thought this was a serious thing; I didn't know you were going to turn it into a burlesque!"

"Perhaps M'sieu Thayer has studied the practice of medicine?"

"No. But—"

"Nor, pardon, the practice of politeness. Ba'teese will not need your help."

"Whether you need it or not, I'll come back when you're through with this infernal horseplay. I—"

"Ba'teese choose his guests."

"You mean—"

"Ba'teese mean what he say."

"Very well, then. Come on, Medaine."

The girl, apparently without a thought of the air of proprietorship in the man's tone, rose, only to face Ba'tiste. The Canadian glowered at her.

"And are you chattel?" he stormed. "Do you stand in the cup of his hand that he shall tell you when to rise and when to sit, when to walk and where to go?"

She turned.

"You were abrupt, Fred. I'm glad Ba'tiste reminded me. Personally, I don't see why I should have been drawn into this at all, or why I should be made the butt of a quarrel over some one I never saw before."

"I'm sorry—terribly sorry." Barry was speaking earnestly and holding forth his hand. "I shouldn't have answered you that way—I'm—"

"We'll forget it all." A flashing smile had crossed the girl's lips. "Fred never knows how to take Ba'tiste. They're always quarreling this way. The only trouble is that Fred—" and she turned to face him piquantly—"always takes in the whole world when he gets mad. And that includes me. I think," and the little nose took a more upward turn than ever, "that Ba'tiste is entirely right, Fred. You talked to me as though I were a sack of potatoes. I won't go with you, and I won't see you until you can apologize."

"There's nothing to apologize for!"

Thayer jammed on his hat and stamped angrily out the door. Medaine watched him with laughing eyes.

"He'll write me a letter to-night," came quietly. Then, "Lost Wing!"

"Ugh!" It was a grunt from outside.

"I just wanted to be sure you were there. Call me when Mr. Thayer has passed the ridge."

"Ugh!"

Medaine turned again to Ba'tiste, a childish appearance of confidence in her eyes, her hand lingering on the chair by the bed.

"Were you really fooling, Ba'tiste—or shall we continue?"

"Perhaps—" the twinkle still shone in the old man's eyes— "but not now. Perhaps—sometime. So mebbe sometime you—"

"Wah—hah—hai-i-e-e-e!" The Sioux had called from without. Medaine turned.

"When you need me, Ba'tiste," she answered, with a smile that took in also the eager face on the bed, "I'll be glad to help you. Good-by."

That too included Barry, and he answered it with alacrity. Then for a moment after she had gone, he lay scowling at Ba'tiste, who once more, in a weakened state of merriment, had reeled to the wall, followed as usual by his dog, and leaned there, hugging his sides. Barry growled:

"You're a fine doctor! Just when you had me cured, you quit! I'd forgotten I even had a broken arm."

"So?" Ba'tiste straightened. "You like her, eh? You like the petite Medaine?"

"How can I help it?"

"*Bon*! Good! I like you to like Medaine. You no like Thayer?"

"Less every minute."

"Bon! I no like heem. He try to take Pierre's place with Medaine. And Pierre, he was strong and tall and straight. Pierre, he could smile—*bon*! Like you can smile. You look like my Pierre!" came frankly.

"Thanks, Ba'tiste." Barry said it in wholehearted manner. "You don't know how grateful I am for a little true friendliness."

"Grateful? Peuff! You? Bah, you shall go back, and they will ask who helped you when you were hurt, and you—you will not even remember what is the name."

"Hardly that." Barry pulled thoughtfully at the covers. "In the first place, I'm not going back, and in the second, I haven't enough true friends to forget so easily. I—I—" Then his jaw dropped and he lay staring ahead, out to the shadows beneath the pines and the stalwart cross which kept watch there. "I—"

"You act funny again. You act like you act when I talk about my Julienne. Why you do eet?"

Barry Houston did not answer at once. Old scenes were flooding through his brain, old agonies that reflected themselves upon his features, old sorrows, old horrors. His eyes grew cold and lifeless, his hands white and drawn, his features haggard. The chuckle left the lips of Ba'tiste Renaud. He moved swiftly, almost sinuously to the bed, and gripped the younger man by his uninjured arm. His eyes came close to Barry Houston, his voice was sharp, tense, commanding:

"You! Why you act like that when I talk about murder? Why you get pale, huh? Why you get pale?"

CHAPTER V

The gaze of Ba'tiste Renaud was strained as he asked the question, his manner tense, excited. Through sheer determination, Barry forced a smile and pulled himself back to at least a semblance of composure.

"Maybe you know the reason already—through Thayer. But if you don't—Ba'tiste, how much of it do you mean when you say you are a man's friend?"

"Ba'teese may joke," came quietly, "but Ba'teese no lie. You look like my Pierre—you help where it has been lonesome. You are my frien'."

"Then I know you are not going to ask me for something that hurts in telling. And at least, I can give you my word of honor that it isn't because of my conscience!"

Ba'tiste was silent after that, walking slowly about the room, shaggy head bent, hands clasped behind his back, studious, as though striving to fathom what had been on the man's mind. As for Barry, he stared disconsolately at vacancy, living again a thing which he had striven to forget. It had been forced upon him, this partial admission of a cloud in the past; the geniality, the utter honesty, the friendliness of the old French-Canadian, the evident dislike for a man whom he,

Barry, also thoroughly distrusted, had lowered the younger man's guard. The tragic story of Pierre and Julienne had furthered the merest chance acquaintance into what seemed the beginning, at least, of closest friendship. Houston had known Ba'tiste for only a matter of a few hours,—yet it seemed months since he first had looked upon the funny little blue cap and screaming red shirt of the Canadian; and it was evident that Renaud had felt the same reaction. Barry Houston, to this great, lonely man of the hills, looked like a son who was gone, a son who had grown tall and straight and good to look upon a son upon whom the old man had looked as a companion, and a chum for whom he had searched in every battle-scarred area of a war-stricken nation, only to find him,—too late. And with this viewpoint, there was no shamming about the old man's expressions of friendship. More, he took Barry's admission of a cloud in the past as a father would take it from a son; he paced the floor minute after minute, head bowed, gray eyes half closed, only to turn at last with an expression which told Barry Houston that a friend was his for weal or woe, for fair weather or foul, good or evil.

"Eet is enough!" came abruptly. "There is something you do not want to tell. I like you—I not ask. You look like my Pierre—who could do no wrong. So! *Bon*—good! Ba'teese is your frien'. You have trouble? Ba'teese help."

"I've had plenty of that, in the last two years," came quietly. "I think I've got plenty ahead of me. What do you know about Thayer?"

"He no good."

"Why?"

"Ba'teese don' know. On'y he have narrow eyes too close

together. He have a quirk to his mouth Ba'teese no like. He have habit nev' talkin' about himself—he ask you question an' tell you nothing. He have hatchet-face; Ba'teese no like a man with a hatchet-face. Beside, he make love to Medaine!"

Barry laughed.

"Evidently that's a sore spot with you, Ba'tiste."

"No. Ba'teese no care. But if my Pierre had live, he would have make love to her. She would have marry him. And to have M'sieu Thayer take his place? No! Mebbe—" he said it hopefully, "mebbe you like Medaine, huh?"

"I do! She's pretty, Ba'tiste."

"Mebbe you make love?"

But the man on the bed shook his head.

"I can't make love to anybody, Ba'tiste. Not until I've—I've found something I'm looking for. I'm afraid that's a long way off. I haven't the privileges of most young fellows. I'm a little—what would you call it—hampered by circumstance. I've—besides, if I ever do marry, it won't be for love. There's a girl back East who says she cares for me, and who simply has taken it for granted that I think the same way about her. She stood by me—in some trouble. Out of every one, she didn't believe what they said about me. That means a lot. Some way, she isn't my kind; she just doesn't awaken affection on my part, and I spend most of my time calling myself a cad over it. But she stood by me—and—I guess that's all that's necessary, after all. When I've fulfilled my contract with myself—if I ever do—I'll do the square thing and ask her to marry me."

Ba'tiste scowled.

"You dam' fool," he said. "Buy 'em present. Thank 'em, *merci beaucoup*. But don' marry 'em unless 'you love 'em. Ba'teese, he know. Ba'teese, he been in too many home where there is no love."

"True. But you don't know the story behind it all, Ba'tiste. And I can't tell you except this: I got in some trouble. I'd rather not tell you what it was. It broke my father's heart— and his confidence in me. He—he died shortly afterward."

"And you—was it your fault?"

"If you never believe anything else about me, Ba'tiste, believe this: that it wasn't. And in a way, it was proven to him, before he went. But he had been embittered then. He left a will—with stipulations. I was to have the land he owned out here at Empire Lake; and the flume site leading down the right side of Hawk Creek to the mill. Some one else owns the other side of the lake and the land on the opposite bank of the stream."

"*Oui*. Medaine Robinette."

"Honestly? Is it hers?"

"When she is twenty-one. But go on."

"Father wouldn't leave me the mill. He seemed to have a notion that I'd sell it all off—and he tied everything up in a way to keep me from doing anything like that. The mill is rented to me. The land is mine, and I can do everything but actually dispose of it. But on top of that comes another twist: if I haven't developed the business within five years into double what it was at the peak of its best development, back goes everything into a trust fund, out of which I am to have a hundred dollars a month, nothing more. That's what I'm out here for, Ba'tiste, to find out why, in spite of the fact that I've worked day and night now for a year and a half, in spite of the fact that I've gone out and struggled and fought for contracts, and even beaten down the barriers of dislike and distrust and suspicion to get business—why I can't get it! Something or some one is blocking me, and I'm going to find out what and who it is! I think I know one man—Thayer. But there may be more. That's why I'm playing this game of lost identity. I thought I could get out here and nose around without him knowing it. When he found out at once who I was, and seemed to have had a previous tip that I was coming out here, I had to think fast and take the first scheme that popped into my head. Maybe if I can play the game long enough, it will take him off his guard and cause him to work more in the open. They may give me a chance to know where I stand. And I've got to know that, Ba'tiste. Because—" and his voice was vibrant with determination, "I don't care what happens to me personally. I don't care whether five minutes after I have made it, I lose every cent of what I have worked for. But I do care about this; I'm going to make good to my father's memory. I'm going to be able to stand before a mirror and look myself straight in the eye, knowing that I bucked up against trouble, that it nearly whipped me, that it took the unfairest advantage that Fate can take of a man in allowing my father to die before I could fully right myself in his eyes, but that if there is a Justice, if there is anything fair and decent in this universe, some way he'll know, some way he'll rest in peace, with the understanding that his son took up the gauntlet that death laid down for him, that he made the fight, and that he won!"

"*Bon*—good!" Old Ba'tiste leaned over the foot of the bed. "My Pierre—he would talk like that. *Bon*? Now—what is it you look for?"

Courtney Ryley Cooper

"In the first place, I want to know how so many accidents can happen in a single plant, just at the wrong time. I want to know why it is that I can go out and fight for a contract, and then lose it because a saw has broken, or an off-bearer, lugging slabs away from the big wheel, can allow one to strike at just the wrong moment and let the saw pick it up and drive it through the boiler, laying up the whole plant for three weeks. I want to know why it is that only about one out of three contracts I land are ever filled. Thayer's got something to do with it, I know. Why? That's another question. But there must be others. I want to know who they are and weed them out. I've only got three and a half years left, and things are going backward instead of forward."

"How you intend to fin' this out?"

"I don't know. I've got one lead—as soon as I'm able to get into town. That may give me a good deal of information; I came out here, at least, in the hope that it would. After that, I'm hazy. How big a telegraph office is there at Tabernacle?"

"How big?" Ba'tiste laughed. "How *petite*! Eet is about the size of the—what-you-say—the peanut."

"Is there ever a time when the operator isn't there?"

"At noon. He go out to dinner, and he leave open the door. If eet is something you want, walk in."

"Thanks." A strange eagerness was in Houston's eyes. "I think I'll be able to get up to-morrow. Maybe I can walk over there; it's only a mile or two, isn't it?"

But when to-morrow, came, it found a white, bandaged figure sitting weakly in front of Ba'tiste's cabin, nothing more. Strength of purpose and strength of being had proved two different things, and now he was quite content to rest there in the May sunshine, to watch the chattering magpies as they went about the work of spring house-building, to study the colors of the hills, the mergings of the tintings and deeper hues as the scale ran from brown to green to blue, and finally to the stark red granite and snow whites of Mount Taluchen.

Ba'tiste and his constant companion, Golemar, were making the round of the traps and had been gone for hours. Barry was alone—alone with the beauties of spring in the hills, with the soft call of the meadow lark in the bit of greenery which fringed the still purling stream in the little valley, the song of the breeze through the pines, the sunshine, the warmth—and his problems.

Of these, there were plenty. In the first place, how had Thayer known that he was on the way from the East? He had spoken to only two persons,—Jenkins, his bookkeeper, and one other. To these two persons he merely had given the information that he was going West on a bit of a vacation. He had deliberately chosen to come in his car, so that there might be every indication, should there be such a thing as a spy in his rather diminutive office, that he merely intended a jaunt through a few States, certainly not a journey half across the country. But just the same, the news had leaked; Thayer had been informed, and his arrival had been no surprise.

That there had been need for his coming, Barry felt sure. At the least, there was mismanagement at the mill; contract after contract lost just when it should have been gained told him this, if nothing more. But—and he drew a sheet of yellow paper from his pocket and stared hard at it—there was something else, something which had aroused his curiosity to an extent of suspicion, something which might mean an open book of information to him if only he could reach Tabernacle at the right moment and gain access to the telegraph files without the interference of the agent.

Then suddenly he ceased his study of the message and returned it to his pocket. Two persons were approaching the cabin from the opposite hill,—a girl whom he was glad to see, and a man who walked, or rather rolled, in the background: Medaine Robinette and a sort of rear guard who, twenty or thirty feet behind her, followed her every step, trotted when she ran down the steep side of an embankment, then slowed as she came to a walk again. A bow-legged creature he was, with ill-fitting clothing and a broad "two-gallon" hat which evidently had been bequeathed to him by some cow-puncher, long hair which straggled over his shoulders, and a beaded vest which shone out beneath the scraggly outer coat like a candle on a dark night. Instinctively Barry knew him to be the grunting individual who had waited outside the door the night before,—Lost Wing, Medaine's Sioux servant: evidently a self-constituted bodyguard who traveled more as a shadow than as a human being. Certainly the girl in the foreground gave no indication that she was aware of his presence; nor did she seem to care.

Closer she came, and Barry watched her, taking a strange sort of delight in the skipping grace with which she negotiated the stepping stones of the swollen little stream which intervened between her and the cabin of Ba'tiste Renaud, then clambered over the straggling pile of massed logs and dead timber which strewed the small stretch of flat before the rise began, leading to where he rested. More like some graceful, agile boy was she than a girl. Her clothing was of that type which has all too soon taken the place of the buckskin in the West,—a riding habit, with stout little shoes and leather puttees; her hair was drawn tight upon her head and encased in the shielding confines of a cap, worn low over her forehead, the visor pulled aside by a jutting twig and now slanting out at a rakish angle; her arms full of something pink and soft and pretty. Barry wondered what it could be,—then brightened with sudden hope.

"Wonder if she's bringing them to me?"

The answer came a moment later as she faced him, panting slightly from the exertion of the climb, the natural flush of exercise heightened by her evident embarrassment.

"Oh, you're up!" came in an almost disappointed manner. Then with a glance toward the great cluster of wild roses in her arms, "I don't know what to do with these things now."

"Why?" Barry's embarrassment was as great as hers. "If—if it'll do any good, I'll climb back into bed again."

"No—don't. Only I thought you were really, terribly ill and—"

"I am—I was—I will be. That is—gosh, it's a shame for you to go out and pick all those and then have me sitting up here as strong as an ox. I—"

"Oh, don't worry about that." She smiled at him with that sweetness which only a woman can know when she has the advantage. "I didn't pick them. Lost Wing"—she pointed to the skulking, outlandishly dressed Indian in the background—"attended to that. I was going to send them over by him. But I didn't have anything to do, so I just thought I'd bring them myself."

"Thanks for that, anyway. Can't I keep them just the same— to put on the table or something?"

"Oh, if you care to." Barry felt that she was truly

disappointed that he wasn't at the point of death, or at least somewhere near it. "Where's Ba'tiste."

"Out looking after his traps, picking them up I think, for the summer. He'll be back soon. Is there—"

"No. I usually come over every day to see him, you know." Then the blue eyes lost their diffidence to become serious. "Do you remember yet who you are?"

"Less right at this minute than at any other time!" spoke Barry truthfully. "I'm out of my head entirely!" He reached for the flowers.

"Please don't joke that way. It's really serious. When I was across—army nursing—I saw a lot of just such cases as yours. Shell shock, you know. One has to be awfully careful with it."

"I know. But I'm getting the best of care. I—ouch!" His interest had exceeded his caution. The unbandaged hand had waved the flowers for emphasis and absently gripped the stems. The wild roses fluttered to the ground. "Gosh!" came dolefully, "I'm all full of thorns. Guess I'll have to pick 'em out with my teeth."

"Oh!" Then she picked up the roses and laid them gingerly aside. "You can't use your other hand, can you?"

"No. Arm's broken."

"Then—" she looked back toward Lost Wing, hunched on a stump, and Barry's heart sank. She debated a moment, at last to shake her head. "No—he'd want to dig them out with a knife. If you don't mind." She moved toward Houston and Barry thrust forth his hand.

"If you don't mind," he countered and she sat beside him. A moment later:

"I must look like a fortune teller."

"See anything in my palm besides thorns?"

"Yes. A little dirt. Ba'tiste evidently isn't a very good nurse."

"I did the best I could with one hand. But I was pretty grimy. I—I didn't know," and Barry grinned cheerfully, "I was going to be this lucky."

She pretended not to hear the sally. And in some way Barry was glad. He much rather would have her silent than making some flippant remark, much rather would he prefer to lean comfortably back on the old bench and watch the quiet, almost childish determination of her features as she sought for a grip on the tiny protuberances of the thorns, the soft brownness of the few strands of hair which strayed from beneath the boyish cap, the healthy glow of her complexion, the smallness of the clear-skinned hands, the daintiness of the trim little figure. Much rather would he be silent with the picture than striving for answers to questions that in their very naiveness were an accusation. Quite suddenly Barry felt cheap and mean and dishonest. He felt that he would like to talk about himself,—about home and his reasons for being out here; his hopes for the mill which now was a shambling, unprofitable thing; about the future and—a great many things. It was with an effort, when she queried him again concerning his memory, that he still remained Mr. Nobody. Then he shifted the conversation from himself to her.

"Do you live out here?"

"Yes. Didn't Ba'tiste tell you? My house is just over the

hill—you can just see one edge of the roof through that bent aspen."

Barry stared.

"I'd noticed that. Thought it was a house, but couldn't be sure. I thought I understood Ba'tiste to say you only came out here in the summer."

"I did that when I was going to school. Now I stay here all the year 'round."

"Isn't it lonely?"

"Out here? With a hundred kinds of birds to keep things going? With the trout leaping in the streams in the summer time, and a good gun in the hollow of your arm in the winter? Besides, there's old Lost Wing and his squaw, you know. I get a lot of enjoyment out of them when we're snowed in—in the winter. He's told me fully fifty versions of how the Battle of Wounded Knee was fought, and as for Custer's last battle—it's wonderful!"

"He knows all about it?"

"I'd hardly say that." Medaine reached under her cap for a hairpin, looked quickly at Barry as though to ask him whether he could stand pain, then pressed a recalcitrant thorn into a position where it could be extracted. "I think the best description of Lost Wing is that he's an admirable fiction writer. Ba'tiste says he has more lies than a dog has fleas."

"Then it isn't history?"

"Of course not. Just imagination. But it's well done, with plenty of gestures. He stands in front of the fire and acts it all out while his squaw sits on the floor and grunts and nods and wails at the right time, and it's really entertaining. They're about a million years old, both of them. My father got them when he first came down here from Montreal. He wanted Lost Wing as a sort of bodyguard. It was a good deal wilder in this region then than it is now, and father owned a good deal of land."

"So Ba'tiste tells me. He says that practically all of the forests around here are yours."

"They will be, next year," came simply, "when I'm—"

She stopped and laughed.

"Ba'tiste told me. Twenty-one."

"He never could keep anything to himself."

"What's wrong about that? I'm twenty-seven myself."

"Honestly? You don't look it."

"Don't I? I ought to. I've got a beard and everything. See?" He pulled his hand away for a moment to rub the two-days' growth on his face. "I tried to shave this morning. Couldn't make it. Ba'tiste said he'd play barber for me this afternoon. Next time you come over I'll be all slicked up."

Again she laughed, and once more pursued the remaining thorns.

"How do you know there'll be a next time?"

"If there isn't, I'll drive nails in myself, so you'll have to pull 'em out." Then seriously. "You do come over here often, don't you?"

"Of course—" then, the last thorn disposed of, she rose—"to see Ba'tiste. I look on him as a sort of a guardian. He knew my father. But let's talk about yourself. You seem remarkably clear in your mind to be afflicted with amnesia. Are you sure you don't remember anything—?"

"No—not now. But," and Barry hedged painfully, "I think I will. It acts to me like a momentary thing. Every once in a while I get a flash as though it were all coming back; it was just the fall, I'm sure of that. My head's all right."

"You mean your brain?"

"Yes. I don't act crazy, or anything like that, do I?"

"Well," and she smiled quizzically, "of course, I don't know you, so I have nothing to go by. But I must admit that you say terribly foolish things."

Leaving him to think over that, she turned, laughed a good-by, and with the rolling, bow-legged old Lost Wing in her wake, retraced the path to the top of the hill, there to hesitate a moment, wave her hand quickly, and then, as though hurrying away from her action, disappeared. Barry Houston sat for a long time, visualizing her there on the brow of the hill, her head with its long-visored cap tilted, her hand upraised, her trimness and her beauty silhouetted against the opalesque sky, dreaming,—and with a bit of heartache in it. For this sort of thing had been his hope in younger, fairer days. This sort of a being had been his make-believe companion of a Castle in Spain. This sort of a joking, whimsical girl had been the one who had come to him in the smoke wreaths and tantalized him and promised him—

But now, his life was gray. His heart was not his own. His life was at best only a grim, drab thing of ugly memories and angered determinations. If a home should ever come to him, it must be in company with some one to whom he owed the gratitude of friendship in time of need; not love not affection, but the paying of a debt of deepest honor. Which Barry would do, and faithfully and honestly and truthfully. As for the other—

He leaned against the bark slabs of the cabin. He closed his eyes. He grinned cheerily.

"Well," came at last, "there's no harm in thinking about it!"

CHAPTER VI

It was thus that Ba'tiste found him, still dreaming. The big voice of the Canadian boomed, and he reached forward to nudge Barry on his injured shoulder.

"And who has been bringing you flowers?" he asked.

"Medaine. That is—Miss Robinette."

"Medaine? Oh, ho! You hear, Golemar?" he turned to the fawning wolf-dog. "He calls her Medaine! Oh, ho! And he say he will marry, not for love. Peuff! We shall see, by gar, we shall see! Eh, Golemar?" Then to Barry, "You have sit out here too long."

"I? Nothing of the kind. Where's the axe? I'll do some fancy one-handed woodchopping."

And while Ba'tiste watched, grinning, Barry went about his task, swinging the axe awkwardly, but whistling with the joy of work. Nor did he pause to diagnose his light-heartedness. He only knew that he was in the hills; that the streets and offices and people of the cities, and the memories that they carried, had been left behind for him that he was in a new world to make a new fight and that he was strangely, inordinately happy Time after time the axe glinted, to descend upon the chopping block, until at last the pile of stovewood had reached its proper dimensions, and old Ba'tiste came from the doorway to carry it in. Then, half an hour later, they sat down to their meal of sizzling bacon and steaming coffee,—a great, bearded giant and the younger man whom he, in a moment of impulsiveness, had all but adopted. Ba'tiste was still joking about the visit of Medaine, Houston parrying his thrusts. The meal finished, Ba'tiste went forth once more, to the hunt of a bear trap and its deadfall, dragged away by a mountain lion during the last snow. Barry sought again the bench outside the cabin, to sit there waiting and hoping,—in vain. At last came evening, and he undressed laboriously for a long rest. Something awaited him in Tabernacle,—either the opening of a book of schemes, or at least the explanation of a mystery, and that meant a walk of quite two miles, the exercise of muscles which still ached, the straining of tendons drawn by injury and pain. But when the time came, he was ready.

"*Bon*—good!" came from Ba'tiste, as they turned into the little village of Tabernacle the next day, skirted the two clapboarded stores forming the "main business district," and edged toward the converted box car that passed as a station. "*Bon*—the agent he is leaving."

Barry looked ahead, to see a man crossing an expanse of flat country toward what was evidently a boarding house. Ba'tiste nudged him.

"You will walk slowly, as though going into the station to loaf. Ba'tiste will come behind—and keep watch."

Barry obeyed. A moment more and he was within the converted box car, to find it deserted and silent, except for the constant clackle of the telegraph key, rattling off the business of a mountain railroad system, like some garrulous old woman, to any one who would listen. There was no private office, only a railing and a counter, which Barry crossed easily. A slight crunching of gravel sounded without. It was Ba'tiste, now lounging in the doorway, ready at a moment to give the alarm. Houston turned hastily toward the file hook and began to turn the pages of the original copy which hung there.

A moment of searching and he leaned suddenly forward. Messages were few from Tabernacle; it had been an easy matter for him to come upon the originals of the telegrams he sought, in spite of the fact that they had been sent more than two weeks before. Already he was reading the first of the night letters:

Barry Houston,
Empire Lake Mill and Lumber Co.,
212 Grand Building, Boston, Mass.

Please order six-foot saw as before. Present one broken to-day through crystallization.

F. B. THAYER.

"That's one of 'em." Houston grunted the words, rather than spoke them. "That was meant for me all right—humph!"

The second one was before him now, longer and far more interesting to the man who bent over the telegraph file, while Ba'tiste kept watch at the door. Hastily he pulled a crumpled message from his pocket and compared them,—and grunted again.

"The same thing. Identically the same thing, except for the addresses! Ba'tiste," he called softly, "what kind of an operator is this fellow?"

"No good. A boy. Just out of school. Hasn't been here long."

"That explains it." Houston was talking to himself again. "He got the two messages and—" Suddenly he bent forward and examined a notation in a strange hand:

"Missent Houston. Resent Blackburn."

It explained much to Barry Houston, that scribble of four words. It told him why he had received a telegram which meant nothing to him, yet caused suspicion enough for a two-thousand-mile trip. It explained that the operator, in sending two messages, had, through absent-mindedness, put them both on the wire to the same person, when they were addressed separately, that he later had seen his mistake and corrected it. Barry smiled grimly.

"Thanks very much, Operator," he murmured. "It isn't every mistake that turns out this lucky."

Then slowly, studiously, he compared the messages again, the one he had received, and the one on the hook which read:

J. C. Blackburn,
Deal Building, Chicago, Ill.

Our friend reports Boston deal put over O. K. Everything safe. Suggest start preparations for operations in time compete Boston for the big thing. Have Boston where we want him and will keep him there.

THAYER.

It was the same telegram that Barry Houston had received and puzzled over in Boston, except for the address. He had been right then; the message had not been for him; instead it

had been intended decidedly *not* for him and it meant—
what? Hastily Houston crawled over the railing, and
motioning to Ba'tiste, led him away from the station. Around
the corner of the last store he brought forth his telegram and
placed it in the big man's hands.

"That's addressed to me,—but it should have gone to some
one else. Who's J. C. Blackburn of Chicago?"

"Ba'teese don't know. Try fin' out. Why?"

"Have you read that message?"

The giant traced out the words, almost indecipherable in
places from creasing and handling. He looked up sharply.

"Boston? You came from Boston?"

"Yes. That must refer to me. It must mean what I've been
suspecting all along,—that Thayer's been running my mill
down, to help along some competitor. You'll notice that he
says he has me where he wants me."

"*Oui*—yes. But has he? What was the deal?"

"I don't know. I haven't been in any deal that I know of, yet
he must refer to me. I haven't any idea what he means by the
reference to starting operations, or that sentence about the
'big thing.' There isn't another mill around here?"

"None nearer than the Moscript place at Echo Lake."

"Then what can it be?" Suddenly Houston frowned with
presentiment. "Thayer's been going with Medaine a good
deal, hasn't he?"

"*Oui*—yes. When Ba'teese can think of no way to keep him from it."

"It couldn't be that he's made some arrangement with her—about her forest lands?"

"They are not hers yet. She does not come into them until she is twenty-one."

"But they are available then?"

"*Oui*. And they are as good as yours."

"Practically the same thing, aren't they? How much of the lake does she own?"

"The east quarter, and the forests that front on eet, and the east bank of Hawk Creek."

"Then there would be opportunity for everything, for skidways into the lake, a flume on her side and a mill. That must be—"

"Ba'teese would have hear of eet."

"Surely. But Thayer might have—"

"Ba'teese would have hear of eet," came the repetition. "No, eet is something else. She would have ask Ba'teese and Ba'teese would have said, 'No. Take nothing and give nothing. *M'sieu* Thayer, he is no good.' So eet is not that. You know the way back? *Bon*—good. Go to the cabin. Ba'teese will try to learn who eet is, this Blackburn."

They parted, Ba'teese to lounge back into the tiny town, Houston to take the winding road which led back to the

Courtney Ryley Cooper

cabin. A pretty road it was, too, one which trailed along beside the stream, now clear with that sharp brilliancy which is characteristic of the mountain creek, a road fringed with whispering aspens, bright green in their new foliage, with small spruce and pine. Here and there a few flowers showed; by the side of the road the wild roses peeped up from the denser growths of foliage, and a vagrant butterfly or so made the round of blossom after blossom. It was spring-summer down here, sharp contrast indeed to the winter which lurked above and which would not fade until June had far progressed. But with it all, its beauty, its serenity, its peace and soft moistness, Houston noticed it but slightly. His thoughts were on other things: on Thayer and his duplicity, on the possibilities of the future, and the methods of combating a business enemy he felt sure was lurking in the background.

It meant more to Houston than the mere monetary value of a loss,—should a loss come. Back in the family burying ground in Boston was a mound that was fresher than others, a mound which shielded the form of a man who had died in disappointment, leaving behind an edict which his son had sworn to carry through to its fulfillment. Now there were obstacles, and ones which were shielded by the darkness of connivance and scheming. The outlook was not promising. Yet even in its foreboding, there was consolation.

"I at least know Thayer's a crook. I can fire him and run the mill myself," Barry was murmuring to himself, as he plodded along. "There may be others; I can weed them out. At least saws won't be breaking every two weeks and lumber won't warp for lack of proper handling. Maybe I can get somebody back East to look after the office there and—"

He ceased his soliloquy as he glanced ahead and noticed the trim figure of Medaine Robinette swinging along the road, old Lost Wing, as usual, trailing in her rear, astride a calico pony and leading the saddle horse which she evidently had become tired of riding. A small switch was in one hand, and she flipped it at the new leaves of the aspens and the broad-leafed mullens beside the road. As yet, she had not seen him, and Barry hurried toward her, jamming his cap into a pocket that his hand might be free to greet her. He waved airily as they came closer and called. But if she heard him, she gave no indication. Instead, she turned—swiftly, Houston thought—and mounted her horse. A moment later, she trotted past him, and again he greeted her, to be answered by a nod and a slight movement of the lips. But the eyes had been averted. Barry could see that the thinnest veneer of politeness had shielded something else as she spoke to him,—an expression of distaste, of dislike, almost loathing!

CHAPTER VII

"Why?"

Barry Houston could not answer the self-imposed question. He could only stand and stare after her and the trotting, rolling Indian, as they moved down the road and disappeared in the shadow of the aspens at the next curve. She had seen him; there could be no doubt of that. She had recognized him; more, Houston felt sure that she had mounted her horse that she might better be able to pass him and greet him with a formal nod instead of a more friendly acknowledgment. And this was the girl who, an afternoon before, had sat beside him on the worn old bench at the side of Ba'tiste's cabin and picked thorns from the palm of his hand,—thorns from the stems of wild roses which she had brought him! The enigma was too great for Houston. He could only gasp with the suddenness of it and sink back into a dullness of outlook and viewpoint which he had lost momentarily. It was thus that old friends had passed him by in Boston; it was thus that men who had been glad to borrow money from him in other days had looked the other way when the clouds had come. A strange chill went over him.

"Thayer's told her!"

He spoke the sentence like a man repeating the words of an

execution. His features suddenly had grown haggard. He stumbled slightly as he made the next rise in the road and went on slowly, silently, toward the cabin.

There Ba'tiste found him, slumped on the bench, staring out at the white and rose pinks of Mount Taluchen, yet seeing none of it. The big man boomed a greeting, and Barry, striving for a smile, answered him. The Canadian turned to his wolf-dog.

"*Peuff*! Golemar! Loneliness sits badly upon our friend. He is homesick. Trot over the hill and bring to him the petite Medaine! Ah *oui*," he laughed in immense enjoyment at his raillery, "bring to him the petite Medaine to make him laugh and be happy." Then, seeing that the man was struggling vainly for a semblance of cheeriness, he slid beside him on the bench and tousled his hair with one big hand. "Nev' min' old Ba'teese," he said hurriedly; "he joke when eet is no time. You worry, huh? So, mebbe, Ba'teese help. There are men at the boarding house."

"The Blackburn crowd?"

"So. Seven carpenters, and others. They work for Blackburn, who is in Chicago. They are here to build a mill."

"A mill?" Barry looked up now with new interest. "Where?"

"Near the lake. The mill, eet will be sawing in a month. The rest, the big plant, eet will take time for that."

"On Medaine's land then!" But Ba'tiste shook his head.

"No. Eet is on the five acres own' by Jerry Martin. He has been try' to sell eet for five year. Eet is no good—rocks and rocks—and rocks. They build eet there."

"But what can they do on five acres? Where will they get their lumber?"

The trapper shrugged his shoulders.

"Ba'teese on'y know what they tell heem."

"But surely, there must be some mistake about it. You say they are going to start sawing in a month, and that a bigger plant is going up. Do you mean a complete outfit,—planers and all that sort of thing?"

"So!"

Houston shook his head.

"For the life of me, I can't see it. In the first place, I have the only timber around here with the exception of Medaine's land, and you say that she doesn't come into that until next year. But they're going to start sawing at this new mill within a month. My timber stretches back from the lake for eight miles; they either will have to go beyond that and truck in the logs for that distance, which would be ruinous as far as profits are concerned, or content themselves with scrub pine and sapling spruce. I don't see what they can make out of that. Isn't that right? All I know about it is from what I've heard. I've never made a cruise of the territory around here. But it's always been my belief that with the exception of the land on the other quarter of the lake—"

"That is all."

"Then where—"

But again Ba'tiste shrugged his shoulders. Then he pulled long at his grizzled beard, regarding the wolf-dog which sat between his legs, staring up at him.

"Golemar," came at last. "There is something strange. Peuff! We shall fin' out, you and me and *mon ami*." Suddenly he turned. "M'sieu Thayer, he gone."

"Gone? You mean he's run away?"

"By gar, no. But he leave hurried. He get a telephone from long distance. Chicago."

"Then—"

"Ba'teese not know. M'sieu Shuler in the telephone office, he tell me. Eet is a long call, M'sieu Shuler is curious, and he listen in while they, what-you-say, chew up the rag. Eet is a woman. She say to meet her in Denver. This morning M'sieu Thayer take the train. *Bon*—good!"

"Good? Why?"

"What you know about lumber?"

Houston shook his head.

"A lot less than I should. It wasn't my business, you know. My father started this mill out here during boom times, when it looked as though the railroad over Crestline would make the distance between Denver and Salt Lake so short that the country would build up like wild fire. He got them to put in a switch from above Tabernacle to the mill and figured on making a lot of money out of it all. But it didn't pan out, Ba'tiste. First of all, the railroad didn't go to Salt Lake and in the second—"

"The new road will," said the French-Canadian. "Peuff!

When they start to build eet, blooey! Eet will be no time."

"The new road? I didn't know there was to be one."

"*Ah, oui, oui, oui!*" Ba'tiste became enthusiastic. "They shall make eet a road! Eet will not wind over the range like this one. Eet shall come through the mountains with a six-mile tunnel, at Carrow Peak where they have work already one, two, t'ree year. Then eet will start out straight, and peuff! Eet will cut off a hundred mile to Salt Lake. Then we will see!"

"When is all this going to happen?"

The giant shrugged his shoulders.

"When the railroad, eet is ready, and the tunnel, eet is done. When that shall be? No one know. But the survey, eet is made. The land, eet is condem'. So it must be soon. But you say you no know lumber?"

"Not more than any office man could learn in a year and a half. It wasn't my business, Ba'tiste. Father thought less and less of the mill every year. Once or twice, he was all but ready to sell it to Thayer, and would have done it, I guess, if Thayer could have raised the money. He was sick of the thing and wanted to get rid of it. I had gone into the real estate business, never dreaming but that some day the mill would be sold and off our hands. Then—then my trouble came along, and my father—left this will. Since then, I've been busy trying to stir up business. Oh, I guess I could tell a weathered scantling from a green one, and a long time ago, when I was out here, my father taught me how to scale a log. That's about all."

"Could you tell if a man cut a tree to get the greatest footage? If you should say to a lumberjack to fell a tree at the spring of the root, would you know whether he did it or not? Heh? Could you know if the sawyer robbed you of fifty feet on ever' log? No? Then we shall learn. To-morrow, we shall go to the mill. M'sieu Thayer shall not be there. Perhaps Ba'tiste can tell you much. *Bien*! We shall take Medaine, *oui*? Yes?"

"I—I don't think she'd go."

"Why not?"

"I'd rather—" Houston was thinking of a curt nod and averted eyes. "Maybe we'd better just go alone, Ba'tiste."

"*Tres bien*. We shall go into the forest. We shall learn much."

And the next morning the old French-Canadian lived true to his promise. Behind a plodding pair of horses hitched to a jolting wagon, they made the journey, far out across the hills and plateau flats from Tabernacle, gradually winding into a shallow canon which led to places which Houston remembered from years long gone. Beside the road ran the rickety track which served as a spur from the main line of the railroad, five miles from camp,—the ties rotten, the plates loosened and the rails but faintly free from rust; silent testimony of the fact that cars traveled but seldom toward the market, that the hopes of distant years had not been fulfilled. Ahead of them, a white-faced peak reared itself against the sky, as though a sentinel against further progress,—Bear Mountain, three miles beyond the farthest stretch of Empire Lake. Nearer, a slight trail of smoke curled upward, and Ba'tiste pointed.

"The mill," he said. "Two mile yet."

"Yes, I remember in a hazy sort of way." Then he laughed

shortly. "Things will have to happen and happen fast if I ever live up to my contract, Ba'tiste."

"So?"

"Yes, I put too much confidence in Thayer. I thought he was honest. When my father died, he came back to Boston, of course, and we had a long talk. I agreed that I was not to interfere out here any more than was necessary, spending my time, instead, in rounding up business. He had been my father's manager, and I naturally felt that he would give every bit of his attention to my business. I didn't know that he had other schemes, and I didn't begin to get on to the fact until I started losing contracts. That wasn't so long ago. Now I'm out here, and if necessary, I'll stay here and be everything from manager to lumberjack, to pull through."

"*Bon*! My Pierre, he would talk like that." Then the old man was silent for a moment. "Old Ba'tiste, he has notice some things. He will show you. Golemar! Whee!"

In answer to the whining call of the giant, the wolf-dog, trotting beside the lazy team, swerved and nipped at the horses' heels. The pace became a jogging trot. Soon they were in view of the long, smooth mound of sawdust leading to the squat, rambling saw shed. A moment more and the bunk house, its unpainted clapboards blackened by the rain and sun and snows, showed ahead. A half-mile, then Ba'tiste left the wagon and, Barry following him, walked toward the mill and its whining, groaning saws.

"Watch close!" he ordered. "See ever'thing they do. Then remember. Ba'tiste tell you about it when we come out."

Within they went, where hulking, strong-shouldered men were turning the logs from the piles without, along the skidways and to the carriage of the mill, their cant hooks working in smooth precision, their muscles bulging as they rolled the great cylinders of wood into place, steadied them, then stood aside until the carriages should shunt them toward the sawyer and the tremendous, revolving wheel which was to convert them into "board feet" of lumber. Hurrying "off-bearers", or slab-carriers, white with sawdust, scampered away from the consuming saw, dragging the bark and slab-sides to a smaller blade, there to be converted into boiler fuel and to be fed to the crackling fire of the stationary engine, far at one end of the mill. Leather belts whirred and slapped; there was noise everywhere, except from the lips of men. For they, these men of the forest, were silent, almost taciturn.

To Barry, it all seemed a smooth-working, perfectly aligned thing: the big sixteen-foot logs went forward, rough, uncouth things, to be dragged into the consuming teeth of the saw; then, through the sheer force of the blade, pulled on until brownness became whiteness, the cylindrical shape a lopsided thing with one long, glaring, white mark; to be shunted back upon the automatic carriage, notched over for a second incision, and started forward again, while the newly sawn boards traveled on to the trimmers and edgers, and thence to the drying racks.

Log after log skidded upon the carriage and was brought forward, while Houston, fascinated, watched the kerf mark of the blade as it tore away a slab-side. Then a touch on the arm and he followed Ba'tiste without. The Canadian wandered thoughtfully about a moment, at last to approach a newly stacked pile of lumber and lean against it. A second more and he drew something to his side and stared at it.

"Oh, ho!" came at last. "M'sieu Houston, he will, what-you-say, fix the can on the sawyer."

"Why?"

"First," said Ba'tiste quietly, "he waste a six-inch board on each slab-side he take off. Un'stand? The first cut—when the bark, eet is sliced off. He take too much. Eet is so easy. And then—look." He drew his hand from its place of conceal-ment, displaying a big thumb measuring upon a small ruler. "See? Eet is an inch and a quarter. Too thick."

"I know that much at least. Lumber should be cut at the mill an inch and an eighth thick to allow for shrinkage to an inch—but not an inch and a quarter."

"Bon!" Ba'tiste grinned. "Eet make a difference on a big log. Eight cuts of the saw and a good board, eet is gone."

"No wonder I don't make money."

"There is much more. The trimmer and the edger, they take off too much. They make eight-inch boards where there should be ten, and ten where there should be twelve. You shall have a new crew."

"And a new manager," Houston said it quietly. The necessity for his masquerade was fading swiftly now.

"And new men on the kilns. See!"

Far to one side, a great mass of lumber reared itself against the sky, twisted and warped, the offal of the drying kilns. Ba'tiste shrugged his shoulders.

"So! When the heat, eet is made too quick, the lumber twist. Eet is so easy—when one wants some one to be tired and quit!"

To quit! It was all plain to Barry Houston now. Thayer had tried to buy the mill when the elder Houston was alive. He had failed. Now, he was striving for something else to make Houston the newcomer, Houston, who was striving to succeed without the fundamentals of actual logging experience, disgusted with the business and his contract with the dead. The first year and a half of the fight had passed,—a losing proposition; Barry could see why now, in warped lumber and thick-cut boards, in broken machinery and unfulfilled contracts. Thayer wanted him to quit; his father's death had tied up the mill proper to such an extent that it could neither be leased nor sold for a long time. But the timber could be bought on a stumpage basis, the lake and flume leased, and with a new mill—

"I understand the whole thing now!" There was excitement in the tone. "They can't get this mill—on account of the way the will reads. I can't dispose of it. But they know that with the mill out of the way, and the whole thing a disappointment, that I should be willing to contract my timber to them and lease the flume. Then they can go ahead with their own plans and their own schemes. It's the lake and flume and timber that counts, anyway; this mill's the cheapest part of it all."

"Ah, *oui!*" The big man wagged his head in sage approval. "But it shall not be, eh?"

Houston's lips went into a line,

"Not until the last dog dies!"

CHAPTER VIII

"Ah, *oui!*" Evidently Ba'tiste liked the expression. "Eet shall not be until—what-you-say—the last dog, eet is dead. Come! We will go into the forest. Ba'tiste will show you things you should know."

And to the old wagon again they went, to trail their way up the narrow road along the bubbling, wooden flume which led from the lake, to swerve off at the dam and turn into the hills again. Below them, the great expanse of water ruffled and shimmered in the May sun; away off at the far end, a log slid down a skidway, and with a booming splash struck the water, to bury itself for a hundred feet, only to rise at last, and bobbing, go to join others of its kind, drifting toward the dam with the current of the stream which formed the lake. In the smoother spaces, trout splashed; the reflections of the hills showed in the great expanse as the light wind lessened, allowing the surface to become glass-like, revealing also the twisted roots and dead branches of trees long inundated in forming the big basin of water.

Evidently only a few men were working in the hills; the descent of the logs was a thing spaced by many minutes, and the booming of the splash struck forth into the hills to be echoed and re-echoed. Houston stared gloomily at the skid, at the lake and the small parcel of logs drifting there.

"All for nothing," came at last. "It takes about three logs to make one—the way they're working."

"*Oui*! But M'sieu Houston shall learn."

Barry did not answer. He had learned a great deal already. He knew enough to realize that his new effort must be a clean sweep,—from the manager down. Distrust had enveloped him completely; even to the last lumberjack must the camp be cleaned, and the start made anew with a crew upon whom he could depend for honesty, at least. How the rest of the system was to work out, he did not know. How he was to sell the lumber which he intended milling, how he was to look after both the manufacturing and the disposing of his product was something beyond him, just at this moment. But there would be a way; there must be. Besides, there was Ba'tiste, heavy-shouldered, giant Ba'tiste, leaning over the side of the wagon, whistling and chiding the faithful old Golemar, and some way Houston felt that he would be an ally always.

The wagon had turned into the deeper forest now redolent with the heavy odor of the coniferous woods, and Ba'tiste straightened. Soon he was talking and pointing,—now to describe the spruce and its short, stubby, upturned needles; the lodgepole pines with their straighter, longer leaves and more brownish, scaly bark; the Englemann spruce; the red fir and limber pine; each had its characteristic, to be pointed out in the simple words of the big Canadian, and to be catalogued by the man at his side. A moment before, they had been only pines, only so many trees. Now each was different, each had its place in the mind of the man who studied them with a new interest and a new enthusiasm, even though they might fall, one after another, into the maw of the saw for the same purpose.

"They are like people, *oui!*" Old Ba'tiste was gesticulating. "They have their, what-you-say, make-ups. The lodgepole, he is like the man who runs up and looks on when the crowd, eet gathers about some one who has been hurt. He waits until there had been a fire, and then he comes in and grows first, along with the aspens, so he can get all the room he wants. The spruce, he is like a woman, yes, *oui.* He looks better than the rest—but he is not. Sometime, he is not so good. Whoa!"

The road had narrowed to a mere trail; Ba'tiste tugged on the reins, and motioning to Barry, left the wagon, pulling forth an axe and heavy, cross-cut saw as he did so. A half-hour later, Golemar preceding them, they were deep in the forest. Ba'tiste stopped and motioned toward a tall spruce.

"See?" he ordered, as he nicked it with his axe, "you cut heem as far above the ground as he is thick through. Now, first, the undercut."

"Looks like an overcut to me."

"Oh, ho! Ah, *oui,* so eet is! But eet is called the undercut. Eet makes the tree fall the way you want heem!"

The axe gleamed in blow after blow. A deep incision appeared in the trunk of the tree, and at the base of it Ba'tiste started the saw, Barry working on the other end with his good arm. Ten minutes of work and they switched to the other side. Here no "undercut" was made; the saw bit into the bark and deep toward the heart of the tree in a smooth, sharp line that progressed farther, farther—

"*Look out!*"

A crackling sound had come from above. Ba'tiste abandoned

the saw, and with one great leap caught Houston and pulled him far to one side, as with a roar, the spruce seemed to veritably disintegrate, its trunk spreading in great, splintered slabs, and the tree proper crashing to the ground in the opposite direction to which it should have fallen, breaking as it came. A moment Ba'tiste stood, with his arm still about the younger man, waiting for the dead branches, severed from other trees, to cease falling, and the disturbed needles and dust of the forest to settle. Then, pulling his funny little knit cap far down over his straggly hair, he came forth, to stand in meditation upon the largest portion of the shattered tree.

"Eet break up like an ice jam!" came at last. "That tree, he is not made of wood. Peuff! He is of glass!"

Barry joined him, studying the splintered fragments of the spruce, suddenly to bend forward in wonderment.

"That's queer. Here's a railroad spike driven clear into the heart."

"Huh? What's that?" Ba'tiste bent beside him to examine the rusty spike, then hurried to a minute examination of the rest of the tree. "And another," came at last. "And more!"

Four heavy spikes had revealed themselves now, each jutting forth at a place where the tree had split. Ba'tiste straightened.

"Ah, *oui*! Eet is no wonder! See? The spike, they have been in the tree for mebbe one, two, t'ree year. And the tree, he is not strong. When the winter come, last year, he split inside, from the frost, where the spike, he spread the grain. But the split, he does not show. When we try to cut heem down and the strain come, blooey, he, what-you-say, bust!"

"But why the spikes?"

"Wait!" Ba'tiste, suddenly serious, turned away into the woods, to go slowly from tree to tree, to dig at them with his knife, to squint and stare, to shin a few feet up a trunk now and then, examining every protuberance, every round, bulbous scar. At last he shouted, and Houston hurried to him, to find the giant digging excitedly at a lodgepole. "I have foun' another!"

The knife, deep in the tree, had scratched on metal. Five minutes more and they had discovered a third one, farther away. Then a fourth, a fifth; soon the number had run to a score, all within a small radius. Ba'tiste, more excited than ever, ranged off into the woods, leaving Barry to dig at the trees about him and to discover even more metal buried in the hearts of the standing lumber. For an hour he was gone, to return at last and stand staring about him.

"The spike, they are all in this little section," he said finally. "I have cruise' all about here—there are no more."

"But why should trees grow spikes?"

"Ah, why? So that saws will break at the right time! Eet is easy for the iron hunter at the mill to look the other way— eef he knows what the boss want. Eet is easy for the sawyer to step out of the way while the blade, he hit a spike!"

A long whistle traveled over Houston's lips. This was the explanation of broken saws, just at the crucial moment!

"Simple, isn't it?" he asked caustically. "Whenever it's necessary for an 'accident' to happen, merely send out into the woods for a load of timber from a certain place."

"Then the iron hunter—the man who look for metal in the wood—he look some other place. Beside," and Ba'tiste looked almost admiringly at a spike-filled tree. "Eet is a good job. The spike, they are driven deep in the wood, they are punched away in, so the bark, eet will close over them. If the iron hunter is not, what-you-say, full of pepper, and if he is lazy, then he not find heem, whether he want to or not. M'sieu Thayer, he have a head on him."

"Then Thayer—"

"Why not?"

"But why? He was the only man on the job out here. He didn't have to fill a whole section of a forest full of spikes when he wanted to break a saw or cause me trouble."

"Ah, no. But M'sieu—that is, whoever did eet—maybe he figure on the time when you yourself try to run the mill. Eh?"

"Well, if he did," came sharply, "he's figured on this exact moment. I've seen enough, Ba'tiste. I'm going to Denver and contract myself an entirely new crew. Then I'm coming back to drop this masquerade I've been carrying on—and if you'll help me—run this place myself. Thayer's out—from the minute I can get a new outfit. I'm not going to take any chances. When he goes, the whole bunch here goes with him!"

"Ah, *oui*!" Ba'tiste grinned with enthusiasm. "You said a what-you-say—large bite! Now," he walked toward the saw, "we shall fell a tree that shall not split."

"If you don't mind, I'd rather go back and look around the place. I want to get lined up on everything before I start to Denver."

"Ah, *oui*." Together, led by the wolf-dog, they made their

Courtney Ryley Cooper

way to the wagon again, once more to skirt the lake and to start down the narrow roadway leading beside the flume. A half-hour more and there came the sound of hammers and of saws. They stopped, and staring through the scraggly trees, made out the figures of half a dozen men busily at work upon the erection of a low, rambling building. All about them were vast piles of lumber, two-by-fours, scantlings, boardings, shingles,—everything that possibly could be needed in the building of not one, but many structures. Ba'tiste nodded.

"The new mill."

"Yes. Probably being built out of my lumber. It's a cinch they didn't transport it all the way from Tabernacle."

"Nor pay M'sieu Houston. Many things can happen when one is the manager."

Barry made no answer. For another mile they drove in silence, at last to come into the clearing of Barry's mill, with its bunk house, its cook house, its diminutive commissary, its mill and kilns and sheds. Houston leaped from the wagon to start a census and to begin his preparations for a cleaning-out of the whole establishment. But at the door of the commissary he whirled, staring. A buggy was just coming over the brow of the little hill which led to the mill property. Some one had called to him,—a woman whose voice had caused him to start, then, a second later, to go running forward.

She was beside Thayer in the buggy, leaning forth, one hand extended as Barry hurried toward her, her black eyes flashing eagerness, her full, yet cold lips parted, her olive-skinned cheeks enlivened by a flush of excitement as Houston came to her, forgetful of the sneer of the man at her side, forgetful of the staring Ba'tiste in the background, forgetful of his masquerade, of everything.

"Agnes!" he gasped. "Why did you—"

"I thought—" and the drawling voice of Fred Thayer had a suddenly sobering effect on Houston, "that you weren't hurt very bad. Your memory came back awful quick, didn't it? I thought she'd bring you to your senses!"

CHAPTER IX

Houston pretended not to hear the remark. The woman in the buggy was holding forth her hands to him and he assisted her to the ground.

"Well," she asked, in a sudden fawning manner, "aren't you glad to see me, Barry? Aren't you going to kiss me?"

"Of course." He took her in his arms. "I—I was so surprised, Agnes. I never thought of you—"

"Naturally you didn't." It was Thayer again. "That's why I sent for her. Thought you'd get your memory back when—"

"I've had my memory for long enough—" Houston had turned upon him coldly—"to know that from now on I'll run this place. You're through!"

"Barry!" The woman had grasped his arm. "Don't talk like that. You don't know what you're saying!"

"Please, Agnes—"

"Let him rave, if that's the way he wants to repay faithfulness."

"Wait until I've talked to you, Barry. You haven't had time to think. You've jumped at conclusions. Fred just thought that I could—"

"This hasn't anything to do with you, Agnes. There hasn't been anything wrong with me. My brain's been all right; I've known every minute what I've been doing. This man's crooked, and I know he's crooked. I needed time, and I shammed forgetfulness. I've gotten the information I need now—and I'm repeating that he's through! And every one else in this camp goes with him!"

"I'm not in the habit of taking insults! I—"

Thayer moved forward belligerently, one hand reaching toward a cant hook near by. But suddenly he ceased. Ba'tiste, quite naturally, had strolled between them.

"M'sieu Houston have a broke' arm," had come very quietly. Thayer grunted.

"Maybe that's the reason he thinks he can insult every one around here."

Ba'tiste looked down upon him, as a Newfoundland would look upon a snapping terrier.

"M'sieu Houston insult nobody."

"But—"

The voice of the big man rose to a roar.

"Ba'teese say, M'sieu Houston insult nobody. Un'stan'? Ba'teese say that! Ba'teese got no broke' arm!"

"Who is this man?" The woman had turned angrily toward Barry; "What right has he to talk this way? The whole thing's silly, as far as I can see, Barry. This man, whoever he is, has been stuffing you full of stories. There—"

"This man, Agnes," and Barry Houston's voice carried a quality he never before had used with Agnes Jierdon, "is the best friend I ever had. You'll realize it before long. He not only has saved my life, but he's going to help me save my business. I want you to know him and to like him."

A quick smile flashed over the full lips.

"I didn't know, Barry. Pardon me."

Houston turned to the introduction, while Agnes Jierdon held forth a rather limp hand and while Ba'tiste, knit cap suddenly pulled from straggly gray hair, bent low in acknowledgment. Thayer, grumbling under his breath, started away. Houston went quickly toward him.

"You understood me?"

"Perfectly. I'm fired. I was good enough for your father, but you know more than he did. I was—"

"We won't go into that."

"There's nothing about it that I'm ashamed of."

Still the sneer was there, causing Barry's bandaged arm to ache for freedom and strength. "I don't have to go around hiding my past."

Houston bit down a retort and forced himself to the question:

"How long will it take you to get out of here?"

"I'll be out to-night. I don't stay where I'm not wanted. Needn't think I'll hang around begging you for a job. There are plenty of 'em, for men like me."

"One that I know of, in particular. I asked you when you could get out."

"An hour, if you're so impatient about it. But I want my check first."

"You'll get it, and everybody else connected with you. So you might as well give the word."

For a moment, Thayer stared at him in malignant hate, his gnarled hands twisting and knotting. Then, with a sudden impulse, he turned away toward the mill. A moment later the whistle blew and the saws ceased to snarl. Barry turned back to Agnes and Ba'tiste. The woman caught impulsively at his arm.

"Where on earth am I going to live, Barry?" she questioned. "I don't want to go back to town. And I can't stay in this deserted place, if every one is leaving it."

"I'll keep the cook. She can fix you a room in one of the cottages and stay there with you. However, it would be best to go back."

"But I won't." She shook her head with an attempt at levity. "I've come all this distance, worried to death every moment over you, and now I'm going to stay until I'm sure that everything's all right. Besides, Barry," she moved close to him, "you'll need me. Won't you? Haven't I always been near you when you've needed me? And aren't you taking on the biggest sort of job now?"

Houston smiled at her. True, she had always been near in time of trouble and it was only natural that now—

"Of course," came his answer. "Come, I'll have you made comfortable in the cottage." Then, as he started away, "May I see you, Ba'tiste, sometime to-night?"

"Ah, *oui*." The Canadian was moving toward his wagon and the waiting dog. "In the cabin."

Three hours later, the last of the men paid off, Agnes installed in the best of three little cottages in care of the motherly old cook, Barry Houston approached the door of Ba'tiste's cabin, the wolf-dog, who had picked him up a hundred yards away, trotting beside him. There was a light within; in the shadows by the grave, a form moved,—old Lost Wing. Medaine was there, then. Barry raised his hand to knock,—and halted. His name had been mentioned angrily; then again,—followed by the voice of the girl:

"I don't know what it is, Ba'tiste. Fred wouldn't tell me, except that it was something too horrible for me to know. And I simply can't do what you say. I can't be pleasant to him when I feel this way."

"But—"

"Oh, I know. I want to be fair, and I try to be. I speak to him when I meet him; isn't that enough? We're not old friends; we're hardly even acquaintances. And if there is something in his past to be ashamed of, isn't it best that we simply remain that way? I—"

Then she ceased. Houston had knocked on the door. A

second later, he entered the cabin, to return Medaine Robinette's cool but polite greeting in kind, and to look apprehensively toward Ba'tiste Renaud. But the old man's smile was genuine.

"We have been talk' about you, *oui*, yes!" he said. "Eh, Medaine?"

It was one of his thrusts. The girl colored, then turned toward the door.

"I'm afraid I've stayed longer than I intended," she apologized. "It's late. Good night."

Then she was gone. Houston looked at Ba'tiste, but the old French-Canadian merely waved a big hand.

"Woman," he said airily, "peuff! She is strange. Eet is nothing. Eet will pass. Now," as though the subject had been dismissed, "what mus' Ba'teese do?"

"At the mill? I wish, if you don't mind, that you'd guard it for me. I'm going to Denver on the morning train to hire a new crew. I don't want Thayer to do anything to the mill in my absence."

"Ah, *oui*. It shall be. You will sleep here?"

"If you don't mind? It's nearer Tabernacle."

"Bon—good! Golemar!" And the dog scratched at the door. "Come, we shall go to the mill. We are the watchmen, yes?"

"But I didn't mean for you to start to-night. I just thought—"

"There is no time like the minute," answered the Canadian

quietly. "To-night, you shall be Ba'teese, *oui*, yes. Ba'teese shall be you."

Pulling his knit cap on his head, he went out into the darkness and to the guardianship of the mill that belonged— to a man who looked like his Pierre. As for Houston, the next morning found him on the uncomfortable red cushions of the smoking car as the puffing train pulled its weary, way through the snowsheds of Crestline Mountain, on the way over the range. Evening brought him to Denver, and the three days which followed carried with them the sweaty smell of the employment offices and the gathering of a new crew. Then, tired, anxious with an eagerness that he never before had known, he turned back to the hills.

Before, in the days agone, they had been only mountains, reminders of an eruptive time in the cooling of the earth,—so many bumpy places upon a topographical railroad map. But now,—now they were different. They seemed like home. They were the future. They were the housing place of the wide spaces where the streams ran through green valleys, where the sagebrush dotted the plateau plains, and where the world was a thing with a rim about it; hills soft blue and brown and gray and burning red in the sunlight, black, crumpled velvet beneath the moon and stars; hills where the pines grew, where his life awaited him, a new thing to be remolded nearer to his own desires, and where lived Ba'tiste, Agnes—and Medaine.

Houston thought of her with a sudden cringing.

In that moment as he stood outside the door of Ba'tiste's cabin, he had heard himself sealed and delivered to oblivion as far as she was concerned. He was only an acquaintance— one with a grisly shadow in his past—and it was best that he remain such. Grudgingly, Barry admitted the fact to himself, as he sat once more in the red-plush smoking car, surrounded by heavy-shouldered, sodden-faced men, his new crew, en route to Empire Lake. It was best. There was Agnes, with her debt of gratitude to be paid and with her affection for him, which in its blindness could not discern the fact that it was repaid only as a sense of duty. There was the fight to be made,—and the past. Houston shuddered with the thought of it. Things were only as they should be; grimly he told himself that he had erred in even thinking of happiness such as comes to other men. His life had been drab and gray; it must remain so.

Past the gleaming lakes and eternal banks of snow the train crawled to the top of the world at Crestline, puffed and clattered through the snowsheds, then clambered down the mountain side to Tabernacle. With his dough-faced men about him, Houston sought transportation, at last to obtain it, then started the journey to the mill.

Into the canon and to the last rise. Then a figure showed before him, a gigantic form, running and tumbling through the underbrush at one side of the road, a dog bounding beside him. It was Ba'tiste, excited, red-faced, his arms waving like windmills, his voice booming even from a distance:

"M'sieu Houston! M'sieu Houston! Ba'teese have fail! Ba'teese no good! He watch for you—he is glad you come! Ba'teese ashame'! Ashame'!"

He had reached the wagon now, panting, still striving to talk and failing for lack of breath, his big hands seeking to fill in the spaces where words had departed. Houston leaned toward him, gripping him by a massive shoulder.

"What's happened? What's—"

"Ba'teese ashame'!" came again between puffs of the big lungs. "Ba'teese watch one, two, t'ree night. Nothin' happen. Ba'teese think about his lost trap. He think mebbe there is one place where he have not look'. He say to Golemar he will go for jus' one, two hour. Nobody see, he think. So he go. And he come back. Blooey! Eet is done! Ba'teese have fail!"

"But what, Ba'tiste? It wasn't your fault. Don't feel that way about it? Has anything happened to Agnes?"

"No. The mill."

"They've—?"

"Look!"

They had reached the top of the rise. Below them lay something which caused Barry Houston to leap to his feet unmindful of the jolting wagon, to stand weaving with white-gripped hands, to stare with suddenly deadened eyes—

Upon a blackened, smoldering mass of charred timbers and twisted machinery. The remainder of all that once had been his mill!

CHAPTER X

Words would not come for a moment. Houston could only stare and realize that his burden had become greater than ever. In the wagons behind him were twenty men, guaranteed at least a month of labor, and now there was nothing to provide it. The mill was gone; the blade was still hanging in its sockets, a useless, distempered thing; the boiler was bent and blackened, the belting burned; the carriages and muley saws and edgers and trimmers were only so much junk. He turned at last to Ba'tiste, to ask tritely what he knew could not be answered:

"But how did it happen, Ba'tiste? Didn't any one see?"

The Canadian shrugged his shoulders.

"Ba'teese come back. Eet is done."

"Let's see Agnes. Maybe she can tell us something."

But the woman, her arms about Houston's neck, could only announce hysterically that she had seen the mill burning, that she had sought help and had failed to find it.

"Then you noticed no one around the place?"

"Only Ba'tiste."

"But that was an hour or so before."

The big French-Canadian had moved away, to stand in doleful contemplation of the charred mass. The voice of Agnes Jierdon sank low:

"I don't know, Barry. I don't want to accuse—"

"You don't mean—"

"All I know is that I saw him leave the place and go over the hill. Fifteen minutes later, I saw the mill burning and ran down there. All about the place rags were burning and I could smell kerosene. That's all I saw. But in the absence of any one else, what should a person think?"

Houston's lips pressed tight. He turned angrily, the old grip of suspicion upon him,—suspicion that would point in time of stress to every one about him, suspicion engendered by black days of hopelessness, of despair. But in an instant, it all was gone; the picture of Ba'tiste Renaud, standing there by the embers, the honesty of his expression of sorrow, the slump of his shoulders, while the dog, unnoticed, nuzzled its cold nose in a limp hand, was enough to wipe it all out forever. Houston's eyes went straight to those of Agnes Jierdon and centered there.

"Agnes," came slowly, "I want to ask a favor. No matter what may happen, no matter what you may think personally, there is one man who trusts me as much as you have trusted me, and whom I shall trust in return. That man is Ba'tiste Renaud, my friend. I hope you can find a friend in him too; but if you can't, please, for me, never mention it."

"Why, of course not, Barry." She laughed in an embarrassed manner and drew away from him. "I just thought I'd tell you what I knew. I didn't have any idea you were such warm comrades. We'll forget the whole incident."

"Thank you." Then to Ba'tiste he went, to bang him on the shoulder, and with an effort to whirl him about. "Well!" he demanded, in an echo of Ba'tiste's own thundering manner, "shall we stand here and weep? Or—"

"Eet was my fault!" The French-Canadian still stared at the ruins. "Eet is all Ba'teese' fault—"

"I thought you were my friend, Ba'tiste."

"*Sacre*! I am."

"Then show it! We'll not be able to make a case against the firebugs—even though you and I may be fairly sure who did it. Anyway, it isn't going to break us. I've got about fifteen thousand in the bank. There's enough lumber around here to build a new saw-shed of a sort, and money to buy a few saws, even if we can't have as good a place as we had before. We can manage. And I need help—I won't be able to move without you. But—"

"*Oui*?"

"But," and Barry smiled at him, "if you ever mention any responsibility for this thing again—you're fired. Do we understand each other?"

Very slowly the big trapper turned and looked down into the frank, friendly eyes of the younger man. He blinked slightly, and then one tremendous arm encircled Houston's shoulder for just a moment. At last a smile came, to grow stronger.

Courtney Ryley Cooper

The grip about the shoulders tightened, suddenly to give way to a whanging blow, as Batiste, jovial now, drew away, pulled back his shoulders and squared himself as though for some physical encounter.

"Ah, *oui!*" He bellowed. "*Oui, oui, oui! Bon*—good! Ba'teese, he un'stan'. Now what you want me to do?"

"Take this bunch of men and turn to at clearing away this wreckage. Then," and he smiled his confidence at Renaud, "make your plans for the building of a saw-shed. That is—if you really want to go through with it?"

"Ah, *oui—oui!*" The Canadian waved his arms excitedly and summoned his men. For a moment, Barry stood watching, then returning to Agnes, escorted her toward her cottage.

"Don't you think," he asked, as they walked along, "that you'd better be going back? This isn't just the place for a woman, Agnes."

"Why not?"

"Because—well for one thing, this is a man's life out here, not a woman's. There's no place for you—nothing to interest you or hold you. I can't guarantee you any company except that of a cook—or some one like that."

"But Mr. Thayer—" and Houston detected a strange tone in the voice—"spoke of a very dear friend of yours, in whom I might be greatly interested."

"A friend of mine?"

"Yes—a Miss Robinette. Fred said that she was quite interested in you."

Houston laughed.

"She is—by the inverse ratio. So much, in fact, that she doesn't care to be anywhere near me. She knows—" and he sobered, "that there's something—back there."

"Indeed?" They had reached the cottage and the subject was discontinued. Agnes lingered a moment on the veranda. "I suppose I'm never to see anything of you?"

"That's just it, Agnes. It makes me feel like a cad to have you out here—and then not to be able to provide any entertainment for you. And, really, there's no need to worry about me. I'm all right—with the exception of this broken arm. And it'll be all right in a couple of weeks. Besides, there's no telling what may happen. You can see from the burning of this mill that there isn't any love lost between Thayer and myself."

"Why, Barry! You don't think he had anything to do with it?"

"I know he did. Directly or indirectly, he was back of it. I haven't had much of a chance to talk to you, Agnes, but this much is a certainty: Thayer is my enemy, for business reasons. I know of no other. He believes that if he can make the going rough enough for me that I'll quit, lease him my stumpage, and let him go into business for himself. So far, he hasn't had much luck—except to tie me up. He may beat me; I don't know. Then again, he may not. But in the meanwhile, you can see, Agnes, that the battlefield is going to be no place for a woman."

"But, Barry, you're wrong. I think you've done an injustice to—"

"Please don't tell me that, Agnes. I put so much faith in your beliefs. But in this case, I've heard it from his own lips—I've seen his telegrams. I know!"

The woman turned quickly. For a moment she examined, in an absent sort of way, the blossoms of a climbing rose, growing, quite uninvited, up the porch pillar of the cottage. Then:

"Maybe you're right, Barry. Probably I will go away. But I want to be sure that you're all right first."

"Would you care to go to the village to-night? There's a picture show there—and we could at least get a dish of ice cream and some candy."

"I think not," came the answer in a tired voice. "It's so far; besides, all this excitement has given me a headache. Go back to your work and forget about me. I think that I'll go to bed immediately I've had something to eat."

"You're not ill?"

"Only a headache—and with me, bed is always the best place for that. I suppose you'll go to Denver in the morning for new saws?"

"Yes."

"Then I'll wait until you return before I make up my mind. Good-by." She bent forward to be kissed, and Barry obeyed the command of her lips with less of alacrity than ever before. Nor could he tell the reason. Five minutes more and he was back at the mill, giving what aid he could with his uninjured arm.

Night, and he traveled with Ba'tiste to his cabin, only to fret nervously about the place and at last to strike out once more, on foot, for the lumber camp. He was worried, nervous; in a vague way he realized that he had been curt, almost brusque, with a woman for whom he felt every possible gratitude and consideration. Nor had he inquired about her when work had ended for the day. Had the excuse of a headache been made only to cover feelings that had been deeply injured? Or had it meant a blind to veil real, serious illness? For three years, Barry Houston had known Agnes Jierdon in day-to-day association. But never had he remembered her in exactly the light that he had seen her to-day. There had been a strangeness about her, a sharpness that he could not understand.

He stopped just at the entrance to the mill clearing and looked toward the cottage. It was darkened. Barry felt that without at least the beckoning of a light to denote the wakefulness of the cook, he could not in propriety go there, even for an inquiry regarding the condition of the woman whom he felt that some day he would marry. Aimlessly he wandered about, staring in the moonlight at the piled-up remains of his mill, then at last he seated himself on a stack of lumber, to rest a moment before the return journey to Ba'tiste's cabin. But suddenly he tensed. A low whistle had come from the edge of the woods, a hundred yards away, and Barry listened attentively for its repetition, but it did not come. Fifteen minutes he waited, then rose, the better to watch two figures that had appeared for just a moment silhouetted in the moonlight at the bald top of a small hill. A man and a woman were walking close together,—the woman, it seemed, with her head against the man's shoulder; the man evidently with his arm about her.

There was no time for identities. A second more and they had faded into the shadows. Barry rose and started toward the darkened cottage, only to turn again into the road.

"Foolishness!" he chided himself as he plodded along. "She

doesn't know any one but Thayer—and what if she does? It's none of my business. She's the one who has the claim on me; I have none on her!"

And with this decision he walked on. A mile—two. Then a figure came out of the woods just ahead of him, cut across the road and detoured into the scraggly hills on the other side, without noticing the approaching Houston in the shadows. But Barry had been more fortunate. The moonlight had shown full on the man's lean face and gangling form; it was undoubtedly Fred Thayer. He was still in the neighborhood, then.

Had he been the man in the woods,—the one who had stood silhouetted on the hill top? Barry could only guess. Again he chided himself for his inquisitiveness and walked on. Almost to Ba'tiste's cabin he went; at last to turn from the road at the sound of hoofbeats, then to stare as Medaine Robinette, on horseback, passed him at a trot, headed toward her home, the shadowy Lost Wing, on his calico pony, straggling along in the rear. The next morning he went to Denver, still wondering, as he sought to make himself comfortable on the old red plush seats, wondering whether the girl he had seen in the forest with the man he now felt sure was Fred Thayer had been Agnes Jierdon or Medaine Robinette, whom, in spite of her coldness to him, in spite of her evident distaste and revulsion that was so apparent in their meetings, had awakened within him a thing he had believed, in the drabness of his gray, harassed life, could never exist,—the thrill and the yearnings of love.

It was a question which haunted him during the days in which he cut into his bank account with the purchase of the bare necessities of a sawmill. It was a question which followed him back to Tabernacle, thence across country to camp. But it was one that was not to be answered. Things had happened again.

Ba'tiste was not at the mill, where new foundations had appeared in Houston's absence. A workman pointed vaguely upward, and Barry hurried on toward the lake, clambering up the hill nearest the clearing, that he might take the higher and shorter road.

He found no Ba'tiste but there was something else which held Houston's interest for a moment and which stopped him, staring wonderingly into the distance. A new skidway had made its appearance on the side of the jutting mountain nearest the dam. Logs were tumbling downward in slow, but steady succession, to disappear, then to show themselves, bobbing jerkily outward toward the center of the lake. That skidway had not been there before. Certainly, work at the mill had not progressed to such an extent that Ba'tiste could afford to start cutting timber already. Houston turned back toward the lower camp road, wondering vaguely what it all could mean, striving to figure why Ba'tiste should have turned to logging operations instead of continuing to stress every workman's ability on the rebuilding of the burned structure. A mile he went—two—then halted.

A thunderous voice was booming belligerently from the distance:

"You lie—un'stan'? Ba'teese say you lie—if you no like eet, jus'—what-you-say—climb up me! Un'stan'? Climb up me!"

Houston broke into a run, racing along the flume with constantly increasing speed as he heard outburst after outburst from the giant trapper, interjected by the lesser sounds of argumentative voices in reply. Faintly he heard a woman's voice, then Ba'tiste's in sudden command:

"Go on—you no belong here. Ba'tiste, he handle this. Go 'long!"

Faster than ever went Barry Houston, at last to make the turn of the road as it followed the flume, and to stop, breathless, just in time to escape colliding with the broad back of the gigantic Canadian, squared as he was, half across the road. Facing him were five men with shovels and hammers, workmen of the Blackburn camp, interrupted evidently in the building of some sort of contraption which led away into the woods. Houston looked more closely, then gasped. It was another flume; they were making a connection with his own; already water had been diverted from the main flume and was flowing down the newly boarded conduit which led to the Blackburn mill. A lunge and he had taken his place beside Renaud.

"What's this mean?" he demanded angrily, to hear his words echoed by the booming voice of his big companion:

"Ah, *oui*! Yes—what this mean? Huh?"

The foreman looked up caustically.

"I've told you about ten times," he answered, addressing himself to Ba'tiste. "We're building a connection on our flume."

"Our flume?" Houston gasped the words. "Where do you get that 'our' idea? I own this flume and this lake and this flume site—"

"If your name's Houston, I guess you do," came the answer. "But if you can read and write, you ought to know that while you may own it, you don't use it. That's our privilege from now on, in cold black and white. As far as the law is concerned, this is our flume, and our water, and our lake, and our woods back there. And we're going to use all of 'em, as much as we please—and it's your business to stay out of our way!"

Courtney Ryley Cooper

CHAPTER XI

The statement took Houston off his feet for a moment; but recovery came just as quickly, a recoil with the red splotches of anger blazing before his eyes, the surge of hot blood sweeping through his veins, the heat of conflict in his brain. His good hand clenched. A leap and he had struck the foreman on the point of the chin, sending him reeling backward, while the other men rushed to his assistance.

"That's my answer to you!" shouted Houston. "This is my flume and—"

"Run tell Thayer!" shouted the foreman, and then with recovering strength, he turned for a cant hook. But Ba'tiste seized it first, and with a great wrench, threw it far out of the way. Then, like some great, human trip hammer, he swung into action, spinning Houston out of the way as he went forward, his big fists churning, his voice bellowing his call of battle:

"Climb up me! Climb up me!"

The foreman stooped for a club,—and rose just in time to be lifted even higher, at the point of Ba'tiste's right fist then to drop in a lump. Then they were all about him, seeking for an opening, fists pounding, heavy shoes kicking at shins, while in the rear, Houston, scrambling around with his one arm, almost happy with the enthusiasm of battle, swung hard and often at every opportunity, then swerved and covered until he could bring his fist into action again.

The fight grew more intense with a last spurt, then died out, as Ba'tiste, seizing the smallest of the men, lifted him bodily and swinging him much after the fashion of a sack of meal, literally used him as a battering ram against the rest of the attacking forces. For a last time, Houston hit a skirmisher and was hit in return. Then Ba'tiste threw his human weapon from him, straight into the mass of men whom he had driven back for a second, tumbling them all in a scrambling, writhing heap at the edge of the flume.

"Climb up me!" he bellowed, as they struggled to their feet. "Ah, *oui*?" And the big arms moved threateningly. "Climb up me!"

But the invitation was not accepted. Bloody, eyes discolored, mouth and nose steadily swelling, the foreman moved away with his battered crew, finally to disappear in the forest. Ba'tiste reached for the cant hook, and balancing it lightly in one hand, sought a resting place on the edge of the flume. Houston sat beside him.

"What on earth can it all mean?" he asked, after a moment of thought.

"They go back—get more men. Mebbe they think they whip us, *oui*? Yes? Ba'teese use this, nex' time." He balanced the cant hook, examining it carefully as though for flaws which might cause it to break in contact with a human target. Barry went on:

"I was talking about the flume. You heard what that fellow

said—that they had the woods, the lake and the flume to use as they pleased? How—"

"Mebbe they think they jus' take it."

"Which they can't. I'm going back to the camp and get more men."

"No." Ba'tiste grinned. "We got enough—you an' Ba'teese. I catch 'em with this. You take that club. If they get 'round me, you, what-you-say, pickle 'em off."

But the expected attack did not come. An hour they waited, and a hour after that. Still no crowd of burly men came surging toward them from the Blackburn camp, still no attempt was made to wrest from their possession the waterway which they had taken over as their rightful property.

Houston studied the flume.

"We'll have to get some men up here and rip out this connection," came at last. "They've broken off our end entirely."

"Ah, *oui*! But we will stay here. By'm'by, Medaine come. We will send her for men."

"Medaine? That was she I heard talking?"

"*Oui*. She had come to ask me if she should bring me food. She was riding. Ba'teese sen' her away. But she say she come back to see if Ba'teese is all right."

Houston shook his head.

"That's good. But I'm afraid that you won't find her doing anything to help me out."

"She will help Ba'teese," came simply from the big man, as the iron-bound cant hook was examined for the fiftieth time. "Why they no come, huh?"

"Search me. Do you suppose they've given it up? It's a bluff on their part, you know, Ba'tiste. They haven't any legal right to this land or flume or anything else; they just figured that my mill was burned and that I wouldn't be in a position to fight them. So they decided to take over the flume and try to force us into letting them have it."

"Here comes somebody!" Ba'tiste's grip tightened about the cant hook and he rose, squaring himself. Houston seized the club and stood waiting a few feet in the rear, in readiness for any one who might evade the bulwark of blows which Ba'tiste evidently intended to set up. Far in the woods showed the shadowy forms of three men, approaching steadily and apparently without any desire for battle. Ba'tiste turned sharply. "Your eye, keep heem open. Eet may be a blind."

But Houston searched the woods in vain. There were no supporters following the three men, no deploying groups seeking to flank them. A moment more, and Ba'tiste, with a sudden exclamation, allowed his cant hook to drop to the ground.

"Wade!"

"Who?" Houston came closer.

"Eet is Thayer and Wade, the sheriff from Montview, and his deputy. Peuff! Have he fool heem too?"

Closer they came, and the sheriff waved a hand in friendly greeting. Ba'tiste returned the gesture. Thayer, scowling, black-faced, dropped slightly to the rear, allowing the two officials to take the lead—and evidently do the talking. The sheriff grinned as he noticed the cant hook on the ground. Then he looked up at Ba'tiste Renaud.

"What's been going on here?"

"This man," Ba'tiste nodded grudgingly toward the angular form of Fred Thayer, "heem a what-you-say a big bomb. This my frien', M'sieu Houston. He own this flume. This Thayer's men, they try to jump it."

"From the looks of them," chuckled the sheriff, "you jumped them. They've got a young hospital over at camp. But seriously, Ba'tiste, I think you're on the wrong track. Thayer and Blackburn have a perfect right to this flume and to the use of the lake and what stumpage they want from the Houston woods."

"A right?" Barry went forward. "What right? I haven't given them—"

"You're the owner of the land, aren't you?"

"Yes, in a way. It was left to me conditionally."

"You can let it out and sell the stumpage if you want to?"

"Of course."

"Then, what are you kicking about?"

"I—simply on account of the fact that these men have no right to be on the land, or to use it in any way. I haven't given them permission."

"That's funny," the sheriff scratched his head; "they've just proved in court that you have."

"In court? I—?"

"Yeh. I've got an injunction in my pocket to prevent you from interfering with them. Judge Bardley gave it in Montview about an hour ago, and we came over by automobile."

"But why?"

"Why?" the sheriff stared at him. "When you give a man a lease, you have to live up to it in this country."

"But I've given no one—"

"Oh, show it to him, sheriff." Thayer came angrily forward. "No use to let him stand there and lie."

"That's what I want to see!" Houston squared himself grimly. "If you've got a lease, or anything else, I want to look at it."

"You know your own writing, don't you?" The sheriff was fishing in his pockets.

"Of course."

"You'd admit it if you saw it?"

"I'm not trying to hide anything. But I know that I've not given any lease, and I've not sold any stumpage and—"

"Then, what's this?" The sheriff had pulled two legal

documents from his pocket, and unfolding them, had shown Houston the bottom of each. Barry's eyes opened wide.

"That's—that's my signature," came at last.

"This one's the same, isn't it?" The second paper was shoved forward.

"Yes."

"Then I don't see what you're kicking about. Do you know any one named Jenkins, who is a notary public?"

"He works in my office in Boston."

"That's his writing, isn't it?"

"Yes."

"And his seal."

"I suppose so." Bewildered, Houston was looking at the papers with glazed eyes. "It looks like it."

"Then," and the sheriff's voice went brusque, "what right have you to try to run these men off of property for which you've given them a bona-fide lease, and to which you've just admitted your signature as genuine?"

"I've—I've given no lease. I—"

"Then look 'em over. If that isn't a lease to the lake and flume and flume site, and if the second one isn't a contract for stumpage at a dollar and a half a thousand feet,—well, then, I can't read."

"But I'm telling you that I didn't give it to them." Houston had reached for the papers with a trembling hand. "There's a fraud about it somewhere!"

"I don't see where there can be any fraud when you admit your signature, and there's a notary's seal attached."

"But there is! I can't tell you why—but—"

"Statements like that don't count in law. There are the papers and they're duly signed and you've admitted your signature. If there's any fraud about it, you've got the right to prove it. But in the meanwhile, the court's injunction stands. You've leased this land to these men, and you can't interfere with them. Understand?"

"All right." Houston moved hazily back, away from the flume site. Ba'tiste stood staring glumly, wondering, at the papers which had been returned to the sheriff. "But I know this, that it's a fakery—somehow—and I'll prove it. I have absolutely no memory of ever signing any such papers as that, or of even talking to any one about selling stumpage at a figure that you should know is ridiculous. Why, you can't even buy the worst kind of timber from the government at that price! I don't remember—"

"Didn't I tell you?" Thayer had turned to the sheriff. "There he goes pulling that loss of memory stunt again. That's one of his best little bets," he added sneering, "to lose his memory."

"I've never lost it yet!"

"No—then you can forget things awfully easy. Such as coming out here and pretending not to know who you were. Guess you forgot your identity for a minute, didn't you? Just like you forgot signing this lease and stumpage contract! Yeh, you're good at that—losing your memory. You never remember anything that happens. You can't even remember the night you murdered your own cousin, can you?"

"That's a—"

"See, sheriff? His memory's bad." All the malice and hate of pent-up enmity was in Fred Thayer's voice now. One gnarled hand went forward in accusation. "He can't even remember how he killed his own cousin. But if he can't, I can. Ask him about the time when he slipped that mallet in his pocket at a prize fight and then went on out with his cousin. Ask him what became of Tom Langdon after they left that prize fight. He won't be able to tell you, of course. He loses his memory; all he will be able to remember is that his father spent a lot of money and hired some good lawyers and got him out of it. He won't be able to tell you a thing about how his own cousin was found with his skull crushed in, and the bloody wooden mallet lying beside him—the mallet that this fellow had stolen the night before at a prize fight! He won't—"

White-hot with anger, Barry Houston lurched forward, to find himself caught in the arms of the sheriff and thrown back. He whirled,—and stopped, looking with glazed, deadened eyes into the blanched, horrified features of a girl who evidently had heard the accusation, a girl who stood poised in revulsion a moment before she turned, and, almost running, hurried to mount her horse and ride away. And the strength of anger left the muscles of Barry Houston. The red flame of indignation turned to a sodden, dead thing. He could only realize that Medaine Robinette now knew the story. That Medaine Robinette had heard him accused without a single statement given in his own behalf; that Medaine, the girl of his smoke-wreathed dreams, now fully and thoroughly believed him—a murderer!

CHAPTER XII

Dully Houston turned back to the sheriff and to the goggle-eyed Ba'tiste, trying to fathom it all. Weakly he motioned toward Thayer, and his words, when they came, were hollow and expressionless:

"That's a lie, Sheriff. I'll admit that I have been accused of murder. I was acquitted. You say that nothing counts but the court action—and that's all I have to say in my behalf. The jury found me not guilty. In regard—to this, I'll obey the court order until I can prove to the judge's satisfaction that this whole thing is a fraud and a fake. In the meanwhile—" he turned anxiously, almost piteously, "do you care to go with me, Ba'tiste?"

Heavily, silently, the French-Canadian joined him, and together they walked down the narrow road to the camp. Neither spoke for a long time. Ba'tiste walked with his head deep between his shoulders, and Houston knew that memories were heavy upon him, memories of his Julienne and the day that he came home to find, instead of a waiting wife, only a mound beneath the sighing pines and a stalwart cross above it. As for Houston, his own life had gone gray with the sudden recurrence of the past. He lived again the first days of it all, when life had been one constant repetition of questions, then solitude, questions and solitude, as the homicide squad brought him up from his cell to inquire about some new angle that they had come upon, to question him regarding his actions on the night of the death of Tom Langdon, then to send him back to "think it over" in the hope that the constant tangle of questions might cause him to change his story and give them an opening wedge through which they could force him to a confession. He lived again the black hours in the dingy courtroom, with its shadows and soot spots brushing against the window, the twelve blank-faced men in the jury box, and the witnesses, one after another, who went to the box in an effort to swear his life away. He went again through the agony of the new freedom—the freedom of a man imprisoned by stronger things than mere bars and cells of steel—when first he had gone into the world to strive to fight back to the position he had occupied before the pall of accusation had descended upon him, and to fight seemingly in vain. Friends had vanished, a father had gone to his grave, believing almost to the last that it had been his money and the astuteness of his lawyers that had obtained freedom for a guilty son, certainly not a self-evidence of innocence that had caused the twelve men to report back to the judge that they had been unable to force their convictions "beyond the shadow of a doubt." A nightmare had it been and a nightmare it was again, as drawn-featured, stoop-shouldered, suddenly old and haggard, Barry Houston walked down the logging road beside a man whose mind also had been recalled to thoughts of murder. A sudden fear went over the younger man; he wondered whether this great being who walked at his side had believed, and at last in desperation, he faced him.

"Well, Ba'tiste," came in strained tones, "I might as well hear it now as at any other time. They've about got me whipped, anyway, so you'll only be leaving a sinking ship."

"What you mean?" The French-Canadian stopped.

"Just the plain facts. I'm about at the end of my rope; my mill's all but gone, my flume is in the hands of some one else, my lake is leased, and Thayer can make as many inroads on my timber as he cares to, as long as he appeases the court by paying me the magnificent sum of a dollar and a half a thousand for it. So, you see, there isn't much left for me."

"What you do?"

"That depends entirely on you—and what effect that accusation made. If you're with me, I fight. If not—well frankly—I don't know."

"'Member the mill, when he burn down?"

"Yes."

"You no believe Ba'teese did heem. *Oui*, yes? Well, now I no believe either!"

"Honestly, Ba'tiste?" Houston had gripped the other man's arm. "You don't believe it? You don't—"

"Ba'teese believe M'sieu Houston. You look like my Pierre. My Pierre, he could do no wrong. Ba'teese satisfy."

It sent a new flow of blood through the veins of Barry Houston,—that simple, quiet statement of the old trapper. He felt again a surge of the fighting instinct, the desire to keep on and on, to struggle until the end, and to accept nothing except the bitterest, most absolute defeat. He quickened his pace, the French-Canadian falling in with him. His voice bore a vibrant tone, almost of excitement:

"I'm going back to Boston to-night. I'm going to find out

about this. I can get a machine at Tabernacle to take me over the range; it may save me time in catching a train at Denver. There's some fraud, Ba'tiste. I know it.—and I'll prove it if I can get back to Boston. We'll stop by the cottage down here and see Miss Jierdon; then I'm gone!"

"She no there. She, what-you-say, smash up 'quaintance with Medaine. She ask to go there and stay day or two."

"Then she'll straighten things out, Ba'tiste. I'm glad of it. She knows the truth about this whole thing—every step of the way. Will you tell her?"

"*Oui*. Ba'teese tell her—about the flume and M'sieu Thayer, what he say. But Ba'teese—"

"What?"

The trapper was silent a moment. At last:

"You like her, eh?"

"Medaine?"

"No—the other."

"A great deal, Ba'teese. She has meant everything to me; she was my one friend when I was in trouble. She even went on the stand and testified for me. What were you going to say?"

"Nothing," came the enigmatical reply. "Ba'teese will wait here. You go Boston to-night?"

"Yes."

And that night, in the moonlight, behind the rushing engine

of a motor car, Barry Houston once more rode the heights where Mount Taluchen frowned down from its snowy pinnacles, where the road was narrow and the turns sharp, and where the world beneath was built upon a scale of miniature. But this time, the drifts had faded from beside the highway; nodding flowers showed in the moonlight; the snow flurries were gone. Soon the downward grade had come and after that the straggling little town of Dominion. Early morning found Houston in Denver, searching the train schedules. That night he was far from the mountains, hurrying half across the continent in search of the thing that would give him back his birthright.

Weazened, wrinkle-faced little Jenkins met him at the office, to stare in apparent surprise, then to rush forward with well-simulated enthusiasm.

"You're back, Mr. Houston! I'm so glad. I didn't know whether to send the notice out to you in Colorado, or wire you. It just came yesterday."

"The notice? Of what?"

"The M. P. & S. L. call for bids. You've heard about it."

But Houston shook his head. Jenkins stared.

"I thought you had. The Mountain, Plains and Salt Lake Railroad. I thought you knew all about it."

"The one that's tunneling Carrow Peak? I've heard about the road, but I didn't know they were ready for bids for the western side of the mountain yet. Where's the notice?"

"Right on your desk, sir."

Abstractedly, Houston picked it up and glanced at the specifications,—for railroad ties by the million, for lumber, lathes, station-house material, bridge timbers, and the thousands of other lumber items that go into the making of a road. Hastily he scanned the printed lines, only at last to place it despondently in a pocket.

"Millions of dollars," he murmured. "Millions—for somebody!"

And Houston could not help feeling that it was for the one man he hated, Fred Thayer. The specifications called for freight on board at the spurs at Tabernacle, evidently soon to have competition in the way of railroad lines. And Tabernacle meant just one thing, the output of a mill which could afford to put that lumber at the given point cheaper then any other. The nearest other camp was either a hundred miles away, on the western side, or so far removed over the range in the matter of altitude that the freight rates would be prohibitive to a cheaper bid. Thayer, with his ill-gotten flume, with his lake, with his right to denude Barry Houston's forests at an insignificant cost, could out-bid the others. He would land the contract, unless—

"Jenkins!" Houston's voice was sharp, insistent. The weazened man entered, rubbing his hands.

"Yes, sir. Right here, sir."

"What contracts have we in the files?"

"Several, sir. One for mining timber stulls, logs, and that sort of thing, for the Machol Mine at Idaho Springs; one for the Tramway company in Denver for two thousand ties to be delivered in June; one for—"

"I don't mean that sort. Are there any stumpage contracts?"

"Only one, sir."

"One? What!"

"The one you signed, sir, to Thayer and Blackburn, just a week or so before you started out West. Don't you remember, sir; you signed it, together with a lease for the flume site and lake?"

"I signed nothing of the sort!"

"But you did, sir. I attested it. I'll show it to you in just a moment, sir. I have the copy right here."

A minute later, Barry Houston was staring down at the printed lines of a copy of the contract and lease which had been shown him, days before, out in the mountains of Colorado. Blankly he looked toward the servile Jenkins, awaiting the return of the documents, then toward the papers again.

"And I signed these, did I?"

"You certainly did, sir. It was about five o'clock in the afternoon. I remember it perfectly."

"You're lying!"

"I don't lie, sir. I attested the signature and saw you read both contracts. Pardon, sir, but if any one's lying, sir—it's yourself!"

CHAPTER XIII

Ten minutes after that, Barry Houston was alone in his office. Jenkins was gone, discharged; and Houston felt a sort of relief in the knowledge that he had departed. The last of the Thayer clan, he believed, had been cleaned out of his organization— and it was like lightening a burden to realize it.

That the lease and stumpage contract were fraudulent, Barry Houston was certain. Surely he had seen neither of them; and the signing must have been through some sort of trickery of which he was unaware. But would such a statement hold in court? Houston learned, a half-hour later, that it wouldn't, as he faced the family attorney, in his big, bleak, old-fashioned office.

"It's all right, Barry, for you to tell me that you didn't sign it," came the edict. "I'd believe you—because I feel sure you wouldn't lie to me. But it would be pretty thin stuff to tell to a jury. There is the contract and the lease in black and white. Both bear your signature which, you have declared in the presence of witnesses, to be genuine. Even when a man signs a paper while insane, it's a hard job to pull it back; and we certainly wouldn't have any witnesses who could swear that you had lost your reason."

"Nope," he concluded, giving the papers a flip, as though

disposing of the whole matter, "somebody has just worked the old sewing-machine racket on you—with trimmings. This is an adaptation of a game that is as old as the hills—the one where the solicitors would go up to a farmhouse, sell a man a sewing-machine or a cream separator at a ridiculous figure, let him sign what he thought was a contract to pay a certain amount a month for twelve months—and then take the promissory note which he really had signed down to the bank and discount it. Instead of a promissory note, they made this a contract and a lease. And just to make it good, they had their confederate, a legalized notary public, put his seal upon it as a witness. You can't remember when all this happened?"

"According to Jenkins—who put the notary seal on there—the whole thing was put over about a week or so before I left for the West. That's the date on them too. About that time, I remember, I had a good many papers to sign. A lot of legal stuff, if you'll remember, came up about father's estate, in which my signature was more of a form than anything else. I naturally suspected nothing, and in one or two instances signed without reading."

"And signed away your birthright—to this contract and lease. You did it with no intention of giving your land and flume and flume site away, that's true. If one of the men would be willing to confess to a conspiracy, it would hold water in court. Otherwise not. You've been bunked, and your signature is as legal and as binding as though you had read that contract and lease-form a hundred times over. So I don't see anything to do but to swallow your medicine with as little of a wry face as possible."

It was with this ultimatum that Houston turned again for the West, glad to be out of Boston, glad to be headed back once more for the mountains, in spite of the fact that the shadows of his life had followed him even there, that the ill luck which seemed to have been perched continuously on his shoulders for the past two years still hovered, like a vulture, above him. What he was going to do, how he could hope to combat the obstacles which had arisen was more than he could tell. He had gone into the West, believing, at worst, that he would be forced to become the general factotum of his own business. Now he found there was not even a business; his very foundations had been swept from beneath him, leaving only the determination, the grim, earnest resolution to succeed where all was failure and to fight to victory—but how?

Personally, he could not answer the question, and he longed for the sight of the shambling little station at Tabernacle, with Ba'tiste, in answer to the telegram he had sent from Chicago, awaiting him with the buggy from camp. And Ba'tiste was there, to boom at him, to call Golemar's attention to the fact that a visit to a physician in Boston had relieved the bandaged arm of all except the slightest form of a splint, and to literally lift Houston into the buggy, tossing his baggage in after him, then plump in beside him with excited happiness.

"*Bon*!" he rumbled. "It is good you are back. Ba'teese, he was lonely. Ba'teese, he was so excite' when he hear you come. He have good news!"

"About what?"

"The railroad. They are near' through with the tunnel. Now they shall start upon the main road to Salt Lake. And they shall need timbers—*beaucoup*! Ties and beams and materials! They have ask for bids. Ah, *oui*. Eet is, what-you-say, the swollen chance! M'sieu Houston shall bid lower than—"

"How, Ba'tiste?" Houston asked the question with a dullness that caused the aged trapper to turn almost angrily upon him.

"How? Is eet putty that you are made of? Is eet—but no, Ba'teese, he, what-you-say, misplace his head. You think there is no chance, eh? Mebbe not. Me'bbe—"

"I found a copy of that contract in our files. The clerk I had in the office was in the conspiracy. I fired him and closed everything up there; as far as a Boston end to the business is concerned, there is none. But the damage is done. My lawyer says that there is not a chance to fight this thing in court."

"Ah, *oui*. I expec' that much. But Ba'teese, he think, mebbe, of another way. Eh, Golemar?" He shouted to the dog, trotting, as usual, beside the buggy. "Mebbe we have a, what-you-say, punch of luck."

Then, silent, he leaned over the reins. Houston too was quiet, striving in vain to find a way out of the difficulties that beset him. At the end of half an hour he looked up in surprise. They no longer were on the way to the mill. The road had become rougher, hillier, and Houston recognized the stream and the aspen groves which fringed the highway leading to Ba'tiste's cabin. But the buggy skirted the cabin, at last to bring into sight a snug, well-built, pretty little cottage which Houston knew, instinctively, to be the home of Medaine Robinette. At the veranda, Ba'tiste pulled on the reins and alighted.

"Come," he ordered quietly.

"But—"

"She have land, and she have a part of the lake and a flume site."

Houston hung back.

"Isn't it a bad bet, Ba'tiste? Have you talked to her?"

"No—I have not seen her since the day—at the flume. She is here—Lost Wing is at the back of the cabin. We will talk to her, you and I. Mebbe, when the spring come, she will lease to you the lake and the flume site. Mebbe—"

"Very well." But Houston said it against his will. He felt, in the first place, that he would be presuming to ask it of her,—himself a stranger against whom had come the accusation of murder, hardly denied. Yet, withal, in a way, he welcomed the chance to see her and to seek to explain to her the deadly thrusts which Fred Thayer had sent against him. Then too a sudden hope came; Ba'tiste had said that Agnes Jierdon had become friendly with her; certainly she had told the truth and righted the wrongs of malicious treachery. He joined Ba'tiste with a bound. A moment more and the door had opened, to reveal Medaine, repressed excitement in her eyes, her features a trifle pale, her hand trembling slightly as she extended it to Ba'tiste. Houston she received with a bow,—forced, he thought. They went within, and Ba'tiste pulled his queer little cap from his head, to crush it in the grasp of his massive hands.

"We have come for business, Medaine," he announced, with a slight show of embarrassment. "M'sieu Houston, he have need for a flume site."

"But I don't see where I could be of any assistance. I have no right—"

"Ah! But eet is not for the moment present. Eet is for the springtime."

She seemed to hesitate then and Houston took a sudden resolve. It might as well be now as later.

"Miss Robinette," he began, coming forward, "I realize that all this needs some explanation. Especially," and he halted, "about myself."

"But is that any of my affair?" Her old pertness was gone. She seemed white and frightened, as though about to listen to something she would rather not hear. Houston answered her as best he could:

"That depends upon yourself, Miss Robinette. Naturally, you wouldn't want to have any business dealings with a man who really was all that you must believe me to be. It isn't a pleasant thing for me to talk about—I would like to forget it. But in this case, it has been brought up against my will. You were present a week ago when Thayer accused me of murder."

"Yes."

"Eet was a big lie!"

"Wait just a minute, Ba'tiste." Cold sweat had made its appearance on Barry Houston's forehead. "I—I—am forced to admit that a part of what he said was true. When I first met Ba'tiste here, I told him there was a shadow in my life that I did not like to talk about. He was good enough to say that he didn't want to hear it. I felt that out here, perhaps I would not be harassed by certain memories that have been rather hard for me to bear in the last couple of years. I was wrong. The thing has come up again, in worse form than ever and without giving me a chance to make a denial. But perhaps you know the whole story?"

"Your story?" Medaine Robinette looked at him queerly. "No—I never have heard it."

"Then you've heard—"

"Only accusations."

"Is it fair to believe only one side of a thing?"

"Please, Mr. Houston," and she looked at him with a certain note of pleading, "you must remember that I—well, I didn't feel that it was any of my business. I didn't know that circumstances would throw you at all in my path."

"But they have, Miss Robinette. The land on my side of the creek has been taken from me by fraud. It is absolutely vital that I use every resource to try to make my mill what it should be. It still is possible for me to obtain lumber, but to get it to the mill necessitates a flume and rights in the lake. I've lost that. We've been hoping, Ba'tiste and myself, that we would be able to induce you to lease us your portion of the lake and a flume site. Otherwise, I'm afraid there isn't much hope."

"As I said, that doesn't become my property until late spring, nearly summer, in fact."

"That is time enough. We are hoping to be able to bid for the railroad contract. I believe it calls for the first shipment of ties about June first. That would give us plenty of time. If we had your word, we could go ahead, assemble the necessary machinery, snake a certain amount of logs down through the snow this winter and be in readiness when the right moment came. Without it, however, we can hardly hope for a sufficient supply to carry us through. And so—"

"You want to know—about heem. You have Ba'teese's word—"

"Really—" she seemed to be fencing again.

Houston, with a hard pull at his breath, came directly to the question.

"It's simply this, Miss Robinette. If I am guilty of those things, you don't want to have anything to do with me, and I don't want you to. But I am here to tell you that I am not guilty, and that it all has been a horrible blunder of circumstance. It is very true in one sense—" and his voice lowered—"that about two years ago in Boston, I was arrested and tried for murder."

"So Mr. Thayer said."

"I was acquitted—but not for the reason Thayer gave. They couldn't make a case, they failed absolutely to prove a thing which, had I really been guilty, should have been a simple matter. A worthless cousin, Tom Langdon, was the man who was murdered. They said I did it with a wooden mallet which I had taken from a prize fight, and which had been used to hammer on the gong for the beginning and the end of the rounds. I had been seen to take it from the fight, and it was found the next morning beside Langdon. There was human blood on it. I had been the last person seen with Langdon. They put two and two together—and tried to convict me on circumstantial evidence. But they couldn't convince the jury; I went free, as I should have done. I was innocent!"

Houston, white now with the memories and with the necessity of retailing again in the presence of a girl who, to him, stood for all that could mean happiness, gritted his teeth for the determination to go on with the grisly thing, to hide nothing in the answers to the questions which she might ask. But Medaine Robinette, standing beside the window, the color gone from her cheeks, one hand lingering the curtains, eyes turned without, gave no evidence that she had heard. Ba'tiste, staring at her, waited a moment for her question. It did not come. He turned to Houston.

"You tell eet!" he ordered. There was something of the father about him,—the father with a wayward boy, fearful of the story that might come, yet determined to do everything within his power to aid a person he loved. Houston straightened.

"I'll try not to shield myself in any way," came at last. The words were directed to Ba'tiste, but meant for Medaine Robinette. "There are some things about it that I'd rather not tell—I wish I could leave them out. But—it all goes. My word of honor—if that counts for anything—goes with it. It's the truth, nothing else.

"I had come home from France—invalided back. The records of the Twenty-sixth will prove that. Gas. I was slated for out here—the recuperation hospital at Denver. But we managed to persuade the army authorities that I could get better treatment at home, and they gave me a disability discharge in about ten months—honorable, of course. After a while, I went back to work, still weak, but rather eager to get at it, in an effort to gather up the strands which had become tangled by the war. I was in the real-estate business then, for myself. Then, one afternoon," his breath pulled sharp, "Tom Langdon came into my office."

"He was your cousin?" Ba'tiste's voice was that of a friendly cross-examiner.

"Yes. I hadn't seen him in five years. We had never had

much to do with him; we," and Houston smiled coldly with the turn that Fate had given to conditions in the Houston family, "always had looked on him as a sort of a black sheep. He had been a runaway from home; about the only letters my uncle ever had received from him had asked for money to get him out of trouble. Where he had been this time, I don't know. He asked for my father and appeared anxious to see him. I told him that father was out of town. Then he said he would stay in Boston until he came back, that he had information for him that was of the greatest importance, and that when he told father what it was, that he, Langdon, could have anything my father possessed in the way of a job and a competence for life. It sounded like blackmail—I could think of nothing else coming from Tom Langdon—and I told him so. That was unfortunate. There were several persons in my office at the time. He resented the statement and we quarreled. They heard it and later testified."

Houston halted, tongue licking at dry lips. Medaine still gave no indication that she had heard. Ba'tiste, his knit cap still crushed in his big hands, moved forward.

"Go on."

"Gradually, the quarrel wore off and Tom became more than friendly, still harping, however, on the fact that he had tremendous news for my father. I tried to get rid of him. It was impossible. He suggested that we go to dinner together and insisted upon it. There was nothing to do but acquiesce; especially as I now was trying to draw from him something of what had brought him there. We had wine. I was weak physically. It went to my head, and Tom seemed to take a delight in keeping my glass full. Oh," and he swerved suddenly toward the woman at the window, "I'm not trying to make any excuses for myself. I wanted if—after that first glass or two, it seemed there wasn't enough in the world. He didn't force it on me—he didn't play the part of a tempter or pour it down my throat. I took it readily enough. But I couldn't stand it. We left the cafe, he fairly intoxicated, myself greatly so. We saw the advertisement of a prize fight and went, getting seats near the ring-side. They weren't close enough for me. I bribed a fellow to let me sit at the press stand, next to the timekeeper, and worried him until he let me have the mallet that he was using to strike the gong.

"The fight was exciting—especially to me in my condition. I was standing most of the time, even leaning on the ring. Once, while in this position, one of the men, who was bleeding, was knocked down. He struck the mallet. It became covered with blood. No one seemed to notice that, except myself—every one was too excited. A moment more and the fight was over, through a knock-out. Then I stuck the mallet in my pocket, telling every one who cared to hear that I was carrying away a souvenir. Langdon and I went out together.

"We started home—for he had announced that he was going to spend the night with me. Persons about us heard him. It was not far to the house and we decided to walk. On the way, he demanded the mallet for himself and pulled it out of my pocket. I struggled with him for it, finally however, to be bested, and started away. He followed me a block or so, taunting me with his superior strength and cursing me as the son of a man whom he intended to make bow to his every wish. I ran then and, evading him, went home and to bed. About four o'clock in the morning, I was awakened by the police. They had found Tom Langdon dead, with his skull crushed, evidently by the blow of a club or a hammer. They said I did it."

A slight gasp traveled over the lips of Medaine, still by the window. Ba'tiste, his features old and lined, reached out with one big hand and patted the man on the shoulder. Then for a long time, there was silence.

"Eet is the lie, eh?"

"Ba'tiste," Houston turned appealingly to him "as I live, that's all I know. I never saw Langdon after he took that mallet from me. Some one killed him, evidently while he was wandering around, looking for me. The mallet dropped by his side. It had blood on it—and they accused me. It looked right—there was every form of circumstantial evidence against me. And," the breath pulled hard, "what was worse, everybody believed that I killed him. Even my best friends—even my father."

"Ba'teese no believe it."

"Why?" Houston turned to him in hope,—in the glimmering chance that perhaps there was something in the train of circumstances that would have prevented the actuality of guilt. But the answer, while it cheered him, was rather disconcerting.

"You look like my Pierre. Pierre, he could do no wrong. You look like heem."

It was sufficient for the old French-Canadian. But Houston knew it could carry but little weight with the girl by the window. He went on:

"Only one shred of evidence was presented in my behalf. It was by a woman who had worked for about six months for my father,—Miss Jierdon. She testified to having passed in a taxicab just at the end of our quarrel, and that, while it was true that there was evidence of a struggle, Langdon had the mallet. She was my only witness, besides the experts. But it may help here, Miss Robinette."

It was the first time he had addressed her directly and she turned, half in surprise.

"How," she asked the question as though with an effort, "how were you cleared?"

"Through expert medical testimony that the blow which killed Langdon could not have been struck with that mallet. The whole trial hinged on the experts. The jury didn't believe much of either side. They couldn't decide absolutely that I had killed Langdon. And so they acquitted me. I'm trying to tell you the truth, without any veneer to my advantage."

"*Bon*! Good! Eet is best."

"Miss Jierdon is the same one who is out here?"

"Yes."

"She testified in your behalf?"

"Yes. And Miss Robinette, if you'll only talk to her—if you'll only ask her about it, she'll tell you the story exactly as I've told it. She trusted me; she was the only bright spot in all the blackness. I may not be able to convince you—but she could, Miss Robinette. If you'll only—"

"Would you guarantee the truth of anything she should tell me?"

"Absolutely."

"Even if she told hidden things?"

"Hidden? I don't know what you mean. There's nothing to be hidden. What she tells you will be the truth, the whole truth, the absolute truth."

"I'm—I'm sorry." She turned again to the window. Houston went forward.

"Sorry? Why? There's nothing—"

"Miss Jierdon has told me," came in a strained voice, "things that perhaps you did not mean for her to tell."

"I? Why, I—"

"That she did pass as you were struggling. That she saw the blow struck—and that it was you who struck it."

"Miss Robinette!"

"That further, you confessed to her and told her why you had killed Langdon—because he had discovered something in your own father's life that would serve as blackmail. That she loved you. And that because she loved you, she went on the stand and perjured herself to save you from a conviction of murder—when she knew in her heart that you were guilty!"

CHAPTER XIV

It was a blow greater, far greater than one that could have been struck in mere physical contact. Houston reeled with the effect of it; he gasped, he struggled aimlessly, futilely, for words to answer it. Vaguely, dizzily, knowing nothing except a dim, hazy desire to rid himself of the loathsomeness of it, Houston started to the door, only to be pulled back in the gigantic grip of Ba'tiste Renaud. The old Canadian was glaring now, his voice was thunderous.

"No! No! You shall not go! You hear Ba'teese, huh? You tell Medaine that is a lie! Un'stan'? That is a lie!"

"It is," Houston heard his voice as though coming from far away, "but I don't know how to answer it. I—I—can't answer it. Where is Miss Jierdon? Is she here? May I see her?"

"Miss Jierdon," Medaine Robinette answered him as though with an effort, "went back to camp last night."

"May I bring her here, to repeat that before me? There's been some sort of a horrible mistake—she didn't know what she was saying. She—"

"I'm afraid, Mr. Houston, that I would need stronger evidence—now. Oh, I want to be fair about this," she burst out suddenly. "I—I shouldn't ever have been drawn into it. It's nothing of my concern; certainly, I shouldn't be the one to be called upon to judge the innocence or guilt of some one I hardly know! I—"

"I realize that, Miss Robinette. I withdraw my request for anything you can give me." Again he started toward the door, and this time Ba'tiste did not detain him. But abruptly he halted, a sudden thought searing its way through his brain. "Just one moment more, Miss Robinette. Then I'll go. But this question means a great deal. You passed me one night on the road. Would it be impertinent to ask where you had been?"

"Certainly not. To Tabernacle. Lost Wing went with me, as usual. You may ask him."

"Your word is enough. May I inquire if on that night you saw Fred Thayer?"

"I did not."

"Thank you." Dully he reached for the knob. The woman who had appeared that night in the clearing, her head upon a man's shoulder, had been Agnes Jierdon!

He stepped to the veranda, waiting for Ba'tiste, who was making a last effort in his behalf. Then he called:

"I'd rather you'd not say anything more, Ba'tiste. Words aren't much use—without something to back them up."

And he knew that this possibility was all but gone. Tricked! For now he realized that Agnes Jierdon had stood by him at a time when her supposed confidence and trust could do no more for him than cheer him and cause him to trust her to the end that,—what?

Had it been she who had slipped the necessary papers of the contract and the lease into the mass of formalities which he had signed without even looking at the contents of more than the first page or two of the pile? They had been so many technical details, merely there for signature; he had signed dozens before. It would have been easy.

But Houston forced back the thought. He himself knew what it meant to be unjustly accused. Time was but of little moment now; his theories could wait until he had seen Agnes Jierdon, until he had talked to her and questioned her regarding the statements made to Medaine Robinette. Besides, Ba'tiste already was in the buggy, striving to cover his feelings by a stream of badinage directed toward Golemar, the wolf-dog, and waiting for Houston to take his place beside him. A moment more and they were driving away, Ba'tiste humped over the reins as usual, Houston striving to put from him the agony of the new accusation. Finally, the trapper cocked his head and spoke, rather to the horse and Golemar than to Houston.

"Eet is the one, big lie!"

"Yes, but there's not much way of proving it, Ba'tiste."

"Proof? Bah! And does Ba'teese need proof? Ba'teese no like this woman, Jierdon. She say Ba'teese burn the mill."

"I didn't know you heard that."

"She have a bad mouth. She have a bad eye. She have a bad tongue. Yes, *oui*! She have a bad tongue!"

"Let's wait, Ba'tiste. There may be some mistake about it. Of course, it's possible. She had worked for my father for six months at the time—she could have been placed there for a purpose. Her testimony was of the sort that the jury could take either as for me or against me; she established, as an eyewitness, that we had quarreled and that the mallet played a part in it. Naturally, though, I looked to her as my friend. I thought that her testimony helped me."

"And the taxi-driver? What did he say? Eh?"

"We never were able to find him."

"Oh, ho! Golemar! You hear?" The old trapper's voice was stinging with sarcasm. "They nev' fin' heem. But the woman she was in a taxi. Ah, *oui*. She could pass, just at the moment. She could put in the mind of the jury the fact that there was a quarrel, while she preten' to help M'sieu Houston. But the taxi-driver—no, they nev' fin' heem!"

"Let's wait, Ba'tiste."

"Oh—ah, *oui*."

On they drove in silence, talking of trivial things, each fencing away from the subject that was on their minds and from mention of the unfortunate interview with Medaine Robinette. The miles faded slowly, at last to bring the camp into view. Ten minutes later, Houston leaped from the buggy and knocked at the door of the cottage.

"I want to see Miss Jierdon," he told the cook who had opened the door. That person shook her head.

"She's gone."

"Gone? Where?"

"To town, I guess. She came back here from Miss Robinette's last night and packed her things and left. She didn't say where she was going. She left a note for you."

"Let me have it!" There was anxiety in the command. The cook bustled back into the house, to return with a sealed envelope addressed to Houston. He slit it with a trembling finger.

"What she say?" Ba'tiste was leaning from the buggy. Houston took his place beside him, and as the horse was turned back toward the trapper's cabin, read aloud:

"Dearest Barry:

"Hate awfully to run away like this without seeing you, but it can't be helped. Have an offer of a position in St. Louis that I can't very well refuse. Will write you from there.

"Love and kisses.

"AGNES."

Ba'tiste slapped the reins on the horse's back.

"She is like the Judas, eh?" he asked quietly, and Houston cringed with the realization that he had spoken the truth. Judas! A feminine Judas, who had come to him when his guard had been lowered, who had pretended that she believed in him, that she even loved him, that she might wreck his every plan and hope in life. A Judas, a—

"Let's don't talk about it, Ba'tiste!" Houston's voice was hoarse, weary. "It's a little too much to take, all in one day."

"*Tres bien,*" answered the old French-Canadian, not to speak again until they had reached his cabin and, red-faced, he had turned from the stove to place the evening meal on the table. Then, his mouth full of crisply fried bacon, he waved a hand and spluttered with a sudden inspiration:

"What you do, now?"

"Queer question, isn't it?" The grim humor of it brought a smile, in spite of the lead in Houston's heart. "What is there to do?"

"What?" Ba'tiste gulped his food, rose and waved a hand with a sudden flash of emphasis. "Peuff! And there is ever'thin'. You have a mill."

"Such as it is."

"But eet is a mill. And eet can saw timber—enough to keep the wolf from the door. You have yourself. Your arm, he is near' well. And there is alway'—" he gestured profoundly— "the future. He is like a woman, the future," he added, with a little smile. "He always look good when he is in the far away."

The enthusiasm of the trapper found a faint echo in Houston's heart. "I'm not whipped yet, Ba'tiste. But I'm near it. I've had some pretty hard knocks."

"Ah, *oui*! But so have Ba'teese!" The shadows were falling, and the old French-Canadian walked to the window. "*Oui, oui, oui*! Look." And he pointed to the white cross, still faintly visible, like a luminous thing, beneath the pines. "Ev' day, Ba'teese, he see that. Ev' day Ba'teese remember—how he work for others, how he is *L' M'sieu Doctaire*, how he help and help and help—but how he cannot help his own. Ev' day, Ba'teese, he live again that night in the cathedral when he call, so, 'Pierre! Pierre!' But Pierre does not answer. Ev' day, he remind how he come home, and how his heart, eet is cold, but how he hope that his Julienne, she will warm eet again—to fin' that. But does Ba'teese stop? Does Ba'teese fol' his hands? No! No!" He thundered the words and beat his heavy chest. "Some day, Ba'teese will fin' what he look for! When the cloud, he get heavy, Ba'teese, he go out there—out to his Julienne—and he kneel down and he pray that she give to heem the strength to go on—to look and look and look until he find eet—the thing he is want'! Ba'teese, he too have had his trouble. Ba'teese, he too would like to quit! But no, he shall not! And you shall not! By the cross of my Julienne, you shall not! Eet is to the end—and not before! You look like my Pierre! My Pierre had in heem the blood of Ba'teese—Ba'teese, who had broke' the way. And Pierre would not quit, and you will not quit. And—"

"I will not quit!" Barry Houston said the words slowly, in a voice heightened by feeling and by a new strength, a sudden flooding of a reserve power that he did not know he possessed. "That is my absolute promise to you, Ba'tiste. I will not quit!"

"*Bon*! Good! Golemar, you hear, eh? *Mon ami*, he come to the barrier, and he look at the trouble, but he say he will not quit. *Veritas*! *Bon*! He is my Pierre! He speak like my Pierre would speak! He will not quit!"

"No," and then Houston repeated it, a strange light shining in his eyes, his hands clenched, breath pulling deep into his lungs. "I will not quit."

"Ah, *oui*! Eet is now the, what-you-say, the swing-around point. To-night Ba'teese go out. Where? Ah, you shall wait an' see. Ba'teese go—Ba'teese come back. Then you shall see. Ah, *oui*! Then you shall see."

For an hour or so after that he boomed about the cabin, singing queer old songs in a *patois*, rumbling to the faithful Golemar, washing the dishes while Houston wiped them, joking, talking of everything but the troubles of the day and the plans of the night. Outside the shadows grew heavier, finally to turn to pitch darkness. The bull bats began to circle about the cabin. Ba'tiste walked to the door.

"*Bon*! Good!" he exclaimed. "The sky, he is full of cloud'. The star, he do not shine. *Bon*! Ba'teese shall go."

And with a final wave of the hand, still keeping his journey a mystery, he went forth into the night.

Long Houston waited for his return, but he did not come. The old, creaking clock on the rustic ledge ticked away the minutes and the hours until midnight, but still no crunching of gravel relieved his anxious ears, still no gigantic form of the grizzled, bearded trapper showed in the doorway. One o'clock came and went. Two—three. Houston still waited. Four—and a scratch on the door. It was Golemar, followed a moment later by a grinning, twinkling-eyed Ba'tiste.

"*Bon*! Good!" he exclaimed. "See, Golemar? What I say to you? He wait up for Ba'teese. *Bon*! Now—*alert, mon ami*! The pencil and the paper!"

He slumped into a chair and dived into a pocket of his red shirt, to bring forth a mass of scribbled sheets, to stare at them, striving studiously to make out the writing.

"Ba'teese, he put eet down by a match in the shelter of a lumber pile," came at last. "Eet is all, what-you-say, scramble up. But we shall see—ah, *oui*—we shall see. Now," he looked toward Houston, waiting anxiously with paper and pencil, "we shall put eet in the list. So. One million ties, seven by eight by eight feet, at the one dollar and the forty cents. Put that down."

"I have it. But what—"

"Wait! Five thousan' bridge timber, ten by ten by sixteen feet, at the three dollar and ninety cents."

"Yes—"

"Ten thousand feet of the four by four, at—"

"Ba'tiste!" Houston had risen suddenly. "What have you got there?"

The trapper grinned and pulled at his gray-splotched beard.

"Oh, ho! Golemar! He wan' to know. Shall we tell heem, eh? Ah, *oui*—" he shook his big shoulders and spread his hands. "Eet is—the copy of the bid!"

"The copy? The bid?"

"From the Blackburn mill. There is no one aroun'. Ba'teese, he go through a window. Ba'teese, he find heem—in a file. And he bring back the copy."

"Then—"

"M'sieu Houston, he too will bid. But he will make it lower. And this," he tapped the scribbled scraps of paper, "is cheaper than any one else. Eet is because of the location. M'sieu Houston—he know what they bid. He will make eet cheaper."

"But what with, Ba'tiste? We haven't a mill to saw the stuff, in the first place. This ramshackle thing we're setting up now couldn't even begin to turn out the ties alone. The bid calls for ten thousand laid down at Tabernacle, the first of June. We might do that, but how on earth would we ever keep up with the rest? The boxings, the rough lumber, the two by fourteen's finished, the dropped sidings and groved roofing, and lath and ceiling and rough fencings and all the rest? What on earth will we do it with?"

"What with?" Ba'tiste waved an arm grandiloquently. "With the future!"

"It's taking the longest kind of a chance—"

"Ah, *oui*! But the man who is drowning, he will, what-you-say, grab at a haystack."

"True enough. Go ahead. I'll mark our figures down too, as you read."

And together they settled to the making of a bid that ran into the millions, an overture for a contract for which they had neither mill, nor timber, nor flume, nor resources to complete!

CHAPTER XV

Time dragged after that. Once the bid was on its way to Chicago, there was nothing to do but wait. It was a delay which lengthened from June until July, thence into late summer and early autumn, while the hills turned brown with the colorings of the aspens, while Mount Taluchen and its surrounding mountains once more became grim and forbidding with the early fall of snow.

The time for the opening of the bids had passed, far in the distance, but there had come no word. Ba'tiste, long since taken into as much of a partnership agreement as was possible, went day after day to the post office, only to return empty-handed, while Houston watched with more intensity than ever the commercial columns of the lumber journals in the fear that the contract, after all, had gone somewhere else. But no notice appeared. Nothing but blankness as concerned the plans of the Mountain Plains and Salt Lake Railroad.

Medaine he saw but seldom,—then only to avoid her as she strove to avoid him. Houston's work was now in the hills and at the camp, doing exactly what the Blackburn mill was doing, storing up a reasonable supply of timber and sawing at what might or might not be the first consignment of ties for the fulfillment of the contract. But day after day he realized that he was all but beaten.

His arm had healed now and returned to the strength that had existed before the fracture. Far greater in strength, in fact, for Houston had taken his place in the woods side by side with the few lumberjacks whom he could afford to carry on his pay roll. There, at least, he had right of way. He had sold only stumpage, which meant that the Blackburn camp had the right to take out as much timber as it cared to, as long as it was paid for at the insignificant rate of one dollar and fifty cents a thousand feet. Thayer and the men in his employ could not keep him out of his own woods, or prevent him from cutting his own timber. But they could prevent him from getting it to the mill by an inexpensive process.

From dawn until dusk he labored, sometimes with Ba'tiste singing lustily beside him, sometimes alone. The task was a hard one; the snaking of timber through the forest to the high-line roadway, there to be loaded upon two-wheeled carts and dragged, by a slow, laborious, costly process, to the mill. For every log that he sent to the saw in this wise, he knew that Thayer was sending ten,—and at a tenth of the cost. But Houston was fighting the last fight,—a fight that could not end until absolute, utter failure stood stark before him at the end of the road.

September became October with its rains, and its last flash of brilliant coloring from the lower hills, and then whiteness. November had arrived, bringing with it the first snow and turning the whole, great, already desolate country into a desert of white.

It was cold now; the cook took on a new duty of the maintenance of hot pails of bran mash and salt water for the relief of frozen hands. Heavy gum-shoes, worn over lighter footgear and reaching with felt-padded thickness far toward the knee, encased the feet. Hands numbed, in spite of thick mittens; each week saw a new snowfall, bringing with it the consequent thaws and the hardening of the surface. The snowshoe rabbit made its appearance, tracking the shadowy, silent woods with great, outlandish marks. The coyotes howled o' nights; now and then Houston, as he worked, saw the tracks of a bear, or the bloody imprints of a mountain lion, its paws cut by the icy crust of the snow as it trailed the elk or deer. The world was a quiet thing, a white thing, a cold, unrelenting thing, to be fought only by thick garments and snowshoes. But with it all, it gave Houston and Ba'tiste a new enthusiasm. They at least could get their logs to the mill now swiftly and with comparative ease.

Short, awkward-appearing sleds creaked and sang along the icy, hard-packed road of snow, to approach the piles of logs snaked out of the timber, to be loaded high beyond all seeming regard for gravitation or consideration for the broad-backed, patient horses, to be secured at one end by heavy chains leading to a patent binder which cinched them to the sled, and started down the precipitous road toward the mill. Once in a while Houston rode the sleds, merely for the thrill of it; for the singing and crunching of the logs against the snow, the grinding of bark against bark, the quick surge as the horses struck a sharp decline and galloped down it, the driver shouting, the logs kicking up the snow behind the sled in a swirling, feathery wake.

At times he stayed at the bunk house with the lumberjacks, silent as they were silent, or talking of trivial things which were mighty to them,—the quality of the food, the depth of the snow, the fact that the little gray squirrels were more plentiful in one part of the woods than another, or that they chattered more in the morning than in the afternoon. Hours he spent in watching Old Bill, a lumberjack who, in his few moments of leisure between the supper table and bed, whittled laboriously upon a wooden chain, which with dogged persistence he had lugged with him for months. Or perhaps staring over the shoulder of Jade Hains, striving to copy the picture of a motion-picture star from a worn, dirty, months-old magazine; as excited as they over the tiny things in life, as eager to seek a bunk when eight o'clock came, as grudging to hear the clatter of alarm clocks in the black coldness before dawn and to creak forth to the watering and harnessing of the horses for the work of the day. Some way, it all seemed to be natural to Barry Houston, natural that he should accept this sort of dogged, humdrum, eventless life and strive to think of nothing more. The other existence, for him, had ended in a blackened waste; even the one person in whom he had trusted, the woman he would have been glad to marry, if that could have repaid her in any way for what he thought she had done for him, had proved traitorous. His letters, written to her at general delivery, St. Louis, had been returned, uncalled for. From the moment that he had received that light, taunting note, he had heard nothing more. She had done her work; she was gone.

December came. Christmas, and with it Ba'tiste, with flour in his hair and beard, his red shirt pulled out over his trousers, distributing the presents which Houston had bought for the few men in his employ. January wore on, bringing with it more snow. February and then—

"Eet is come! Eet is come!" Ba'tiste, waving his arms wildly, in spite of the stuffiness of his heavy mackinaw, and the broad belt which sank into layer after layer of clothing at his waist, came over the brow of the raise into camp, to seize Houston in his arms and dance him about, to lift him and literally throw him high upon his chest as one would toss a child, to roar at Golemar, then to stand back, brandishing an opened letter above his head. "Eet is come! I have open eet—I can not wait. Eet say we shall have the contract! Ah, *oui! oui! oui! oui!* We shall have the contract!"

Houston, suddenly awake to what the message meant, reached for the letter. It was there in black and white. The bid had been accepted. There need now be but the conference in Chicago, the posting of the forfeit money, and the deal was made.

"Eet say five thousand dollars cash, and the rest in a bond!" came enthusiastically from Ba'tiste. "Eet is simple. You have the mill, you have the timber. Ba'teese, he have the friend in Denver who will make the bond."

"But how about the machinery; we'll need a hundred-thousand-dollar plant before we're through, Ba'tiste."

"Ah!" The old French-Canadian's jaw dropped. "Ba'teese, he is like the child. He have not think of that. He have figure he can borrow ten thousand dollar in his own name. But he have not think about the machinery."

"But we must think about it, Ba'tiste. We've got to get it. With the equipment that's here, we never could hope to keep up with the contract. And if we can't do that, we lose everything. Understand me, I'm not thinking of quitting; I merely want to look over the battlefield first. Shall we take the chance?"

Big Ba'tiste shrugged his shoulders.

"Ba'teese, he always try to break the way," came at last. "Ba'teese, he have trouble—but he have nev' been beat. You ask Ba'teese—Ba'teese say go ahead. Somehow we make it."

"Then to-morrow morning we take the train to Denver, and from there I'll go on to Boston. I'll raise the money some way. I don't know how. If I don't, we're only beaten in the beginning instead of at the end. We'll simply have to trust to the future—on everything, Ba'tiste. There are so many things that can whip us, that—" Houston laughed shortly—"we might as well be gamblers all the way through. We'll never fulfill the contract, even with the machinery, unless we can get the use of the lake and a flume to the mill. We may be able to keep it up for a month or two, but that will be all. The expense will eat us up. But one chance is no greater than the other, and personally, I'm at the point where I don't care."

"*Oui*! Ba'teese, he have nothing. Ba'teese he only fight for the excitement. So, to-morrow we go!"

And on the next day they went, again to go over all the details of their mad, foundationless escapade with Chance, to talk it all over in the old smoking car, to weigh the balance against them from every angle, and to see failure on every side. But they had become gamblers with Fate; for one, it was his final opportunity, to take or disregard, with a faint glimmer of success at one end of the vista, with the wiping out of every hope at the other. They tried not to look at the gloomy side, but that was impossible. As the train ground its way up the circuitous grades, Houston felt that he was headed finally for the dissolution. But there was at least the consolation about it that within a short time the uncertainty of his life would be ended; the hopes either crushed forever, or realized, that—

"Ba'tiste!" They were in the snowsheds at Crestline, and Houston had pointed excitedly toward a window of the west-bound train, just pulling past them on the way down the slope. A woman was there, a woman who had turned her head sharply, but with not enough speed to prevent a sight of her by the French-Canadian who glanced quickly and gasped:

"The Judas!"

Houston leaped from his seat and ran to the vestibule of the car, but in vain. It was closed; already the other last coach of the other train was pulling past and gaining headway with the easier grade. Wondering, he returned to his seat beside his partner.

"It was she, Ba'tiste," came with conviction. "I got a good look at her before she noticed me. Then, when I pointed— she turned her head away."

"But Ba'teese, he see her."

"She's going back. What do you suppose it can mean? Can she be—"

"Ba'teese catch the nex' train to Tabernacle so soon as we have finish our business. Eet is for no good."

"I wonder—" it was a hope, but a faint one—"if she could be coming back to make amends, Ba'tiste? That—that other thing seemed so unlike the person who had been so good to me, so apart from the side of her nature that I knew—"

"She have a bad mouth," Ba'tiste repeated grimly. "She have a bad eye, she have a bad tongue. A woman with a bad tongue, she is a devil. You—you no see it, because she come to you with a smile, when every one else, he frown. You think she is the angel, yes, *oui*? But she come to Ba'teese different. She talk to you sof' and she try to turn you against your frien'. Yes. *Oui? Ne c'est pas?* Ba'teese see her with the selfish mouth. Peuff! He see her when she look to heem out from the corner of her eye—so. Ba'teese know. Ba'teese come back quick, to keep watch!"

"I guess you're right, Ba'tiste. It won't do any harm. If she's returned for a good purpose, very well. If not, we're at least prepared for her."

With that resolution they went on to Denver, there to seek out the few friends Ba'tiste possessed, to argue one of them into a loan of ten thousand dollars on the land and trustworthy qualities which formed the total of Ba'tiste's resources, to gain from the other the necessary bond to cover the contract,—a contract which Barry Houston knew only too well might never be fulfilled. But against this fear was the booming enthusiasm of Ba'tiste Renaud:

"Nev' min'. Somehow we do eet. Ah, *oui*! Somehow. If we make the failure, then it shall be Ba'teese who will fin' the way to pay the bond. Now, Ba'teese, he go back."

"Yes, and keep watch on that woman. She's out here for something'—I feel sure of it—something that has to do with Thayer. Before you go, however, make the rounds of the employment agencies and tell them to send you every man they can spare, up to a hundred. We'll give them work to the extent of five thousand dollars. They ought to be able to get enough timber down to keep us going for a while anyway—especially with the roads iced."

"Ah. *Oui*. It is the three o'clock. *Bon voyage, mon* Baree!"

It was the first time Ba'tiste Renaud ever had dropped the conventional "M'sieu" in addressing Houston, and Barry knew, without the telling, without the glowing light in the old man's eyes, that at least a part of the great loneliness in the trapper's heart had departed, that he had found a place there in a portion of the aching spot left void by a shrapnel-shattered son to whom a father had called that night in the ruined cathedral,—and called in vain. It caused a queer pang of exquisite pain in Houston's heart, a joy too great to be expressed by the reflexes of mere pleasure. Long after the train had left Denver, he still thought of it, he still heard the old man's words, he still sat quiet and peaceful in a new enthusiasm of hope. The world was not so blank, after all. One man, at least, believed in him fully.

Came Chicago and the technicalities of ironing out the final details of the contract. Then, dealer in millions and the possessor of nothing, Houston went onward toward Boston.

And Ba'tiste was not there to boom enthusiastically regarding the chances of the future, to enlarge upon the opportunities which might arise for the fulfillment of a thing which seemed impossible.

Coldly, dispassionately, now that it was done, that the word of the Empire Lake Mill and Lumber Company had been given to deliver the materials for the making of a great railroad, had guaranteed its resources and furnished the necessary bond for the fulfillment of a promise, Barry Houston could not help but feel that it all had been rash, to say the least. Where was the machinery to be obtained? Where the money to keep things going? True, there would be spot cash awaiting the delivery of every installment of the huge order, enough, in fact, to furnish the necessary running expenses of a mill under ordinary circumstances. But the circumstances which surrounded the workings of the Empire Lake project were far from ordinary. No easy skidways to a lake, no flume, no aerials; there was nothing to cut expenses. Unless a miracle should happen, and Houston reflected that miracles were few and far between, that timber must be brought to the mill by a system that would be disastrous as far as costs were concerned. Yet, the contract had been made!

He wandered the aisle of the sleeper, fidgeting from one end to the other, as neither magazines, nor the spinning scenery without held a counter-attraction for his gloomy thoughts. When night at last came, he entered the smoking compartment and slumped into a seat in a far corner, smoking in a detached manner, often pulling on his cigar long after lengthy minutes of reflection had allowed its ashes to cool.

About him the usual conversation raged, the settling of a nation's problems, the discussion of crime waves, Bolshevism and the whatnot that goes with an hour of smoking on a tiresome journey. From Washington and governmental affairs, it veered to the West and dry farming, thence to the cattle business; to anecdotes, and finally to ghost stories. And then, with a sudden interest, Houston forgot his own problems to listen attentively, tensely, almost fearfully. A man whom he never before had seen, and whom he probably never would see again, was talking,—about something which might be as remote to Houston as the poles. Yet it held him, it fascinated, it gripped him!

"Speaking of gruesome things," the talker had said, "reminds me. I'm a doctor—not quite full fledged, I'll admit, but with the right to put M. D. after my name. Spent a couple of years as an interne in Bellstrand Hospital in New York. Big place. Any of you ever been there?"

No one had. The young doctor went on.

"Quite a place for experiments. They've got a big room on the fifth floor where somebody is always dissecting, or carrying out some kind of investigations into this bodily thing we call a home. My work led me past there a good deal, and I'd gotten so I hardly noticed it. But one Sunday night, I guess it was along toward midnight, I saw something that brought me up short. I happened to look in and saw a man in there, murdering another one with a wooden mallet."

"Murdering him?" The statement had caused a rise from the rest of the auditors. The doctor laughed.

"Well, perhaps I used too sentimental a phrase. I should have said, acting out a murder. You can't very well murder a dead man. The fellow he was killing already was a corpse.

"You mean—"

"Just what I'm saying. There were two or three assistants. Pretty big doctors, I learned later, all of them from Boston. They had taken a cadaver from the refrigerator and stood it in a certain position. Then the one man had struck it on the head with the mallet with all the force he could summon. Of course it knocked the corpse down—I'm telling you, it was gruesome, even to an interne! The last I saw of them, the doctors were working with their microscopes—evidently to see what effect the blow had produced."

"What was the idea?"

"Never found out. They're pretty close-mouthed about that sort of thing. You see, opposite sides in a trial are always carrying out experiments and trying their level best to keep the other fellow from knowing what's going on. I found out later that the door was supposed to have been locked. I passed through about ten minutes later and saw them working on another human body—evidently one of a number that they had been trying the tests on. About that time some one heard me and came out like a bullet. The next thing I knew, everything was closed. How long the experiments had been going on, I couldn't say. I do know, however, that they didn't leave there until about three o'clock in the morning."

"You—you don't know who the men were?" Houston, forcing himself to be casual, had asked the question. The young doctor shook his head.

"No—except that they were from Boston. At least, the doctors were. One of the nurses knew them. I suppose the other man was a district attorney—they usually are around somewhere during an experiment."

"You never learned with what murder case it was connected?"

"No—the fact is, it passed pretty much out of my mind, as far as the details were concerned. Although I'll never forget the picture."

"Pardon me for asking questions. I—I—just happen to come from Boston and was trying to recall such a case. You don't remember what time of the year it was, or how long ago?"

"Yes, I do. It was in the summer, along about two or two and a half years ago."

Houston slumped back into his corner. Ten minutes later, he found an opportunity to exchange cards with the young physician and sought his berth. To himself, he could give no reason for establishing the identity of the smoking-compartment informant. He had acted from some sort of subconscious compulsion, without reasoning, without knowing why he had catalogued the information or of what possible use it could be to him. But once in his berth, the picture continued to rise before him; of a big room in a hospital, of doctors gathered about, and of a man "killing" another with a mallet. Had it been Worthington? Worthington, the tired-eyed, determined, over-zealous district attorney, who, day after day, had struggled and fought to send him to the penitentiary for life? Had it been Worthington, striving to reproduce the murder of Tom

Langdon as he evidently had reconstructed it, experimenting with his experts in the safety of a different city, for points of evidence that would clinch the case against the accused man beyond all shadow of a doubt? Instinctively Houston felt that he just had heard an unwritten, unmentioned phase of his own murder case. Yet—if that had been Worthington, if those experts had found evidence against him, if the theories of the district attorney had been verified on that gruesome night in the "dead ward" of Bellstrand Hospital—

Why had this damning evidence been allowed to sink into oblivion? Why had it not been used against him?

CHAPTER XVI

It was a problem which Barry Houston, in spite of wakefulness, failed to solve. Next morning, eager for a repetition of the recital, in the hope of some forgotten detail, some clue which might lead him to an absolute decision, he sought the young doctor, only to find that he had left the train at dawn. A doorway of the past had been opened to Houston, only to be closed again before he could clearly discern beyond. He went on to Boston, still struggling to reconstruct it all, striving to figure what connection it might have had, but in vain. And with his departure from the train, new thoughts, new problems, arose to take the place of memories. His purposes now were of the future, not of the past.

And naturally, he turned first to the office of his father's attorney,—the bleak place where he had conferred so many times in the black days. Old Judge Mason, accustomed to seeing Barry in time of stress, tried his best to be jovial.

"Well, boy, what is it this time?"

"Money." Houston came directly to the point. "I've come back to Boston to find out if any one will trust me."

"With or without security."

"With it—the best in the world." Then he brought forward a copy of the contract. Mason studied it at length, then, with a slow gesture, raised his glasses to a resting place on his forehead.

"I—I don't know, boy," he said at last. "It's a rather hard problem to crack. I wish there was some one in the family we could go to for the money."

"But there isn't."

"No. Your uncle Walt might have it. But I'm afraid that he wouldn't feel like lending it to you. He still believes—well, you know how fathers are about their boys. He's forgotten most of Tom's bad points by now."

"We'll drop him from the list. How about the bankers."

"We'll have to see. I'm a little afraid there. I know you'll pardon me for saying it, Barry, but they like to have a man come to them with clean hands. Not that you haven't got them," he interjected, "but—well, you know bankers. What's the money for; running expenses?"

"No. Machinery. The other mill burned down, you know— and as usual, without insurance. We have a makeshift thing set up there now—but it's nothing to what will be needed. I've got to have a good, smooth-working plant—otherwise I won't be able to live up to specifications."

"You're not," and the old lawyer smiled quizzically, "going to favor your dearly beloved friend with the order, are you?"

"Who?"

"Worthington."

"The district attorney?"

"That was. Plutocrat now, and member of society, you know. He came into his father's money, just after he went out of office, and bought into the East Coast Machinery Company when it was on its last legs. His money was like new blood. They've got a good big plant. He's president," again the smile, "and I know he'd be glad to have your order."

Houston continued the sarcasm.

"I'd be overjoyed to give it to him. In fact, I think I'd refuse to buy any machinery if I couldn't get it from such a dear friend as Worthington was. It wasn't his fault that I wasn't sent to the penitentiary."

"No, that's right, boy." Old Lawyer Mason was quietly reminiscent. "He tried his best. It seemed to me in those days he was more of a persecutor than prosecutor."

"Let's forget it." Houston laughed uneasily.

"Now, to go back to the bankers—"

"There isn't much for us to do but to try them, one after another. I guess we might as well start now as any time."

Late that afternoon they were again in the office, the features of Mason wrinkled with thought, those of Barry Houston plainly discouraged. They had failed. The refusals had been courteous, fraught with many apologies for a tight market, and effusive regrets that it would be impossible to loan money on such a gilt-edged proposition as the contract seemed to hold forth, but—There had always been that one word, that stumbling-block against which they had run time after time, shielded and padded by courtesy, but present nevertheless. Nor were Houston and Mason unaware of the real fact which lay behind it all; that the bankers did not care to trust their money in the hands of a man who had been accused of murder and who had escaped the penalty of such a charge by a margin, which to Boston, at least, had seemed exceedingly slight. One after another, there in the office, Mason went over the list of his business acquaintances, seeking for some name that might mean magic to them. But no such inspiration came.

"Drop back to-morrow, boy," he said at last. "I'll think over the thing to-night, and I may be able to get a bright idea. It's going to be tough sledding—too tough, I'm afraid. If only we didn't have to buck up against that trial, and the ideas people seem to have gotten of it, we'd be all right. But—"

There it was again, that one word, that immutable obstacle which seemed to arise always. Houston reached for his hat.

"I'm going to keep on trying, anyway, Mr. Mason. I'll be back to-morrow. I'm going to get that money if I have to make a canvass of Boston, if I have to go out and sell shares at a dollar apiece and if I go broke paying dividends. I've made my promise to go through—and I'm going!"

"Good. I'll be looking for you."

But half an hour later, following a wandering, aimless journey through the crooked streets, Barry Houston suddenly straightened with an inspiration. He whirled, he dived for a cigar store and for a telephone.

"Hello!" he called, after the long wait for connections. "Mr. Mason? Don't look for me tomorrow—I believe I'll not be there."

"But you haven't given it up?"

"Given up?" Houston laughed with sudden enthusiasm. "No—I've just started. Put the date off a day or two until I can try something that's buzzing around in my head. It's a wild idea—but it may work. If it doesn't, I'll see you Thursday."

Then he turned from the telephone and toward the railroad station.

"One, to New York," he ordered hurriedly through the ticket window. "I've got time to make that seven-forty, if you rush it."

And the next morning, Barry Houston was in New York, swirling along Seventh Avenue toward Bellstrand Hospital. There he sought the executive offices and told his story. "Five minutes later he was looking at the books of the institution, searching, searching,—at last to stifle a cry of excitement and bend closer to a closely written page.

"August second," he read. "Kilbane Worthington, district attorney, Boston, Mass. Acc by Drs. Horton, Mayer and Brensteam. Investigations into effect of blows on skull. Eight cadavers."

With fingers that were almost frenzied, Houston copied the notation, closed the book, and hurried again for a taxicab. It yet was only nine o'clock. It the traffic were not too thick, if the driver were skilful—

He raced through the gate at Grand Central just as it was closing. He made the train in unison with the last drawling cry of the conductor. Then for hours, in the Pullman chair car, he fidgeted, counting the telegraph posts, checking off the stations as they flipped past the windows, through a day of eagerness, of excited, racking anticipation. It was night when he reached Boston, but Houston did not hesitate. A glance at a telephone book, another rocking ride in a taxicab, and Barry stood on the veranda of a large house, awaiting the answer to his ring at the bell. Finally it came.

"Mr. Worthington," he demanded. The butler arched his eyebrows.

"Sorry, but Mr. Worthington has left orders not to be—"

"Tell him that it is a matter of urgent business. That it is something of the utmost importance to him."

A wait. The butler returned.

"Sorry, sir. But Mr. Worthington is just ready to retire."

"You tell Mr. Worthington," answered Houston in a crisp voice, "that he either will see me or regret it. Tell him that I am very sorry, but that just now, I am forced to use his own methods—and that if he doesn't see me within five minutes, there will be something in the morning papers that will be, to say the least, extremely distasteful to him."

"The name, please?"

"It doesn't matter."

"Are you from a newspaper?"

"I'm not saying. Whether I go to one directly from here, depends entirely upon Mr. Worthington. Will you please take my message?"

"I'm afraid—"

"Take my message!"

"Directly, sir!"

Another wait. Then:

"Mr. Worthington will see you in the library, sir."

"Thanks." Houston almost bounded into the hall. A moment later, in the dimness of the heavily furnished, somewhat mysterious appearing library, Barry Houston again faced the man whom, at one time, he had hoped never again to see. Kilbane Worthington was seated at the large table, much in the manner which he had affected in court, elbows on the surface, chin cupped in his thin, nervous hands. The light was not good for recognizing faces; without realizing it, the former district attorney had placed himself at a disadvantage. Squinting, he sought to make out the features of the man who had hurried into the room, and failing, rose.

"Well," he asked somewhat brusquely, "may I inquire—"

"Certainly. My name's Houston."

"Houston—Houston—it seems to me—"

"Maybe your memory needs refreshing. Such little things as I figured in probably slipped your mind the minute you were through with them. To be explicit, my name is Barry Houston, son of the late William K. Houston. You and I met—in the courtroom. You once did me the very high honor to accuse me of murder and then tried your level best to send me to the penitentiary for life when you knew, absolutely and thoroughly, that I was an innocent man!"

CHAPTER XVII

The former district attorney started slightly. Then, coming still closer, he peered into the tense, angry features of Barry Houston.

"A bit melodramatic, aren't you?" he asked in a sneering tone.

"Perhaps so. But then murder is always melodramatic."

"Murder? You don't intend—"

"No. I simply referred to the past. I should have said 'reference to murder.' I hope you will pardon me if any inelegance of language should offend you."

"Sarcastic, aren't you?"

"I have a right to be. Knowing what I know—I should use more than sarcasm."

"If I'm not mistaken, you have. The butler spoke of some threat."

"Hardly a threat, Mr. Worthington." Houston was speaking coldly, incisively. "Merely what I have heard you often call in court a statement of fact. In case it wasn't repeated to you correctly, I'll bore you with it again. I said that if you didn't see me immediately, there would be something extremely distasteful to you in the morning papers."

"Well? I've seen you. Now—"

"Wait just a moment, Mr. Worthington. I thought it was only civil lawyers who indulged in technicalities. I didn't know that criminal," and he put emphasis on the word, then repeated it, "that criminal lawyers had the habit also."

"If you'll cease this insulting—"

"Oh, I think I have a right to that. To tell the truth, I've only begun to insult you. That is—if you call this sort of a thing an insult. To get at the point of the matter, Mr. Worthington, I want to be fair with you. I've come here to ask something—I'll admit that—but it is something that should benefit you in a number of ways. But we'll speak of that later. The main point is this: I am thinking very seriously of suing the city of Boston for a million dollars."

"Well? What's that to me?" Worthington sighed, with a bit of relief, Houston thought, and walked back to the table for a cigarette. "I haven't anything to do with the city. Go as far as you like. I'm out of politics; in case you don't know, I'm in business for myself and haven't the least interest in what the city does, or what any one does to it."

"Even though you should happen to be the bone of contention—and the butt of what may be a good deal of unpleasant newspaper notoriety?"

"You're talking blackmail!"

"I beg your pardon. Blackmail is something by which one extorts money. I'm here to try to give you money—or at least the promise of it—and at the same time allow you to make up for something that should, whether it does or not, weigh rather heavily on your conscience."

"If you'll come to the point."

"Exactly. Do you remember my case?"

"In a way. I had a good many of them."

"Which, I hope, you did not handle in the same way that you did mine. But to recall it all to your recollection, I was accused of having killed my own cousin, Tom Langdon, with a mallet."

"Yes—I remember now. You two had some kind of a drunken fight."

"And you, at the time, if I remember correctly, had a fight of your own. It was nearing election time."

"Correct. I remember now." Then, with a little smile, "Quite luckily, I was beaten."

"I agree with you there. But to return to the original statement. Am I right, or am I wrong, when I say that you were striving very hard, for a record that would aid you in the election?"

"Every official tries to make the best possible record. Especially at election time."

"No matter whom it injures."

"I didn't say that."

"But I did—and I repeat it. No matter whom it injures! Now, to be plain and frank and brutal with you to-night as you were with me in the courtroom, Mr. Worthington, I have pretty convincing evidence that you knew I was innocent. Further, that you knew it almost at the beginning of the trial. But that in spite of this knowledge, you continued to persecute me—notice, I don't say prosecute—to persecute me in a hope of gaining a conviction, simply that you might go before the voters and point to me in prison as a recommendation of your efficiency as a district attorney."

"Oh!" Worthington threw away his cigarette with an angry gesture, and came forward. "You fellows are all the same. You're always squealing about your innocence. I never saw a man yet who wasn't innocent in one way or another. Even when they confess, they've got some kind of an alibi for their act. They didn't know the gun was loaded, or the other fellow hit them first or—"

"In my case I have no alibis. And this isn't simply my own statement. I have sufficient witnesses."

"Then why didn't you produce them at the trial?"

"I couldn't. You had them."

"I?"

"Yes. I don't mind giving you the names. One of them was Doctor Horton. Another was Doctor Mayer. A third was Doctor Brensteam, all physicians of the highest reputation. I would like, Mr. Worthington, to know why you did not make use of them in the trial instead of the expert Hamon, and that other one, Jaggerston, who, as every one knows, are professional expert witnesses, ready at all times to testify upon anything from handwriting to the velocity of a rifle bullet, providing they are sufficiently paid."

"Why? Simply because I figured they would make the best witnesses."

"It couldn't have been," and Houston's voice was more coldly caustic than ever, "that it was because they would be willing to perjure themselves, while the real doctors wouldn't?"

"Of course not! This whole thing is silly. Besides, I'm out of it entirely. I'm—"

"Mr. Worthington," and Houston's tone changed. "Your manner and your words indicate very plainly that you're not out of it—that you merely wish you were. Isn't that the truth? Don't you?"

"Well," and the man lit a fresh cigarette, "I feel that way about every murder case."

"But especially about this one. You're not naturally a persecutor. You don't naturally want to railroad men to the penitentiary. And I believe that, as a general thing, you didn't do it. You tried it in my case; election was coming on, you had just run up against two or three acquittals, and you had made up your mind that in my case you were going to run the gauntlet to get a conviction. I don't believe you wanted to send me up simply for the joy of seeing an innocent man confined in prison. You wanted a conviction—wasn't that it?"

"Every prosecutor works for that."

"Not when he knows the man is innocent, Mr. Worthington. You knew that—I have proof. I have evidence that you found it out almost at the beginning of my trial—August second, to be exact—and that you used this information to your own ends. In other words, it told you what the defense would testify; and you built up, with your professional experts, a wall to combat it. Now, isn't that the truth?"

"Why—" The former district attorney took more time than usual to knock the ashes from his cigarette, then suddenly changed the subject.

"You spoke of a suit you might bring when you came in here?"

"Yes. Against the city. I have a perfect one. I was persecuted when the official in charge of the case knew that I was not guilty. To that end I can call the three doctors I've mentioned and put them on the stand and ask them why they did not testify in the case. I also can call the officials of Bellstrand Hospital in New York where you conducted certain experiments on cadavers on the night of August second; also a doctor who saw you working in there and who watched you personally strike the blows with a mallet; further, I can produce the records of the hospital which state that you were there, give the names of the entire party, together with the number of corpses experimented upon. Is that sufficient evidence that I know what I'm talking about?"

Worthington examined his cigarette again.

"I suppose it's on the books down there. But there's nothing to state of what the experiments consisted."

"I have just told you that I have an eye-witness. Further, there are the three doctors."

"Have you seen them?"

Houston thought quickly. It was his only chance.

"I know exactly what their testimony will be."

"You've made arrangements for your suit then." Worthington's color had changed. Houston noticed that the hand which held the cigarette trembled slightly.

"No, I haven't. I'm not here to browbeat you, Mr. Worthington, or lie to you. It came to me simply as a ruse to get in to see you. But the more I think of it, the more I know that I could go through with it and possibly win it. I might get my million. I might not. I don't want money gained in that way. The taxpayers would have to foot the bill, not yourself."

"Oh, I guess I'd pay enough," Worthington had assumed an entirely different attitude now. "It would hurt me worse in business than it would if I were still in office. Whether it's true or not."

"You know in your heart that there's no doubt of that."

Worthington did not answer. Houston waited a moment, then went on.

"But personally, I don't want to file the suit. I don't want any money—that way. I don't want any bribes, or exculpations, or statements from you that you know me to be innocent. Some might believe it; others would only ask how much I paid to have that statement given out. The damage has been done and is next to irreparable. You could have cleared me easily enough by dropping the case, or making your investigations before ever an indictment was issued. You didn't, and I remain guilty in the minds of most of Boston, in spite of what the jury said. A man is not guilty until convicted—under the law. He is guilty as soon as accused, with the lay mind. So you can't help me much there; my only chance for freedom lies in finding the man who actually committed that murder. But that's something else. We won't talk about it. You owe me something. And I'm here to-night to ask you for it."

"I thought you said you didn't want any bribes."

"I don't. May I ask you what your margin of profit is at your machinery company?"

"My margin of profit? What's that? Well, I suppose it runs around twelve per cent."

"Then will you please allow me to give you twelve thousand dollars in profits? I'm in the lumber business. I have a contract that runs into the millions; surely that is good enough security to a man"—he couldn't resist the temptation—"who knows my absolute innocence. It isn't good enough for the bankers, who still believe me guilty, so I've come directly to you. I need one hundred thousand dollars' worth of lumber-mill machinery, blade saws, crosscuts, jackers, planers, kickers, chain belting, leather belting, and everything else that goes to make up a first-class plant. I can pay for it—in installments. I guarantee to give you every cent above my current running expenses until the bill is disposed of. My contract with the Mountain, Plains and Salt Lake Railroad is my bond. I don't even ask a discount, or for you to lose any of your profits. I don't even ask any public statement by you regarding my innocence. All I want is to have you do what you would do to any reputable business man who came to you with a contract running into the millions of dollars—to give me credit for that machinery. It's a fair proposition. Come in with me on it, and we'll forget the rest. Stay out—and I fight!"

For a long moment, Kilbane Worthington paced the floor, his hands clasped behind him, his rather thin head low upon his chest. Then, at last, he looked up.

"How long are you going to be in town?"

"Until this matter's settled."

"Where are you staying?"

"The Touraine."

"Very well. I'll have a machine there to pick you up at ten o'clock to-morrow morning and take you to my office. In the meanwhile—I'll think it over."

CHAPTER XVIII

It was a grinning Barry Houston who leaped from the train at Tabernacle a week later and ran open-armed through the snow toward the waiting Ba'tiste.

"You got my telegram?" He asked it almost breathlessly.

"Ah, *oui! oui, oui, oui! Sacre*, and you are the wizard!"

"Hardly that." They were climbing into the bobsled. "I just had enough sense to put two and two together. On the train to Boston I got a tip about my case, something that led me to believe that the district attorney knew all the time that I was innocent. He had conducted experiments at the Bellstrand Hospital of which nothing had been said in the trial. Three famous doctors had been with him. As soon as I saw their names, I instinctively knew that if the experiments had turned out the way the district attorney had wanted them, he would have used them in the trial against me, but that their silence meant the testimony was favorable to me."

"*Bon*!" Ba'tiste grinned happily. "And he?"

"It just happened that he is now in the mill machinery business. I," and Houston smiled with the memory of his victory, "I convinced him that he should give me credit."

"Eet is good. In the woods, there are many men. The log, he is pile all about the mill. Three thousand tie, already they are stack up."

"And the woman—she has caused no trouble?"

"No. Peuff! I have no see her. Mebbe so, eet was a mistake."

"Maybe, Ba'tiste, but I was sure I recognized her. The Blackburn crowd hasn't given up the ghost yet?"

"Ah, no. But eet will. Still they think that we cannot fill the contract. They think that after the first shipment or so, then we will have to quit."

"They may be right, Ba'tiste. It would require nearly two thousand men to keep that mill supplied with logs, once we get into production, outside of the regular mill force, under conditions such as they are now. It would be ruinous. We've got to find some other way, Ba'tiste, of getting our product to the mill. That's all there is to it."

"Ba'teese, he have think of a way—that he have keep secret. Ba'teese, he have a, what-you-say, hump."

"Hunch, you mean?"

"Ah, *oui*. Eet is this. We will not bring the log to the mill. We will bring the mill to the log. We have to build the new plant, yes, *oui*? Then, *bon*, we shall build eet in the forest, where there is the lumber."

"Quite so. And then who will build a railroad switch that can negotiate the hills to the mill?"

"Ah!" Ba'tiste clapped a hand to his forehead. "*Veritas*? I am the prize, what-you-say, squash! Ba'teese, he never think of eet!" A moment he sat glum, only to surge with another idea. "But, now, Ba'teese have eet! He shall go to Medaine! He shall tell her to write to the district attorney of Boston—that he will tell her—"

"It was part of my agreement, Ba'tiste, that he be forced to make no statements regarding my innocence."

"Ah, but—"

"It was either that, or lose the machinery. He's in business. He's afraid of notoriety. The plain, cold truth is that he tried to railroad me, and only my knowledge of that fact led him into doing a decent and honorable thing. But I sealed any chance of his moral aid when I made my bargain. It was my only chance."

Slowly Ba'tiste nodded and slapped the reins on the back of the horse.

"Ba'teese will not see Medaine," came at last, and they went on.

Again the waiting game, but a busy game however, one which kept the ice roads polished and slippery; which resulted, day by day, in a constantly growing mountain of logs about the diminutive sawmill. One in which plans were drawn, and shell-like buildings of mere slats and slab sidings erected, while heavy, stone foundations were laid in the firm, rocky soil to support the machinery, when it arrived. A game in which Houston hurried from the forests to the mill and back again, now riding the log sheds as a matter of swifter locomotion, instead of for the thrill, as he once had done. Another month went by, to bring with it the bill of lading which told that the saws, the beltings, the planers and edgers and trimmers, and the half hundred other items of machinery were at last on their way, a month of activities and—of hopes.

For to Ba'tiste Renaud and Barry Houston there yet remained one faint chance. The Blackburn crowd had taken on a gamble, one which, at the time, had seemed safe enough; the investment of thousands of dollars for a plant which they had believed firmly would be free of competition. That plant could not hope for sufficient business to keep it alive, with the railroad contract gone, and the bigger mill of Houston and Renaud in successful operation. There would come the time when they must forfeit that lease and contract through non-payment, or agree to re-lease them to the original owner. But would that time arrive soon enough? It was a grim possibility,—a gambling wager that held forth hope, and at the same time threatened them with extinction. For the same thing applied to Houston and Ba'tiste that applied to Blackburn and Thayer. If they could not make good on their contract, the other mill was ever ready to step in.

"Eet all depen'," said Ba'tiste more than once during the snowy, frost-caked days in which they watched every freight train that pulled, white-coated, over the range into Tabernacle. "Eet all depen' on the future. Mebbe so, we make eet. Mebbe so, we do not. But we gamble, eh, *mon Baree?*"

"With our last cent," came the answer of the other man, and in the voice was grimness and enthusiasm. It was a game of life or extinction now.

March, and a few warm days, which melted the snows only that they might crust again. Back and forth traveled the bobsled to Tabernacle, only to meet with disappointment.

"I've wired the agent at Denver three times about that stuff," came the announcement of the combined telegrapher and general supervisor of freight at the little station. "He's told me that he'd let me know as soon as it got in. But nothing's come yet."

A week more, and another week after that, in which spring taunted the hills, causing the streams to run bank-full with the melting waters of the snow, in which a lone robin made his appearance about the camp,—only to fade as quickly as he had come. For winter, tenacious, grim, hateful winter, had returned for a last fling, a final outburst of frigid viciousness that was destined to wrap the whole range country in a grip of terror.

They tried the bobsled, Ba'tiste and Houston, only to give it up. All night had the snow fallen, in a thick, curtain-like shield which blotted out even the silhouettes of the heaviest pines at the brow of the hill, which piled high upon the ridges, and with great sweeps of the wind drifted every cut of the road to almost unfathomable depths. The horses floundered and plowed about in vain efforts at locomotion, at last to plunge in the terror of a bottomless road. They whinnied and snorted, as though in appeal to the men on the sled behind,—a sled that worked on its runners no longer, but that sunk with every fresh drift to the main-boards themselves. Wadded with clothing, shouting in a mixture of French and English and his own peculiar form of slang, Ba'tiste tried in vain to force the laboring animals onward. But they only churned uselessly in the drift; their hoofs could find no footing, save the yielding masses of snow. Puffing, as though the exertion had been his own, the trapper turned and stared down at his companion.

"Eet is no use," came finally. "The horse, he can not pull. We must make the trip on the snowshoe."

They turned back for the bunk house, to emerge a few moments later,—bent, padded forms, fighting clumsily against the sweep of the storm. Ghosts they became almost immediately, snow-covered things that hardly could be discerned a few feet away, one hand of each holding tight to the stout cord which led from waist-belt to waist-belt, their only insurance against being parted from each other in the blinding swirl of winter.

Hours, stopping at short intervals to seek for some land-mark—for the road long ago had become obliterated—at last to see faintly before them the little box-car station house, and to hurry toward it in a fear that neither of them dared to express to the other. Snow in the mountains is not a gentle thing, nor one that comes by fits and gusts. The blizzard does not sweep away its vengeful enthusiasm in a day or a night. It comes and it stays—departing for a time, it seems—that it may gather new strength and fury for an even fiercer attack. And the features of the agent, as he stared up from the rattling telegraph key, were not conducive to relief.

"Your stuff's on the way, if that's any news to you," came with a worried laugh. "It left Denver on Number 312 at five o'clock this morning behind Number Eight. That's no sign that it's going to get here. Eight isn't past Tollifer yet."

"Not past Tollifer?" Houston stared anxiously. "Why, it should be at the top of the range by now. It hasn't even begun to climb."

"Good reason. They're getting this over there too."

"The snow?"

"Worse than here, if anything. Denver reported ten inches at eleven o'clock—and it's fifteen miles from the range. There was three inches when the train started. Lord knows where that freight is—I can't get any word from it."

"But—"

"Gone out again!" The telegrapher hammered disgustedly on the key. "The darned line grounds on me about every five minutes. I—"

"Do you hear anything from Crestline—about conditions up there?"

"Bad. It's even drifting in the snowsheds. They've got two plows working in 'em keeping 'em open, and another down at Crystal Lake. If things let up, they're all right. If not—they'll run out of coal by to-morrow morning and be worse than useless. There's only about a hundred tons at Crestline—and it takes fuel to feed them babies. But so far—"

"Yes?"

"They're keeping things halfway open. Wait a minute—" he bent over the key again—"it's opened up. Number Eight's left Tollifer. The freight's behind it, and three more following that. I guess they're going to try to run them through in a bunch. They'll be all right—if they can only get past Crestline. But if they don't—"

He rattled and banged at the key for a long moment, cursing softly. Only the dead "cluck" of a grounded line answered him. Houston turned to Ba'tiste.

"It looks bad."

"*Oui*! But eet depen'—on the storm. Eet come this way, near' ev' spring. Las' year the road tie up—and the year before.

Oh," he shrugged his shoulders, "that is what one get for living in a country where the railroad eet chase eetself all over the mountain before eet get here."

"There wouldn't be any chance at the tunnel either, would there? They haven't cut through yet."

"No—and they won' finish until June. That is when they figure—"

"That's a long way off."

"Too long," agreed Ba'tiste, and turned again toward the telegrapher, once more alert over a speaking key. But before it could carry anything but a fragmentary message, life was gone again, and the operator turned to the snow-caked window, with its dreary exterior of whirling snow that seemed to come ever faster.

"Things are going to get bad in this country if this keeps up," came at last. "There ain't any too great a stock of food."

"How about hay for the cattle?"

"All right. I guess. If the ranchers can get to it. But that's the trouble about this snow. It ain't like the usual spring blizzard. It's dry as a January fall, and it's sure drifting. Keeps up for four or five days; they'll be lucky to find the haystacks."

For a long time then, the three stood looking out the window, striving—merely for the sake of passing time—to identify the almost hidden buildings of the little town, scarcely more than a hundred yards away. At last the wire opened again, and the operator went once more to his desk. Ba'tiste and Houston waited for him to give some report. But there was none. At last:

"What is it?" Houston was at his side. The operator looked up.

"Denver asking Marionville if it can put its snowplow through and try to buck the drifts from this side. No answer yet."

A long wait. Then:

"Well, that's done. Only got one Mallett engine at Marionville. Other two are in the shop. One engine couldn't—"

He stopped. He bent over the key. His face went white—tense.

"God!"

"What's wrong?" The two men were close beside him now.

"Number one-eleven's kicked over the hill!"

"One-eleven—kicked over?"

"Yes. Snowplow. They're wiring Denver, from Crestline. The second plow's up there in the snowshed with the crew. One of 'em's dead. The other's—wait a minute, I have to piece it together."

A silence, except for the rattling of the key, broken, jagged, a clattering voice of the distance, faint in the roar and whine of the storm, yet penetrating as it carried the news of a far-away world,—a world where the three waiting men knew that all had turned to a white hell of wintry fury; where the grim, forbidding mountains were now the abiding place of the snow-ledge and the avalanche; where even steel and the highest product of invention counted for nothing against the blast of the wind and the swirl of the tempest. Then finally, as from far away, a strained voice came, the operator's:

"Ice had gotten packed on the rails already. One-eleven tried to keep on without a pick and shovel gang. Got derailed on a curve just below Crestline and went over. One-twelve's crew got the men up. The plow's smashed to nothing. Fifty-three thousand dollars' worth of junk now. Wait a minute—here's Denver."

Again one of those agonizing waits, racking to the two men whose future depended largely upon the happenings atop the range. Far on the other side, fighting slowly upward, was a freight train containing flatcar after flatcar loaded with the necessary materials of a large sawmill. True, June was yet two months away. But months are short when there is work to do, when machinery must be installed, and when contracts are waiting. Every day, every hour, every minute counted now. And as if in answer to their thoughts, the operator straightened, with a little gesture of hopelessness.

"Guess it's all off," came at last. "The general superintendent in Denver's on the wire. Says to back up everything to Tollifer, including the plows, and give up the ghost."

"Give it up?" Houston stared blankly at the telegrapher. "But that's not railroading!"

"It is when you're with a concern that's all but broke," answered the operator. "It's cheaper for this old wooden-axle outfit to quit than to go on fighting—"

"That mean six weeks eef this storm keep up two days longer!" Ba'tiste broke in excitedly. "By to-morrow morning, ever' snowshed, he will be bank-full of snow. The track, he will be four inches in ice. Six week—this country, he can not stand it! Tell him so on the telegraph! Tell him the cattle, he will starve! Peuff! No longer do I think of our machinery! Eef it is los'—we are los'. But let eet go. Say to heem nothing of that. Say to heem that there are the cattle that will starve, that in the stores there is not enough provision. That—"

"I know. I'll call Denver. But I don't know what chance there is—the road's been waiting for a chance to go into bankruptcy, anyway—since this new Carrow Point deal is about through. They haven't got any money—you know that, Ba'tiste. It's cheaper for them to shut down for six weeks than to try to keep running. That fifty thousand they lost on that snowplow just about put the crimp in 'em. It might cost a couple of hundred thousand more to keep the road open. What's the result? It's easier to quit. But I'll try 'em—"

He turned to the key and hammered doggedly. Only soggy deadness answered. He tested his plugs and tried again. In vain. An hour later, he still was there, fighting for the impossible, striving to gain an answer from vacancy, struggling to instil life into a thing deadened by ice, and drifts, and wind, and broken, sagging telegraph poles. The line was gone!

CHAPTER XIX

Until dusk they remained in the boxlike station, hoping against hope. But the whine and snarl of the wind were the only sounds that came to them, the steady banking of the snow against the windows the only evidence of life. The telegraph line, somewhere between Tabernacle and the country which lay over the bleak, now deadly range, was a shattered thing, with poles buried in drifts, with loose strands of wire swinging in the gusts of the blizzard, with ice coated upon the insulations, and repair—until the sun should come and the snows melt—an almost impossible task.

"It'd take a guy with a diving suit to find some of them wires, I guess," the operator hazarded, as he finally ceased his efforts and reached for his coat and hat and snowshoes. "There ain't no use staying here. You fellows are going to sleep in town to-night, ain't you?"

There was little else to do. They fought their way to the rambling boarding house, there to join the loafing group in what passed for a lobby and to watch with them the lingering death of day in a shroud of white. Night brought no cessation of the wind, no lessening of the banks of snow which now were drifting high against the first-story windows; the door was only kept in working order through constant sallies of the bent old boarding-house keeper, with his snow shovel.

Windows banged and rattled, with a muffled, eerie sound; snow sifted through the tiniest cracks, spraying upon those who sat near them. The old cannon-ball stove, crammed with coal, reached the point where dull red spots enlivened its bulging belly; yet the big room was cold with non-detectable drafts, the men shivered in spite of their heavy clothing, and the region outside the immediate radius of the heater was barn-like with frigidity. Midnight came, and the group about the stove slept in their chairs, rather than undergo the discomfort and coldness of bed.

Morning brought no relief. The storm was worse, if anything, and the boarding-house keeper faced drifts waist high at the doorway with his first shoveling expedition of the day. The telegrapher, at the frost-caked window, rubbed a spot with his hand and stared into the dimness of the flying snow, toward his station.

"Guess I'll have t' call for volunteers if I get in there to-day. We'll have to tunnel."

Ba'tiste and Houston joined him. The box car that served as a station house—always an object of the heaviest drifts—was buried! The big French-Canadian pulled at his beard.

"Peuff! Eet is like the ground hog," he announced. "Eet is underground already."

"Yeh. But I've got to get in there. The wire might be working."

"So? We will help, Baree and Ba'teese. Come—we get the shovels."

Even that was work. The town simply had ceased to be; the stores were closed, solitude was everywhere. They forced a window and climbed into the little general merchandise establishment, simply because it was easier than striving to get in through the door. Then, armed with their shovels, they began the work of tunneling to the station. Two hours later, the agent once more at his dead key, Ba'tiste turned to Houston.

"Eet is the no use here," he announced. "We must get to camp and assemble the men that are strong and willing to help. Then—"

"Yes?"

"Then, eet will be the battle to help those who are not fortunate. There is death in this storm."

Again with their waist-belt guide lines, they started forth, to bend against the storm in a struggle that was to last for hours; to lose their trail, to find it again, through the straggling poles that in the old days had carried telephone wires, and at last to reach the squat, snowed-in buildings of camp. There, Ba'tiste assembled the workmen in the bunk house.

"There are greater things than this now," he announced. "We want the strong men—who will go back with us to Tabernacle, and who will be willing to take the risk to help the countryside. Ah, *oui*, eet is the danger that is ahead. How many of you will go?"

One after another they readied for their snowshoes, silent men who acted, rather than spoke. A few were left behind, to care for the camp in case of emergencies, to keep the roofs as free from snow as possible and to avoid cave-ins. The rest filed outside, one by one, awkwardly testing the bindings of their snowshoes, and awaiting the command. At the doorway, Ba'tiste, his big hands fumbling, caught the paws of Golemar, his wolf-dog, and raised the great, shaggy creature against his breast.

"No," he said in kindly, indulgent fashion. "Eet is not for Golemar to go with us. The drift, they are deep. There is no crust on the snow. Golemar, he would sink above his head. Then blooey! There would be no Golemar!"

Guide lines were affixed. Once more, huddled, clumsy figures of white, one following the other, they made the gruelling trip back to Tabernacle and the duties which they knew lay before them. For already the reports were beginning to come in, brought by storm-weakened, blizzard-battered men, of houses where the roofs had crashed beneath the weight of snow, of lost ranchmen, of bawling cattle, drifting before the storm,—to death. It was the beginning of a two-weeks' siege of a white inferno.

Little time did Barry Houston have for thought in those weeks. There were too many other things to crowd upon him; too many cold, horrible hours in blinding snow, or in the faint glare of a ruddy sun which only broke through the clouds that it might jeer at the stricken country beneath it, then fade again in the whipping gusts of wind and its attendant clouds, giving way once more to the surging sweep of white and the howl of a freshened blizzard.

Telegraph poles reared only their cross-arms above the mammoth drifts. Haystacks became buried, lost things. The trees of the forest, literally harnessed with snow, dropped their branches like tired arms too weary to longer bear their burdens. The whole world, it seemed, was one great, bleak thing of dreary white,—a desert in which there was life only that there might be death, where the battle for existence continued only as a matter of instinct.

And through—or rather over—this bleak desert went the men of the West Country, silent, frost-burned men, their lips cracked from the cut of wind, their eyes blood-red with inflammation, struggling here and there with a pack of food upon their back that they might reach some desolate home where there were women and children; or stopping to pull and tug at a snow-trapped steer and by main effort, drag him into a barren spot where the sweep of the gale had kept the ground fairly clear of snow; at times also, they halted to dig into a haystack, and through long hours scattered the welcome food about for the bawling cattle; or gathered wood, where such a thing was possible, and lighting great fires, left them, that they might melt the snows about a spot near a supply of feed, where the famished cattle could gather and await the next trip of the rescuers, bearing them sustenance.

Oftimes they stopped in vain—the beast which they sought to succor was beyond aid—and a revolver shot sounded, muffled in the thickness of the storm. Then, with knives and axes, the attack came, and struggling forms bore to a ranch house the smoking portions of a newly butchered beef; food at least for one family until the relief of sun and warmth would come. It was a never-ending agony of long hours and muscle-straining work. But the men who partook—were men.

And side by side with the others, with giant Ba'tiste, with the silent woodsmen, with the angular, wiry ranchmen, was Barry Houston. His muscles ached. His head was ablaze with the eye-strain of constant white; his body numbed with cold from the time that he left the old cannon-ball stove of the boarding house in the early morning until he returned to it at night. Long ago had he lost hope,—so far as personal aims and desires were concerned. The Crestline road was tied up; it had quit completely; Barry Houston knew that the fury of the storm in this basin country below the hills was as nothing compared to the terror of those crag tops where altitude added to the frigidity, and where from mountain peak to mountain peak the blizzard leaped with ever-increasing ferocity. Far out on the level stretches leading up to the plains of Wyoming, other men were working, struggling doggedly from telegraph pole to telegraph pole, in an effort to repair the lines so that connection might be made to Rawlins, and thence to Cheyenne and Denver,—to apprise the world that a great section of the country had been cut off from aid, that women and children were suffering from lack of food, that every day brought the news of a black splotch in the snow,—the form of a man, arms outstretched, face buried in the drift, who had fought and lost. But so far, there had been only failure. It was a struggle that made men grim and dogged; Barry Houston no less than the rest. He had ceased to think of the simpler things of life, of the ordinary problems, the usual worries or likes and dislikes. His path led once by the home of Medaine Robinette, and he clambered toward the little house with little more of feeling than of approaching that of the most unfamiliar ranchman.

Smoke was coming from the chimney. There were the marks of snowshoes. But they might mean nothing in the battle for existence. Houston scrambled up to the veranda and banged on the door. A moment more, and he faced Medaine Robinette.

"Just wanted to see if you're all right," came almost curtly.

"Yes—thank you."

"Need any food?"

"I have plenty."

"Anybody sick?"

"No. Lost Wing has found wood. We're keeping warm. Tell me—" and there was the politeness of emergency in her tones—"is there any need for women in Tabernacle? I am willing to go if—"

"Not yet. Besides, a woman couldn't get in there alone."

"I could. I'm strong enough. Besides, I've been out—I went to the Hurd Ranch yesterday. Mrs. Hurd's sick—Lost Wing brought me the word."

"Then keep on with that. There's nothing in Tabernacle—and no place for any one who isn't destitute. Stay here. Have you food enough for Hurd's?"

"Yes. That is—"

"I'll leave my pack. Take that over as you need it. There's enough for a week there. If things don't let up by that time, I'll be by again."

"Thank you."

Then the door was closed, and Houston went his way again, back to Tabernacle and a fresh supply for his pack—hardly realizing the fact that he had talked to the woman he could not help wishing for—the woman he would have liked to have loved. The world was almost too gray, too grim, too horrible for Houston even to remember that there was an estrangement between them. Dully, his intellect numbed as his body was numbed, he went back to his tasks,—tasks that were seemingly endless.

Day after day, the struggle remained the same, the wind, the snow, the drifts, the white fleece flying on the breast of the gale even when there were no storm clouds above, blotting out the light of the sun and causing the great ball to be only a red, ugly, menacing thing in a field of dismal gray. Night after night the drifts swept, changing, deepening in spots where the ground had been clear before, smoothing over the hummocks, weaving across the country like the vagaries of shifting sands before they finally packed into hard, compressed mounds, to form bulwarks for newer drifts when the next storm came. Day after day,—and then quiet, for forty-eight hours.

It caused men to shout,—men who had cursed the sun in the blazing noonday hours of summer, but men who now extended their arms to it, who slapped one another on the back, who watched the snow with blood-red eyes for the first sign of a melting particle, and who became hysterically jubilant when they saw it. Forty-eight hours! Deeper and deeper went the imprints of milder weather upon the high-piled serrations of white, at last to cease. The sun had faded on the afternoon of the second day. The thaw stopped. The snowshoes soon carried a new crunching sound that gradually became softer, more muffled. For the clouds had come again, the wind had risen with a fiercer bite than ever in it; again the snow was falling. But the grim little army of rescuers, plodding from one ranchhouse to another, had less of worriment in their features now,—even though the situation was no less tense, no less dangerous. At least the meager stores of the small merchandise establishment in Tabernacle could be distributed with more ease; a two-inch crust of snow had formed over the main snowfall, permitting small sleds to be pulled behind struggling men; the world beneath had been frozen in, to give place to a new one above. And with that:

"It's open! It's open!" The shout came from the lips of the

telegrapher, waving his arms as he ran from the tunnel that led to the stationhouse. "It's open! I've had Rawlins on the wire!"

Men crowded about him and thumped into the little box car to listen, like children, to the rattling of the telegraph key,— as though they never had heard one before. So soon does civilization feel the need of its inventions, once they are taken away; so soon does the mind become primitive, once the rest of the world has been shut away from it. Eagerly they clustered there, staring with anxious eyes toward the operator as he hammered at the key, talking in whispers lest they disturb him, waiting for his interpretation of the message, like worshippers waiting for the word of an oracle.

"I'm putting it all on the wire!" he announced at last, with feverish intensity. "I'm telling 'em just how it is over here. Maybe they can do something—from Rawlins."

"Rawlins?" Houston had edged forward. "There's not a chance. It's hundreds of miles away; they can't use horses, and they certainly can't walk. Wait—will you give me a chance at something?"

A gleam had come into his eyes. His hands twisted nervously. Voices mumbled about him; suddenly the great hands of Ba'tiste grasped him by the shoulders and literally tossed him toward the telegrapher.

"Ah, *oui*! If eet is the idea—then speak it."

"Go on—" the telegrapher had stopped his key for a moment —"I'll put it through, if it'll help."

"All right. Get Denver on the wire. Then take this message to every newspaper in the city:

"'Can't you help us? Please try to start campaign to force Crestline Road to open the Pass. Women and children are starving here. We have been cut off from the rest of the world for two weeks. We need food—and coal. Road will not be open for four or five weeks more under ordinary circumstances. This will mean death to many of us here, the wiping out of a great timber and agricultural country, and a blot on the history of Colorado. Help us—and we will not forget it."

"THE CITIZENS OF THE WEST COUNTRY."

"Ah, *oui*!" Old Ba'tiste was addressing the rest of the crowd. "The newspapers, they can help, better than any one else. Eet is our chance. *Bon*—good! *Mon* Baree, he have the big, what-you-say, sentiment."

"Sounds good." The telegrapher was busily putting it on the wire. Then a wait of hours,—hours in which the operator varied his routine by sending the word of the stricken country to Cheyenne, to Colorado Springs, to Pueblo, and thence, through the news agencies, to the rest of the world.

"Might as well get everybody in on it," he mused, as he pounded the telegraph instrument; "can't tell—some of those higher-ups might be in New York and think there wasn't anything to it unless they could see it in the New York papers. I—" Then he stopped as the wire cut under his finger and clattered forth a message. He jumped. He grasped Ba'tiste in his lank arms, then turned beaming to the rest of the gaping crowd.

"It's from the papers in Denver!" he shouted. "A joint message. They've taken up the fight!"

A fight which had its echoes in the little railroad box car, the center of the deadened, shrouded West Country, the news of which must travel to Cheyenne, to Rawlins, thence far down through the northern country over illy patched telegraph wires before it reached the place for which it was intended, the box car and its men who came and went, eager for the slightest word from the far-away, yet grudging of their time, lest darkness still find them in the snows, and night come upon them struggling to reach the little town and send them into wandering, aimless journeys that might end in death. For the snows still swirled, the storms still came and went, the red ball of the sun still refused to come forth in its beaming strength. And it was during this period of uncertainty that Houston met Ba'tiste Renaud, returning from a cruising expedition far in the lake region, to find him raging, his fists clenched, his eyes blazing.

"Is eet that the world is all unjust?" he roared, as he faced Houston. "Is eet that some of us do our part, while others store up for emergency? Eh? Bah! I am the mad enough to tear them apart!"

"Who? What's gone wrong?"

"I am the mad! You have no seen the M'sieu Thayer during all the storm?"

"No."

"Nor the M'sieu Blackburn? Nor the men who work for them. Eh? You have no seen them?"

"No, not once."

"Ah! I pass to-day the Blackburn mill. They have shovel out about the sawshed. They have the saw going,—they keep at work, when there are the women and the babies who starve, when there are the cattle who are dying, when there is the country that is like a broken thing. But they work—for themself! They saw the log into the tie—they work from the piles of timber which they have about the sawmill, to store up the supply. They know that we do not get our machinery! They have think they have a chance—for the contract!"

It brought Houston to a sharp knowledge of conditions. They had given, that the rest of the country might not suffer. Their enemies had worked on, fired with the new hope that the road over the mountains would not be opened; that the machinery so necessary to the carrying out of Houston's contract would not arrive in time to be of aid. For without the ability to carry out the first necessities of that agreement, the rest must surely and certainly fail. Long before, Houston had realized the danger that the storm meant; there had been no emergency clause in the contract. Now his hands clenched, his teeth gritted.

"It almost seems that there's a premium on being crooked, Ba'tiste," came at last. "It—"

Then he ceased. A shout had come from the distance. Faintly through the sifting snow they could see figures running. Then the words came,—faint, far-away, shrill shouts forcing their way through the veil of the storm.

"They're going to open the road! They're going to open the road!"

Here, there and back again it came, men calling to men, the few women of the little settlement braving the storm that they too might add to the gladful cry. Already, according to the telegram, snow-fighting machinery and men were being assembled in Denver for the first spurt toward Tollifer, and from there through the drifts and slides of the hills toward

Crestline. Ba'tiste and Houston were running now, as fast as their snowshoes would allow, oblivious for once of the cut of the wind and the icy particles of its frigid breath.

"They open the road!" boomed Ba'tiste in chorus with the rest of the little town. "Ah, *oui*! They open the road. The Crestline Railroad, he have a heart after all, he have a—"

"Any old time!" It was a message bearer coming from the shack of a station. "They're not going to do it—it's the M. P. & S. L."

"Through the tunnel?"

"No. Over the hill. According to the message, the papers hammered the stuffing out of the Crestline road. But you've got to admit that they haven't got either the motive power or the money. The other road saw a great chance to step in and make itself solid with this country over here. It's lending the men and the rolling stock. They're going to open another fellow's road, for the publicity and the good will that's in it."

A grin came to Houston's lips,—the first one in weeks. He banged Ba'tiste on his heavily wadded shoulder.

"That's the kind of railroad to work for!"

"Ah, *oui*! And when eet come through—ah, we shall help to build it."

Two pictures flashed across Houston's brain; one of a snowy sawmill with the force working day and night, when all the surrounding country cried for help, working toward its selfish ends that it might have a supply of necessary lumber in case a more humane organization should fail; another of carload after carload of necessary machinery, snow-covered, ice-bound, on a sidetrack at Tollifer, with the whole, horrible, snow-clutched fierceness of the Continental Divide between it and its goal.

"I hope so!" he exclaimed fervently. "I hope so!"

Then, swept along by hurrying forms, they went on toward the station house, there to receive the confirmation of the glad news, to shout until their throats were raw, and then, still with their duties before them, radiate once more on their missions of mercy. For the announcement of intention was no accomplishment. It was one thing for the snowplows and the gangs and tremendous engines of the M. P. & S. L. to attempt to open the road over the divide. But it was quite another thing to do it!

All that day Houston thought of it, dreamed of it, tried to visualize it,—the fight of a railroad against the snows of the hills. He wondered how the snowplows would work, how they would break through the long, black snowsheds, now crammed with the thing which they had been built to resist. He thought of the laborers; and his breath pulled sharply. Would they have enough men? It would be grueling work up there, terrific work; would there be sufficient laborers who would be willing to undergo the hardships for the money they received? Would—

In the night he awoke, again thinking of it. Every possible hand that could swing a pick or jam a crowbar against grudging ice would be needed up there. Every pair of shoulders willing to assume the burdens of a horrible existence that others might live would be welcomed. A mad desire began to come over him; a strange, impelling scheme took hold of his brain. They would need men,—men who would not be afraid, men who would be willing to slave day and night if necessary to the success of the adventure. And who should be more willing than he? His future, his life, his chance of success, where now was failure, lay at Tollifer. His hands would be more than eager! His muscles more than glad to ache with the fatigue of manual labor! Long before dawn he rose and scribbled a note in the dim light of the old kerosene lamp in the makeshift lobby, a note to Ba'tiste Renaud:

"I'm going over the range. I can't wait. They may need me. I'm writing this, because you would try to dissuade me if I told you personally. Don't be afraid for me—I'll make it somehow. I've got to go. It's easier than standing by.

"HOUSTON."

Then, his snowshoes affixed, he went out into the night. The stars were shining dimly, and Houston noticed them with an air of thankfulness as he took the trail of the telephone poles and started toward the faint outline of the mountains in the distance. It would make things easier; but an hour later, as he looked for a dawn that did not come, he realized that it had been only a jest of the night. The storm clouds were thick on the sky again, the snow was dashing about him once more; half-blindly, gropingly, he sought to force his way from one pole to another,—in vain.

He measured his steps, and stopping, looked about him. He had traveled the distance from one pole to another, yet in the sweep of the darting sheet of white he could discern no landmark, nothing to guide him farther on his journey. He floundered aimlessly, striving by short sallies to recover the path from which the storm had taken him, but all to no purpose. If dawn would only come!

Again and again, hardly realizing the dangers to which he was subjecting himself, Houston sought to regain his lost sense of direction. Once faintly, in the far-away, as the storm lifted for a moment, he thought that he glimpsed a pole and hurried toward it with new hope, only to find it a stalwart trunk of a dead tree, rearing itself above the mound-like drifts. Discouraged, half-beaten, he tried again, only to wander farther than ever from the trail. Dawn found him at last, floundering hopelessly in snow-screened woods, going on toward he knew not where.

A half-hour, then he stopped. Fifty feet away, almost covered by the changing snows, a small cabin showed faintly, as though struggling to free itself from the bonds of white, and Houston turned toward it eagerly. His numbed hands banged at the door, but there came no answer. He shouted; still no sound came from within, and he turned the creaking, protesting knob.

The door yielded, and climbing over the pile of snow at the step, Houston guided his snowshoes through the narrow door, blinking in the half-light in an effort to see about him. There was a stove, but the fire was dead. At the one little window, the curtain was drawn tight and pinned at the sides to the sash. There was a bed—and the form of some one beneath the covers. Houston called again, but still there came no answer. He turned to the window, and ripping the shade from its fastenings, once more sought the bed, to bend over and to stare in dazed, bewildered fashion, as though in a dream. He was looking into the drawn, haggard features of an unconscious woman, the eyes half-open, yet unseeing, one emaciated hand grasped about something that was shielded by the covers. Houston forced himself even closer. He touched the hand. He called:

"Agnes!"

The eyelids moved slightly; it was the only evidence of life, save the labored, irregular breathing. Then the hand moved, clutchingly. Slowly, tremblingly, Houston turned back an edge of the blankets,—and stood aghast.

On her breast was a baby—dead!

CHAPTER XX

There was no time for conjectures. The woman meant a human life,—in deadly need of resuscitation, and Barry leaped to his task.

Warmth was the first consideration, and he hurried to the sheet-iron stove, with its pile of wood stacked behind, noticing, as he built the fire, cans and packages of provisions upon the shelf over the small wooden table, evidence that some one other than the woman herself had looked after the details of stocking the cabin with food and of providing against emergencies. At least a portion of the wood as he shoved it into the stove crackled and spit with the wetness of snow; the box had been replenished, evidently within the last few days.

Soon water was boiling. Hot cloths went to the woman's head; quietly, reverently, Barry had taken the still, small child from the tightly clenched arm and covered it, on the little table. And with the touch of the small, lifeless form, the resentment which had smoldered in Houston's heart for months seemed to disappear. Instinctively he knew what a baby means to a mother,—and she must be its mother. He understood that the agony of loss which was hers was far greater even than the agony which her faithlessness had meant for him. Gently, almost tenderly, he went again to the

Courtney Ryley Cooper

bed, to chafe the cold, thin wrists, to watch anxiously the eyes, then at last to bend forward. The woman was looking at him, staring with fright in her gaze, almost terror.

"Barry—" the word was more of a mumble. "Barry—" then the eyes turned, searching for the form that no longer was beside her. "My—my—" Then, with a spasm of realization, she was silent. Houston strove dully for words.

"I'm sorry—Agnes. Don't be afraid of me. I'll get help for you."

"Don't." The voice was a monotone, minus expression, almost minus life. The face had become blank, so much parchment drawn over bone. "I've been sick—my baby— where's my baby?"

"Don't you know?"

"Yes," came at last. There was the dullness that comes when grief has reached the breaking point. "Dead. It died— yesterday morning."

Houston could say nothing in answer. The simple statement was too tragic, too full of meaning, too fraught with the agony of that long day and night of suffering, for any reply in words that would not jar, or cause even a greater pang. Quietly he turned to the stove, red-hot now, and with snow water began the making of gruel from the supplies on the shelf. Once he turned, suddenly aware that the eyes of the woman were centered in his direction. But they were not upon him; their gaze was for one thing, one alone,—that tiny, covered form on the table.

An hour passed silently, except for the trivialities of speech accompanying the proffered food. Then, at last, forcing himself to the subject, Houston asked a question:

"Where is he?"

"Who?" Sudden fright had come into the woman's eyes. A name formed on Houston's lips, only to be forced back into the more general query:

"Your husband."

She smiled faintly.

"You've got me, haven't you, Barry?" A half-hysterical tone came now. "You know a lot—and you want the rest, so you can pay me back, don't you? Oh," and the thin fingers plucked at the bedclothes, "I expected it! I expected it! I knew sooner or later—"

"If you're talking about me, Agnes—and what I've been led to believe, we'll save that for a future time. I think I'm enough of a man not to harass a person in time of grief."

"Coals of fire, eh?" A tinge of her old expression had come back, with returning strength.

"Nothing of the kind. I simply wanted to help you—because you're a woman in trouble. You're sick. Your baby's—gone. If I can get your husband for you, I—"

But she shook her head, suddenly weak and broken, suddenly only what Barry was trying to make of her in his mind, a grieving woman, in need.

"We're—not married. You'll know it sooner or later. I—I don't know where he is. He was here three days ago and was coming back that night. But he didn't. Maybe he's gone—

he'd threatened it."

"He? You mean—"

She pressed her lips tight.

"I'm not going to tell—yet. You've got to do something for me first. I'm in trouble—" she was speaking rapidly now, the words flooding over her lips between gasps, her eyes set, her hands knitting. "My baby's dead. You know that, don't you?" she asked suddenly, in apparent forgetfulness of any previous conversation. "My baby's dead. It died yesterday morning—all day long I held it in my arms and cried. Then I slept, didn't I?"

"You were unconscious."

"Maybe I'm going to die." There was childishness in the voice. "Like my baby. I baptized her before she went. Maybe I'm going to die too."

"I hope not, Agnes."

"You'd like to see me die!" The frail bonds of an illness-. ridden brain were straining at their leash. "I can see it in your eyes. You'd like to see me die!"

"Why?" he could think of nothing else.

"Because—" and then she stopped. "No—you're trying to get me to tell—but I won't; I'll tell when you come back—I'll tell what I said and did when you bring me the note from the priest. You want me to tell, don't you? Don't you? That's what you came here for. You found out I was here. I—did he tell?" she asked sharply.

Barry shook his head.

"I don't know who you mean, Agnes."

"No? I think you're—"

"I was on my way over the range. I got lost in the storm and stumbled in here." He looked out. "It's let up some now. Maybe I could find my way back to town—you must have a doctor."

"I don't want a doctor! I want to go—with my baby. And I don't want him to know—understand that—" with a struggle she raised to one elbow, eyes suddenly blazing with the flashes of her disordered brain, features strained and excited. "I don't want him to know! He ran away and left me for three days. The fire went out—my baby—" hysterical laughter broke from her dry lips—"My baby died, and still he didn't come. He—"

"Agnes!" Houston grasped her hands. "Try to control yourself! Maybe he couldn't get back. The storm—"

"Yes, the storm! It's always the storm! We would have been married—but there was the storm. He couldn't marry me months ago—when I found out—and when I came back out here! He couldn't marry me then. 'Wait'; that's what he always said—'wait—' and I waited. Now—" then the voice trailed off—"it's been three days. He promised to be back. But—"

Houston sought to end the repetition.

"Perhaps I could find him and bring him here."

But it was useless. The woman drifted back to her rambling

statements. Laughter and tears followed one another in quick succession; the breaking of restraint had come at last. At last she turned, and staring with glazed eyes into those of Houston, burst forth.

"You hate me, don't you?"

"I—"

"Don't deny it!" Querulous imperiousness was in the voice. "You hate me—you'll go back to Boston and tell my mother about this. I know—you've got the upper hand now. You'll tell her why I came out here—you'll tell her about the baby, won't you? Yes, you'll—"

"I'll tell nothing of the sort, Agnes. I don't fight that way. You ought to know that. You've been my enemy, I'll admit. I've felt bitter, terribly so, against you. I believed that you used my trust to betray me. But I believe I know the reason now. Besides, the harm's done. It's in the past. I fight men, not women."

"Do you want help?" A thin hand stretched out. "Will you give me a promise—if I give you one?"

"About what, Agnes?"

"My baby. You—you're not going to let it stay there? You're—"

"I hardly know what to do. I thought after you were better, I'd—"

"I'm better now." She tried to rise. "I'm better—see? I've more strength. You could leave me alone. I—I want you to take my baby."

"Where?"

"Where she can sleep in peace—in hallowed ground. I—I want a priest for her. Tell him that I baptized her Helena."

"Yes. And the other name?"

A weird laugh came from the colorless lips.

"She hasn't one."

"But—"

"Then use mine—so you'll have evidence that I'm not married. Use mine, if that's the kind of a man you are—so you can go back and tell them—back home—that I—I—" The last bond had snapped. She caught at him with clawing hands, her eyes wild, her teeth showing from behind tightly drawn lips. "Torture me—that's it—torture me! At least, I didn't do that to you! I told you that I believed in you—at least that cheered you up when you needed it—I didn't tell you that I believed you guilty. Did I? I didn't continually ask you for the name of the man you'd killed? Oh, there were other things—I know there were other things—" the lips seemed to fairly stream words, "but at least, I didn't torture you. I—I—"

Then she halted, for the briefest part of a moment, to become suddenly madly cajoling, crazily cunning:

"Listen, Barry, listen to me. You want to know things. I can tell them to you—oh, so many of them. I'll tell them too—if you'll only do this for me. It's my baby—my baby. Don't you know what that means? Won't you promise for me? Take her to a priest—please, Barry—for what you once thought I was? Won't you, Barry? Haven't I had punishment enough?

Did you ever lie all day and listen to the wind shriek, waiting for somebody who didn't come—with your dead baby in your arms? Do you want to punish me more? Do you want me to die too—or do you want me to live and tell you why I did the things I did? Do you? Do you want to know who was back of everything? I didn't do it for myself, Barry. It was some one else—I'll help you, Barry, honestly I'll help you."

"About the murder?" Houston was leaning forward now, tense, hopeful. But the woman shook her head.

"No—I don't know about that. Maybe you did it—I can't say. It's about other things—the lease, and the contract. I'll help you about that—if you'll help me. Take my baby—"

"And keep your secret, Agnes? Is that it?"

"Will you?" The woman's eyes were gleaming strangely. "My mother doesn't know. She's old—you know her, Barry. She thinks I'm—what I should have been. That's why I came back out here. I—I—"

The man rose. He walked to the window and stood for a long time looking out, trying to close his ears to the ramblings of the woman on the bed, striving to find a way to keep the promise she sought. For just a moment the old hatred flooded through him, the resentment toward this being who had been an integral factor in all the troubles which had pursued him in his efforts to beat back to a new life. But as swift as they came, they faded. No longer was she an enemy; only a broken, beaten woman, her empty arms aching as her heart ached; harassed by fears of exposure to the one woman in whom she still desired to be held in honor, of the whereabouts of the man who had led her on through the byways of love into a dismal maze of chicanery. Only a woman, ill, perhaps dying. A woman crying out for the one boon that she could ask of a person she knew to distrust and despise her, seeking the thing that now was her greatest desire in the world, and willing to promise—whether truthfully or not, Barry had no way of telling—to reveal to him secrets of the past, if he would but comply. Was she honest? As he stood there looking out at the snow, it seemed to make little difference. Was she sincere? He would strive to aid a dumb brute if he found it in distress. At last he turned and walked to the bed.

"I'll promise, Agnes. If you want to help me afterward, well and good. If not—you are free to do as you please. I suppose you want her dressed before—"

"Yes." The woman had raised eagerly. "There are clothes—she's never had on—in the bottom drawer of that old bureau. Take them with you. Then look in a box in the top drawer. You'll find a crucifix. They—they might want to put it on her."

She sank back in the bed, and Barry went to his task of searching the drawers of the rickety old bureau. In a mass of tangled, old-fashioned jewelry, he found the crucifix, its chain broken and twisted, and placed it in a pocket. Then he turned to the grimmer task,—and the good-by. A half-hour later, white-featured, his arms cupped gently about a blanket-wrapped form, he stepped forth into the storm, and bending against the wind, turned toward the railroad in obedience to the hazy directions of the sobbing woman he had left behind.

The snowfall was lighter now; he could find his way more easily. A half-hour passed, and he stopped, kneeling and resting the tiny, still bundle upon his knees to relieve his aching arms. Then on again in plodding perseverance,—fulfilling a promise to a woman who had done her best to wreck his existence.

A mile farther, and the railroad telegraph poles appeared. Houston saw them with grateful eyes, though with concern. He knew to a certainty that there was no priest in Tabernacle, and what his story would be when he got there was a little more than he could hazard. To Ba'tiste, he would tell the truth; to others, there must simply be some fabrication that would hold for the moment and that would allow him to go on—while Ba'tiste—

But suddenly he ceased his plans. Black splotches against the snow, two figures suddenly had come out of the sweeping veil,—a girl and a man. Something akin to panic seized Houston. The man was Lost Wing, faithfully in the background as usual. The girl was Medaine Robinette.

For once Houston hoped that she would pass him as usual,—with averted eyes. He did not care to make explanations, to be forced to lie to her. But Fate was against him. A moment more and the storm closed in again, with one of its fitful gusts, only to clear at last and to leave them face to face. Medaine's eyes went with womanly instinct to the bundle in his arms. And even though she could see nothing but the roundness of the blankets, the tender manner in which Barry Houston held the poor, inanimate little parcel was enough.

"A baby!" There was surprise in her tone. Forgetting for the moment her aversion to the man himself, she came forward, touching the blankets, then lifting one edge ever so slightly that she might peer beneath. "Where did you find it? Whose is it?"

Houston sought vainly for words. He stammered,—a promise made to an enemy struggling for supremacy. And the words seem to come unbidden:

"Does it matter?"

"Of course not." She looked at him queerly. "I merely thought I could be of assistance."

"You can. Tell me where I can find a priest."

"A priest?"

"Yes, I need him—the baby is dead."

"Oh." She touched the bundle ever so softly. "I didn't know." Then with a sudden thought; "But her mother. She must need—"

"Only a doctor. I will try to get Ba'tiste to come out."

"But couldn't I—"

"I'm sorry." Barry tried in vain for the words that would tell her the truth, yet tell her nothing. He felt that he was miring himself hopelessly, that his denials and his efforts at secrecy could cause only one idea to form in her brain. He wanted to tell her the truth, to ask her aid, to send her back into the woods to the assistance of the stricken woman there. But he could not frame the request. Instead, "I—I can't tell you. I've given a woman my word. She wouldn't understand—if you went there. With Ba'tiste, it is different. He is a doctor. He has a right. I—I—"

"I understand," came quietly, and in those two words Houston felt that her opinion had been formed; that to her, he was the father; the quiet form in his arms his own child! It was like a blow to him; yet it was only what he had expected from the moment that he had recognized her. And after all, he felt that it did not matter; it was only one more false accusation to be added to the total, only one more height to be added to the barrier which already existed between them.

He accepted her attitude—in spite of the pain it brought—and faced her.

"You were willing to help—before you—knew. You would have been glad to help in the case of a stranger. Are you still willing—now?"

She hesitated a moment, her eyes downcast, at last to force a smile.

"Of course. But you are asking something almost impossible. The nearest priest is at Crestline."

"Crestline?" Houston instinctively turned toward the hills, a bleak, forbidding wall against the sky. "I—"

"Rather, a mile below there at the Croatian settlement on Mount Harris. I am afraid you couldn't find it."

"I can try. Will you lend me Lost Wing to run an errand? I want to get Ba'tiste—for her."

"Certainly."

"May I talk to him privately? He understands English?"

She nodded. Then:

"I will tell Lost Wing that anything you have to say to him shall be a secret even from me. I—do not want to know it."

She spoke to the Indian in Sioux then and drew away, her eyes on the tracings of a snowshoe. Houston, pointing with his head, gave the Indian his directions.

"A woman is sick in a cabin, two miles straight west from

here. Get Ba'tiste Renaud and take him there. Turn away from the stream at a tall, dead lodgepole and go to the left. You will see the cabin. I would rather that you would not go in and that you know nothing about the woman. Tell Ba'tiste that her name must stay a secret until she herself is willing that it be otherwise. Do you understand?"

"A'ri." The Indian went then toward his mistress, waiting her sanction to the mission. She looked at Barry Houston.

"Have you given him his directions?"

"Yes."

"Then, Lost Wing, do as he has told you."

The Sioux started on, soon to be engulfed in the swirling veil of the storm. Barry turned again to the girl.

"Just one more request: I can't carry the child up there—this way. Will you help strap her to my pack?"

Silently she assisted him in the grim task of mercy. Then:

"Do you know the Pass?"

"I can find my way."

"Do you know it?"

He shook his head. She tapped one glove against the other.

"It is impossible then. You—"

"I'll make it some way. Thank you—for helping me."

He started on. But she called him back.

"It's dangerous—too dangerous," and there was a note of pity in her voice. "It's bad enough on foot when there's no snow—if you're not familiar with it. I—"

"Tell me the way. Perhaps I could find it. It's not for myself. I made a promise to the child's mother. I'm afraid she's dying."

A new light came into the girl's eyes, a light of compassion, of utmost pity,—the pity that one can feel for some one who has transgressed, some one who faces the penalty, who feels the lash of the whip, yet does not cry out. Slowly she came toward Houston, then bent to tighten the fastenings of her snowshoes.

"I know the way," came quietly. "I have been over it—in summer and winter. I will show you."

"You! Medaine! I—I—beg pardon." The outburst had passed his lips almost before he realized it. "Miss Robinette, you don't know what you're saying. It's all a man could do to make that climb. I—"

"I know the way," she answered, without indicating that she had heard his remonstrance. "I am glad to go—for the sake of—" She nodded slightly toward the tenderly wrapped bundle on the pack. "I would not feel right otherwise."

"But—"

Then she faced him.

"I am not afraid," came with a quiet assurance that spoke more than words. It told Barry Houston that this little woman of the hills was willing to help him, although she loathed him; that she was willing to undergo hardships, to quell her own dislike for the man she aided that she might give him assistance in a time of death. And he thrilled with it, in spite of the false beliefs that he knew existed in the mind of Medaine Robinette. It gave him a pride in her,—even though he knew this pride to be gained at the loss of his own prestige. And more than all, it made him glad that he had played the man back there in the little, lonely cabin, where lay a sorrow-crazed woman, grieving for a child who was gone; that he too had been big enough and strong enough to forget the past in the exigencies of the moment; that he had aided where he might have hindered; that he had soothed where a lesser nature might have stormed. He bowed his head in acknowledgment of her announcement. Then, side by side, affixing the stout cord that was to form a bond of safety between two alien souls, they started forth, a man who had been accused, but who was strong enough to rise above it, and a woman whose woman-heart had dictated that dislike, distrust, even physical fear be subjugated to the greater, nobler purpose of human charity.

CHAPTER XXI

Silence was their portion as they turned toward the mountains. There was little to say. Now and then as Houston, in the lead, got off the trail, Medaine jerked on the cord to draw his attention, then pointed, and Barry obeyed. Thus their pilgrimage progressed.

An hour found them in the hills, plodding steadily upward, following the smoother mounds of snow which indicated heavy, secure drifts, at times progressing easily, almost swiftly, at others veering and tacking, making the precipitous ascent by digging their shoes into the snow and literally pulling themselves up, step by step. Here, where the crags rose about them, where sheer granite walls, too steep, too barren to form a resting place even for the driven snow, rose brown and gaunt above them, where the wind seemed to shriek at them from a hundred places at once, Houston dropped slowly back to watch the effect that it all was having upon the girl, to study her strength and her ability to go on. But there was no weakening in the sturdy little step, no evidence of fatigue. As they went higher, and the wind beat against them with its hail of splintered ice particles, Houston saw her heavily gloved hands go to her face in sudden pain and remain there. The man went to her side, and grasping her by the shoulder, stopped her. Then, without explanation, he brought forth a heavy bandanna handkerchief and tied it about her features, as high as possible without shutting off the sight. Her eyes thanked him. They went on.

Higher—higher! the old cracks of Houston's lips, formed in his days of wandering, opened and began to bleed, the tiny, red drops falling on his clothing and congealing there. The flying ice cut his skin; he knew that his eyeballs were becoming red again, the blood-red where never a speck of white showed, only black pupils staring forth from a sea of carmine. Harder and swifter the wind swept about them; its force greater than the slight form of the woman could resist. Close went Houston to her; his arm encircled her—and she did not resist—she who, down there in the west country in the days that had gone, would have rebelled at the touch of his hand! But now they were in a strange land where personalities had vanished; two beings equipped with human intelligence and the power of locomotion, little more. All else in their natures had become subjugated to the greater tasks which faced them; the primitive had come to life; they were fighting against every vengeful weapon which an outraged Nature could hurl,—fighting at cross-purposes, he to fulfill a promise to a woman who might even now be dead, she to assuage the promptings of a merciful nature, even to the extent of the companionship of a man she had been led to revile.

Afternoon came, and the welcome shelter of a ledge where the snow had drifted far outward, leaving a small space of dry rock,—to them like an island to a drifting victim of shipwreck. There they stopped, to bring food from the small provision pack which had been shifted to Medaine's shoulders, to eat silently, then, without a word, to rise and go onward.

Miles and miles,—rods in fact. Aeons of space after that, in which huddled, bent figures in the grip of stormdom, climbed, veering, swinging about the easier stretches, crawling at painfully slow pace up the steeper inclines. Upward through the stinging blast of the tempest they went, toward the top of a stricken world. Late afternoon; then Medaine turned toward the bleeding man beside her.

"A mile more."

She said no more. He nodded in answer and extended a hand to aid her over a slippery stretch of ice-coated granite. Timber line came and went. The snowfall ceased, to give way to the grayness of heavy, scudding clouds and the spasmodic flurries of driving white, as the gusty wind caught up the loose fall of the drifts and whirled it on, like harassed, lost souls seeking in vain a place they could abide. And it was in one of the moments of quiet that Medaine pointed above.

Five splotches showed on the mountain side,—the roofs of as many cabins; the rest of them were buried in snow. No smoke came from the slanting chimneys; no avenues were shoveled to the doorways; the drifts were unbroken.

"Gone!" Houston voiced the monosyllable.

"Yes. Probably on to Crestline. I was afraid of it."

"Night's coming."

"It's too late to turn back now."

And in spite of the pain of bleeding, snow-burned lips, Houston smiled at her,—the smile that a man might give a sister of whom he was inordinately proud.

"Are you afraid?"

"Of what?"

"Me."

She did not answer for a moment. Then:

"Are you afraid—of yourself?"

"No. Only men with something on their conscience are afraid."

She looked at him queerly, then turned away. Houston again took the lead, rounding the stretches, then waiting for her, halting at the dangerous gulleys and guiding her safely across, but silently. He had said enough; more would require explanations. And there was a pack upon his back which contained a tiny form with tight-curled hands, with eyes that were closed,—a poor, nameless little thing he had sworn to carry to grace and to protection. At last they reached the cabins. Houston untied the bond which connected them and loosened his snowshoes, that he might plunge into the smallest drift before a door and force his way within. There was no wood; he tore the clapboards from a near-by cabin and the tar paper from the wind-swept roof. Five minutes later a fire was booming; a girl tired, bent-shouldered, her eyes drooping from a sudden desire for sleep, huddled near it. Houston walked to the pack and took food.

"You would rather eat alone?"

"Yes."

"I shall be in the next cabin—awake."

"Awake?"

"Yes. I'd rather—keep watch."

"But there is nothing—"

"Illness—a snowslide—a fresh drift. I would feel easier in mind. Good night."

Then with his snowshoes and his pack of death, he went out the door, to plunge through another drift, to force his way into a cabin, and there, a plodding, dumb figure, go soddenly about the duties of comfort. And more than once in the howling, blustery night which followed, Houston shivered, shook himself into action and rose to rebuild a fire that had died while he had sat hunched in the hard, uncomfortable chair beside it, trying to fathom what the day had meant, striving to hope for the keeping of the promises that an hysterical woman had made, struggling for the strength to go on,—on with this cheery, brave little bit of humanity in the next cabin, without a word in self-extenuation, without a hint to break the lack of estimation in which she held him, without a plea in his own defense. And some way, Houston felt that such a plea now would be cheap and tawdry; they were in a world where there were bigger things than human aims and human frailties. Besides, he had locked his lips at the command of a grief-ridden woman. To open them in self-extenuation would mean that she must be brought into it; for she had been the one who had clinched the points of suspicion in the mind of Medaine Robinette. Were he now to speak of proof that she had lied—

It was impossible. The wind-swept night became wind-swept dawn, to find him still huddled there, still thinking, still grim and drawn and haggard with sleeplessness and fatigue. Then he rose at a call from without:

"Are you ready?"

He affixed the pack. Together they went on again, graceless figures in frozen clothing, she pointing the way, he aiding her with his strength, in the final battle toward the summit of the range,—and Crestline.

Hours they plodded and climbed, climbed and plodded, the blood again dripping from his lips, her features again shielded by the heavy folds of the bandanna; the moisture of their breath at times swirling about them like angry steam, at others invisible in the areas of sudden dryness, where the atmosphere lapped up even the vapors of laboring lungs before it could visualize. Snow and cloud and rising walls of granite: this was their world, and they crawling pigmies within it. Once she brushed against the pack on his back and drew away with a sudden recoil. Houston dully realized the reason. The selfish, gripping hands of Winter, holding nothing sacred, had invaded even there.

Noon. And a half-cry from both of them, a burst of energy which soon faded. For above was Crestline—even as the little Croatian settlement had been—smokeless, lifeless. They had gone from here also, hurrying humans fleeing with the last snowplow before the tempest, beings afraid to remain, once the lines of communication were broken. But there was nothing to do but go on.

Roofless houses met them, stacks of crumpled snow, where the beams had cracked beneath the weight of high piled drifts; staring, glassless windows and rooms filled with white; stoves that no longer fought the clasp of winter but huddled instead amid piles of snow; that was all. Crestline had fled; there was no life, no sound, only the angry, wailing cry of the wind through half-frozen roof spouts, the slap of clattering boards, loosened by the storm. Gloomily Houston surveyed the desolate picture, at last to turn to the girl.

"I must go on. I gave my promise."

She nodded.

"It means Tollifer now. The descent is more dangerous."

"Do you know it?"

"Not as well as the other. If I only had something to guide me."

And as if in answer, the storm lifted for a moment. Gradually the wind stilled, in one of those stretches of calm which seem to be only the breeding spots of more terror, more bitterness. But they gave no heed to that, nor to the red ball of the sun, faintly visible through the clouds. Far below, miles in reality, straight jets of steam rose high above black, curling smoke; faintly, distantly, whistles sounded. The snowplows!

He gripped her arm with the sight of it, nor did she resist. Thrilled, enthralled, they watched it: the whirling smoke, the shooting steam, the white spray which indicated the grinding, churning progress of the plows, propelled by the heavy engines behind. Words came from the swollen lips of Houston, but the voice was hoarse, strained, unnatural:

"They've started the fight! They've—"

"It's on the second grade, up from Tollifer. It's fairly easy there, you know, for ten or twelve miles. They're making that without difficulty—their work won't come until they strike the snowsheds at Crystal Lake. Oh—" and there was in the voice all the yearning, the anxiety that a pent-up soul could know—"I wish I were a man now! I wish I were a man—to help!"

"I hope—" and Houston said it without thought of bravado—
"that I may have the strength for both of us. I'm a man—after
a sort. I'm going to work with them."

"But—"

He knew what she meant and shook his head.

"No—she does not need me. My presence would mean
nothing to her. I can't tell you why. My place—is down
there."

For an instant Medaine Robinette looked at him with frankly
questioning eyes, eyes which told that a thought was
beginning to form somewhere back in her brain, a question
arising as to his guilt in at least one of the things which
circumstances had arrayed against him. Some way Barry felt
that she knew that a man willing to encounter the dangers of
a snowy range would hurry again to the side of the woman
for whom he had dared them, unless—But suddenly she was
speaking, as though to divert her thoughts.

"We'll have about three hours—from the looks of the sky.
Unless conditions change quickly, there'll not be another
blow before night. It's our chance. We'd better cut this
cord—the one in the lead may fall and pull the other one
over. We had better make haste."

Houston stepped before her. A moment later they were
edging their way down the declivity of what once had been a
railroad track, at last to veer. The drifts from the mountain
side had become too sharp; it was easier to accept the more
precipitous and shorter journey, straight downward, the
nearest cut toward those welcome spires of smoke.

Gradually the snow shook or was melted from their clothing,

through sheer bodily warmth. Black dots they became,—dots which appeared late in the afternoon to the laboring crews of the snow-fighters far below; dots which appeared and disappeared, edging their way about beetling precipices, plunging forward, then stopping; pulling themselves out of the heavier drifts, where drops of ten and even twenty feet had thrown them; swinging and tacking; scrambling downward in long, almost running descents, then crawling slowly along the ice walls, while the jutting peaks about them seemed to close them in, seemed to threaten and seek to engulf them in their pitfalls, only to break from them at last and allow them once more to resume their journey.

Breaks and stops, falls and plunges into drift after drift; through the glasses the workers below could see that a man was in the lead, with something strapped to his back, which the woman in the rear adjusted now and then, when it became partially displaced by the plunging journey. Banks of snow cut them off; snowshoes sank in air pockets—holes made by protruding limbs of the short, gnarled trees of timber line,—and through these the man fought in short, spasmodic lunges, breaking the way for the woman who came behind, never stopping except to gather strength for a fresh attack, never ceasing for obstacle or for danger. Once, at the edge of an overhanging ledge, he scrambled furiously, failed and fell,—to drop in a drift far below, to crawl painfully back to the waiting dot above, and to guide her, by safer paths, on downward. Hours! The dots grew larger. The glasses no longer were needed. On they came, stumbling, reeling, at last to stagger across the frozen, wind-swept surface of a small lake and toward the bunk cars of the snow crews. The woman wavered and fell; he caught her. Then double-weighted, a pack on his back, a form in his arms, he came on, his blood-red eyes searching almost sightlessly the faces of the waiting, stolid, grease-smeared men, his thick voice drooling over bloody lips:

"Somebody take her—get her into the bunk cars. She's given out. I'm—I'm all right. Take care of her. I've got to go on—to Tollifer!"

Courtney Ryley Cooper

CHAPTER XXII

It was night when Barry Houston limped, muscles cramped and frost-numbed, into the little undertaking shop at Tollifer and deposited his tiny burden. Medaine Robinette had remained behind in the rough care of the snow crews, while he, revived by steaming coffee and hot food, had been brought down on a smaller snowplow, running constantly, and without extra power, between Tollifer and "the front", that the lines of communication be kept open.

"Nameless," he said with an effort, when the lengthy details of certification were asked. "The mother—" and a necessary lie came to his lips—"became unconscious before she could tell me anything except that the baby had been baptized and called Helena. She wanted a priest."

"I'll look after it. There's clothing?"

"Yes. In the pack. But wait—where does the Father live?"

The man pointed the way. Houston went on—to a repetition of his story and a fulfillment of his duties. Then, from far up the mountain side, there came the churning, grinding sound of the snowplow, and he hurried toward the station house to greet it. There on a spur, in the faint glow of an electric light, a short train was side-tracked, engineless, waiting until the time should come when the road again would be open, and the way over the Pass free. One glance told him what it was: the tarpaulin-covered, snow-shielded, bulky forms of his machinery,—machinery that he now felt he could personally aid to its destination. For there was work ahead. Midnight found him in a shack buried in snow and reached only by a circuitous tunnel, a shack where men—no longer Americans, but black-smeared, red-eyed, doddering, stumbling human machines—came and went, their frost-caked Mackinaws steaming as they clustered about the red-hot stove, their faces smudged with engine grease to form a coating against the stinging blast of the ice-laden wind, their cheeks raw and bleeding, their mouths swollen orifices which parted only for mumblings; vikings of another age, the fighters of the ice gangs, of which Houston had become a part.

The floor was their bed; silently, speaking only for the purpose of curses, they gulped the food that was passed out to them, taking the steaming coffee straight down in spite of its burning clutch at tender membranes, gnawing and tearing at their meal like beasts at the kill, then, still wadded in their clothing, sinking to the floor—and to sleep. The air was rancid with the odor of wet, steaming clothing. Men crawled over one another, then dropped to the first open spot, to flounder there a moment, then roar in snoring sleep. Against the wall a bearded giant half leaned, half lay, one tooth touching the ragged lips and breaking the filmy skin, while the blood dripped, slow drop after slow drop, upon his black, tousled beard. But he did not wake.

Of them all, only Houston, tired even as they were tired, yet with something that they had forgotten, a brain, remained open-eyed. What had become of Medaine? Had she recovered? Had she too gone to Tollifer, perhaps on a later trip of the plow? The thoughts ran through his head like the repetition of some weird refrain. He sought sleep in vain.

From far away came the whistles of locomotives, answering the signals of the snowplows ahead. Outside some one shouted, as though calling to him; again he remembered the bulky cars of machinery at Tollifer. It was partially, at least, his battle they were fighting out there, while he remained inactive. He rose and sought the door, fumbling aimlessly in his pockets for his gloves. Something tinkled on the floor as he brought them forth, and he bent to pick up the little crucifix with its twisted, tangled chain, forgotten at Tollifer. Dully, hazily, he stared at it with his red eyes, with the faint feeling of a duty neglected. Then:

"She only said they might want it," he mumbled. "I'm sorry—I should have remembered. I'm always failing—at something."

Then, dully anxious to do his part, to take his place in the fighting line, he replaced the tiny bit of gold in his pocket, and threading his way through the circuitous tunnel of snow, stepped forth into the night.

It was one of those brief spaces of starlight between storms, and the crews were making the most of it. The wind had ceased temporarily, allowing every possible workman to be pulled from the ordinary task of keeping the tracks clear of the "pick-ups" of the wind, blowing the snow down from the drifts of the hill, and to be concentrated upon the primary task of many,—the clearing of the packed sittings which filled the first snowshed.

Atop the oblong shed, swept clear by the wind, a light was signalling, telling the progress of the plow, and its conse-quent engines, within. Even from the distance, Barry could hear the surge of the terrific impact, as the rotary, pushed by the four tremendous "compounds" and Malletts which formed its additional motive power, smashed against the tight-jammed contents of the shed, snarled and tore at its enemy, then, beaten at last by the crusted ice of the rails, came grudgingly back, that the ice crews, with their axes and bars, might break the crystallization from the rails and give traction for another assault. Houston started forward, only to stop. A figure in the dim light of the cook car had caught his eye. Medaine Robinette.

She was helping with the preparation of the midnight meal for the laborers, hurrying from the steaming cauldrons to the benches and baskets, filling the big pots with coffee, arranging the tin cups in their stacks for the various crews, and doing something that Houston knew was of more value than anything else,—bringing a smile to the tired men who labored beside her. And this in spite of the fact that the black rings of fatigue were about her eyes, that the pretty, smoothly rounded features had the suggestion of drawnness, that the lips, when they ceased to move, settled into the slightest bit of a droop. Now and then she stopped by one of the tables and clung to it, as though for support,—only to perk her head with a sudden little motion of determination, to turn, and then with a laugh go on with her work. Presently he heard her singing above the clatter of kitchenware and the scuffling of the men with their heavy, hobnailed shoes. And he knew that it was a song of the lips, not of the heart, that she might lighten the burden of others in forgetfulness of self.

And as he watched her, Houston knew for all time that he loved her, that he wanted her above all things, in spite of what she had been led to believe of him, in spite of everything. His hands extended, as though to reach toward her,—the aching appeal of a lonely, harassed man, striving for a thing he could not touch. Then hope surged in his heart.

If the woman back there in the west country only would tell!

If she would only keep the promise which she had given him in her half-delirium! It meant the world to Barry Houston now,—something far greater even than the success for which he had struggled; she could tell so much!

For Houston felt that Agnes Jierdon knew the details of practically every conspiracy that had been fashioned against him; the substitution of the lease and contract in the pile of technical papers which he had signed, the false story which she had told to Medaine,—suddenly Barry wondered if she really had passed the scene of his struggle with Tom Langdon, if she had seen anything at all; if her whole testimony had not been a manufactured thing, built merely for the purpose of obtaining his utmost confidence. If she only would tell! If she only would stay by her promise to a man who had kept his promise to her! If—

But a call had come from up the line. The whistles no longer were tooting; instead, they were blowing with long foghorn blasts, an eerie sound in the cold, crisp night,—a sound of foreboding, of danger. A dim figure made its appearance, running along the box cars, at last to sight Houston and come toward him.

"Which car does the engine crews sleep in?" came sharply.

Houston shook his head.

"I don't know. Has something gone wrong?"

"Plenty. Both the firemen on Number Six have went out from gas—in the snowshed. We've picked up a guy out of an ice gang that's willin' to stand th' gaff, but we need another one. Guess there ain't nothin' to do but wake up one of th' day crew. Hate t' do it, though—they're all in."

"Don't, then. I'll make a try at it."

"Know anything about firin' an engine?"

"I know enough to shovel coal—and I've got a strong pair of shoulders."

"Come on, then."

Houston followed the figure toward the snowshed on the hill. Ten minutes later he stood beside a great Mallet engine, a sleek, glistening grayhound of the mountains, taking from the superintendent the instructions that would enable him to assist, at least, in the propulsion of the motive power. At the narrow areaway between the track and the high wall of the straightaway drifts through which the plow had cut, four men were lifting a limp figure, to carry it to the cars. The superintendent growled.

"You payin' attention to me—or that guy they're cartin' off? When you get in them gas pockets, stick your nose in the hollow of your elbow and keep it there 'till you've got your breath again. There ain't no fresh air in that there shed; the minute these engines get inside and start throwin' on the juice, it fills up with smoke. That's what gets you. Hold your nose in your arm while you take your breath. Then, if you've got to shovel, keep your mouth and your lungs shut. Got me?"

"Yes, sir."

"Then go to it. Hey, Andy!"

"Yeh." A voice had come from the engine cab.

"Here's a guy that'll swing a shovel. I've told him about

the gas."

Barry climbed to his place on the engine. A whistle sounded, to be echoed and reechoed by the answering blasts of the snowplow train—four engines and the big auger itself—ready now for a fresh sally into the shed. Headlights, extinguished momentarily, were thrown on again, lighting up the dirty, ragged edges of the snow walls, with their black marks of engine soot; throwing into sharp relief the smudge-faced figures of the pick-and-axe crews just emerging from the black maw of the tunnel; playing upon the smooth, white outlines of the forbidding mountains yet beyond, mountains which still must be conquered ere the top of the world was reached. Ahead came the "high-ball" signal from the plow; two sharp blasts, to be repeated by the first, the second, the third and fourth of the engines. Then, throttles open, fire boxes throwing their red, spluttering glare against the black sky as firemen leaped to their task, the great mass of machinery moved forward.

Faster—faster—then the impact, like crashing into a stone wall. They were within the snowshed now, the auger boring and tearing and snarling like some savage, vengeful thing against the solid mass of frigidity which faced it. Inch by inch for eight feet it progressed; the offal of the big blades flying past in the glare of the headlights like swirling rainbows; then progress ceased, while the plow ahead, answered by the engines which backed it, shrilled the triple signal to back up, out into the air again, that the ice crews might hurry to their tasks. The engineer opened the cab window and gratefully sucked in the fresh, clean air.

"Eight feet—that's all," he mused. "Eight feet at a time." Then, noticing Houston's attention, he went on:

"It's all the big screw can make. Got a hood on the front, you know, protecting the blades. It's eight feet from the front of that hood to the first trucks. When it's scooped that out, it's the finish. The wheels hit ice, and it's either back out or get derailed. So we back. Huh! There she goes again. Keep your nose in your elbow, youngster, this time. We're goin' back pretty sudden. We'll get gas."

The screaming of the whistles faded, giving way to the lurching of steel monsters as they once more crawled within the blackness of the smoke-filled, snow-choked shed. Deeper they went and deeper, the shouts from without fading away, the hot, penetrating sulphur smoke seeping in even through the closed cab, blackening it until the electric lights were nothing more than faint pinpoints, sending the faces of the men to their arms, while the two crouched, waiting anxiously until the signal should come from ahead.

A long, long moment, while the smoke cut deeper into protesting lungs, in spite of every effort to evade it, while Old Andy on the engine seat twisted and writhed with the agony of fading breath, at last to reel from his position and stumble about in the throes of suffocation. At last, from ahead, came the welcome signal, the three long-drawn-out blasts, and the engineer waved an arm.

"Pull that rope!" he gasped toward the first fireman. "For God's sake, pull that rope! I'm about gone."

A fumbling hand reached up and missed; the light was nearly gone now, in a swirling cloud of venomous smoke. Again the old engineer stumbled, and Houston, leaping to his side, supported him.

"Find that rope—"

"I can't see! The smoke—"

Desperately Houston released the engineer and climbed upward, groping. Something touched his hand, and he jerked at it. A blast sounded—repeated twice more. In the rear the signal was answered. Out ground the train to freedom again. It was the beginning of a night of an Arctic hell.

Back and forth—back and forth—fresh air and foul air— gleaming lights, then dense blackness—so the hours passed. Sally after sally the snowplow made, only to withdraw to give way to the pick crews, and they in turn, gasping and reeling, hurried out for the attack of the plow again. Men fell grovelling, only to be dragged into the open air and resuscitated, then sent once more into the cruelty of the fight. The hours dragged by like stricken things. Then—with dawn—the plow churned with lesser impact. It surged forward. Gray light broke through at the end of the tunnel. The grip of at least one snowshed was broken; but there remained twenty more—and the Death Trail—beyond!

"That's the baby I'm afraid of!" Old Andy was talking as they went toward the cars, the relief day crew passing them on the way. "We can whip these sheds. But that there Death Trail— there's a million tons of snow above it! Once that there vibration loosens it up—we'd better not be underneath it."

Houston did not answer. The clutch of forty-eight hours of wakeful activity was upon him. The words of Old Andy were only so much of a meaningless jumble to him. Into the car he stumbled, a doddering, red-eyed thing, to drink his coffee as the rest drank it, to shamble to the stove, forgetful of the steaming, rancid air, then like some tired beast, sink to the floor in exhausted, dreamless sleep.

Hours he remained there, while the day crew carried the fight on upward, through three of the smaller snowsheds, at last to halt at the long, curved affair which shielded the jutting edge of Mount Taluchen. Then Houston stirred; some one had caught him by the shoulder and was shaking him gently. A voice was calling, and Houston stirred, dazedly obedient to its command.

"I hate to awaken you—" It was a woman; her tones compassionate, gentle. "But they're whistling for the night crew. They've still got you on the list for firing."

Houston opened his eyes and forced a smile.

"That's all right. Thanks—thanks for waking me."

Then he rose and went forth into the agonies of the night,— willing, eager, almost happy. A few words from a woman had given him strength, had wiped out fatigue and aching muscles, and cramped, lifeless limbs,—a few words from a woman he loved, Medaine Robinette.

CHAPTER XXIII

It was a repetition of the first night,—the same churning of the plows, the same smaller machines working along the right of way to keep the rails clear of drifting snow and ice particles, the wind howling again and carrying the offal of the plows in gigantic spouts of dirty white high into the air, to lash and pulverize it, then swish it away to the icy valleys beneath, where drifts could do no harm, where there were no struggling crews and dogged, half-dead men.

A repetition of the foul-smelling wooden tunnels, the sulphur fumes, the gasping of stricken men. The same long, horrible hours, the same staggering release from labor and the welcome hardness of a sleeping spot on a wooden floor. Night after night it was the same—starlight and snow, fair weather and storm. Barry Houston had become a rough-bearded, tattered piece of human machinery like all the rest. Then, at last—

The sun! Shining faintly through the windows of the bunk car, it caused him to stir in his sleep. Dropping in a flood of ruby red, it still reflected faint streaks of color across the sky, when at last he started forth to what men had mentioned but seldom, and then with fear. For to-night was the last night, the last either in the struggle or in the lives of those who had fought their way upward to the final barricade which yet separated them from the top of the world,—the Death Trail.

Smooth and sleek it showed before Houston in the early moonlight, an icy Niagara, the snow piled high above the railroad tracks, extending upward against an almost sheer wall of granite, in stacks and drifts, banked in places to a depth of a hundred feet. Already the plows were assembled,—four heavy steel monsters, with tremendous beams lashed in place and jutting upward, that they might break the overcasts and knock down the snow roofings that otherwise might form tunnels, breaking the way above as the tremendous fan of the plow would break it below. This was to be the fight of fights, there in the moonlight. Houston could see the engines breathing lazily behind their plows, sixteen great, steel contrivances, their burdens graduated in size from the tremendous auger at the fore to the lesser, almost diminutive one, by comparison, at the rear, designed to take the last of the offal from the track. For there would be no ice here; the drippings of the snowsheds, with their accompanying stalactites and stalagmites, were absent. A quick shoot and a lucky one. Otherwise,—the men who went forward to their engines would not speak of it. But there was one who did.

She was standing beside the cook car as Houston passed, and she looked toward him with a glance that caused Barry to stop and to wait, as though she had called to him. Hesitatingly she came forward, and Houston's dulled mentality at last took cognizance that a hand was extended slightly.

"You're still working on the engine?"

"Yes."

"Then you'll be with them?"

"On the Death Trail? I expect to."

"They talk of it as something terrible. Why?"

Houston pointed to the forbidding wall of snow. His thick, broken lips mumbled in the longest speech he had known in days.

"It's all granite up there. The cut of the roadbed forms a base for the remainder of the snow. It's practically all resting on the tracks; above, there's nothing for the snow to cling to. When we cut out the foundation—they're afraid that the vibration will loosen the rest and start an avalanche. It all depends whether it comes before—or after we've passed through."

"And you are not afraid?" She asked it almost childishly. He shook his head.

"I—don't know. I guess every one is—a bit afraid, when they're going into trouble. I know what I'm doing, if that's what you mean."

She was silent for a long moment, looking up at the packed drifts, at the ragged outlines of the mountains against the moonlit sky, then into the valleys and the shimmering form of the round, icy lake, far below. Her lips moved, and Barry went closer.

"Beg pardon?"

"Nothing—only there are some things I can't understand. It doesn't seem quite natural—"

"What?"

"That things could—" Then she straightened and looked at him with clear, frank eyes. "Mr. Houston," came quietly, "I've been thinking about something all day. I have felt that I haven't been quite fair—that a man who has acted as you have acted since—since I met you this last time—that he deserves more of a chance than I have given him. That—"

"I'm asking nothing of you, Miss Robinette."

"I know. I am asking something of you. I want to tell you that I have been hoping that you can some day furnish me the proof—that you spoke of once. I—that's what I wanted to tell you," she ended quickly and extended her hand. "Good-by. I'll be praying for all of you up there."

Houston answered only with a pressure of his hand. His throat had closed suddenly. His breath jerked into his lungs; his burning, wind-torn lips ached to touch the hand that had lingered for a moment in his. He looked at her with eyes that spoke what his tongue could not say, then he went on,—a shambling, dead-tired man, even on awaking from sleep, but a man whose heart was beating with a new fervor. She would be praying for all of them up there at the Trail. And all of them included him.

At the cab of the engine, he listened to the final instructions of the cursing, anxious superintendent, then went to his black work of the shovel. Higher and higher mounted the steam on the gauge; theirs was the first plow, theirs the greatest task. For if they did not go through, the others could not follow; if their attack were not swift enough, staunch enough, the slide that was sure to come sooner or later would carry with it mangled machinery and the torn forms of men into a chasm of death. One by one the final orders came,—crisp, shouted, cursing commands, answered in kind. Then the last query:

"If there's a damn man of you who's a coward, step out! Hear that? If you're afraid—come on—there's no stopping once you start!"

Engine after engine answered, in jeering, sarcastic tones, the belligerent cries of men hiding what pounded in their hearts, driving down by sheer will-power the primitive desires of self-preservation. Again was the call repeated. Again was it answered by men who snarled, men who cursed that they might not pray. And with it:

"A-w-w-w-w—right! Let 'er go!"

The whistles screamed. Up the grade, four engines to a plow, the jets of steam shrilling upward, coughing columns of smoke leaping blackly up the mountain side, the start was made, as the great, roaring mass of machinery gathered speed for the impact.

A jarring crash that all but threw the men of the first crews from their feet, and the Death Trail had been met. Then churning, snarling, roaring, the snow flying in cloud-like masses past them, the first plow bit its way deep into the tremendous mass, while sweating men, Barry Houston among them, crammed coal into the open, angry fire boxes, the sand streamed on greasy tracks,—and the cavalcade went on.

A hundred yards,—the beams knocking down the snow above and all but covering the engines which forced their way through, only to leave as high a mass behind; while the whole mountain seemed to tremble; while the peaks above sent back roar for roar, and grim, determined men pulled harder than ever at the throttles and waited,—for the breath of night again, or the crash of the avalanche.

A shout from Old Andy. A pull at the whistle, screeching

forth its note of victory. From in front was it answered, then from the rear, and on and on, seemingly through an interminable distance, as moonlit night came again, as the lesser plows in the rear swept their way clear of the Death Trail and ground onward and upward. But only for a moment. Then, the blare of the whistles was drowned in a greater sound, a roar that reverberated through the hills like the bellow of a thousand thunders, the cracking and crashing of trees, the splintering of great rocks as the snows of the granite spires above the Death Trail loosed at last and crashed downward in an all-consuming rush of destruction. Trees gave way before the constantly gathering mass of white, and joined in the downfall. Great boulders, abutting rocks, slides of shale! On it went, thundering toward the valley and the gleaming lake, at last to crash there; to send the ten-foot thicknesses of ice splintering like broken glass; to pyramid, to spray the whole nether world with ice and snow and scattering rock; then to settle, a jumbled conglomerate mass of destructiveness, robbed of its prey.

And the men shouted, and screamed and beat at one another in their frenzy of happiness, in spite of the fact that the track had been torn away from behind them as though it never had existed, and that they now were cut off entirely from the rest of the world. Only one snowshed remained, with but a feeble bulwark of drifts before it. Already lights were gleaming down the back-stretch, engines were puffing upward, bearing ties and rails and ballast and abuttment materials, on toward the expected, with men ready to repair the damage as soon as it was done. There were cries also from there below, the shouts of men who were glad even as the crews of the engines and plows were glad, and the engineers and firemen leaned from their cabs to answer.

Still the whistles screamed; all through the night they screamed, as drift after drift yielded, as the eight-foot bite of the first giant auger gnawed and tore at the packed contents of the last shed atop Crestline; then roared and sang, while the hills sent back their outbursts with echoes that rolled, one into another, until at last the whole world was one terrific out-pouring of explosive sounds and shrill, shrieking blasts, as though the mountains were bellowing their anger, their remonstrance at defeat. Eight feet, then eight feet more; steadily eight feet onward. Nor did the men curse at the sulphur fumes, nor rail at the steel-blue ice. It was the final fight; on the downgrade were lesser drifts, puny in comparison to what they had gone through, simple, easily defeated obstacles to the giant machinery, which would work then with gravity instead of against it. Eight feet more— eight feet after that; they marked it off on the windows of the engine cabs with greasy fingers and counted the hours until success. Night faded. Dawn came and then,—the sun! Clear and brilliant with the promise of spring again and of melting snows. The fight was the same as over.

Sleep,—and men who laughed, even as they snored, laughed with the subconscious knowledge of success, while the bunk cars which sheltered them moved onward, up to the peak, then started down the range. Night again,—and Houston once more in the engine cab. But this time, the red glare of the fire-box did not show as often against the sky; the stops were less frequent for the ice packs; once the men even sang!

Morning of the second day,—and again the sunshine, causing dripping streams from the long, laden branches of the pines and spruce, filling the streams bank-full, here and there cutting through the blanket of white to the dun-brown earth again. Work over, Houston leaned out the door of the bunk car, drinking in the sunshine, warm for the first time in weeks, it seemed,—and warm in heart and spirit. If she would only keep her promise! If she would allow Medaine to see her! If she would tell her the truth,—about the contract, the lease, and most of all that accusation. If—

The whistles again,—and crowded forms at the doors of the cars. Tabernacle was in the distance, while men and women waded through the soggy snows to be the first to reach the train. Happiness gleamed on the features of the inhabitants of a beleagured land shut away from the world for weeks, men and women who saw no shame in the tears which streamed down their cheeks, and who sought not to hide them. Eagerly Barry searched the thronging crowd, at last to catch sight of a gigantic figure, his wolf-dog beside him. He leaped from the car even before it had ceased to move.

"Ba'tiste!" he called. "Ba'tiste!"

Great arms opened wide. A sob came from the throat of a giant.

"*Mon* Baree! *Mon* Baree!" It was all he could say for a moment. Then, "*Mon* Baree, he have come back to Ba'teese. Ah, Golemar! *Mon* Baree, he have come back, he have come back!"

"We've won, Ba'tiste! The line's open—they'll be running trains through before night. And if she keeps her promise—"

"She?" Ba'tiste stared down at him. They had drawn away from the rest of the excited, noisy throng. "She? You mean—"

"Agnes. You've been taking care of her, haven't you? I found her—she promised that she would tell the truth for me when I got back, that she would explain the lease and contract and tell Medaine that it was all a lie. She—"

But Ba'tiste Renaud shook his head.

"No, Baree. Eet is the too late. I have jus' come—from there. I have close her eyes."

CHAPTER XXIV

Dead! Houston saw Medaine Robinette pass in the distance, and his eyes followed her until she had rounded the curve by the dead aspens,—the eyes of lost hope. For it was upon life that he had planned and dreamed; that the woman of the lonely cabin would stand by her promise made in a time of stress and right at least some of the wrongs which had been his burden. But now—

"She—she didn't tell you anything before she went?"

Ba'tiste shook his head.

"She would not speak to me. Nothing would, she tell me. At first I go alone—then yesterday, when the snow, he pack, I take Golemar. Then she is unconscious. All day and night I stay beside the bed, but she do not open her eye. Then, with the morning, she sigh, and peuff! She is gone."

"Without a word." It spelled blackness for Houston where there had been light. "I—I—suppose you've taken charge of everything."

"*Oui*! But I have look at nothing—if that is what you mean."

"No—I just had something here that you ought to have,"

Houston fumbled in his pockets. "She would want it around her neck, I feel sure, I when she is—."

But the sudden glare in Ba'tiste's eyes stopped him as he brought forth the crucifix and its tangled chain. The giant's hands raised. His big lips twisted. A lunge and he had come forward, savage, almost beast-like.

"You!" He bellowed. "Where you get that? Hear me, where you get that?"

"From her. She—"

"Then come! Come—quick with me!" He almost dragged the younger man away, hurrying him toward the sled and its broad-backed old horses. "We must go to the cabin, *oui*—yes! Hurry—" Houston saw that he was trembling. "Eet is the thing I look for—the thing I look for!"

"Ba'tiste! What do you mean?"

"My Julienne," came hoarsely. "Eet is my Julienne's!"

Already they were in the sled, the wolf-dog perched between them, and hurrying along the mushy road, which followed the lesser raises of snow, taking advantage of every windbreak and avoiding the greater drifts of the highway itself. Two miles they went, the horses urged to their greatest speed. Then, with a leap, Ba'tiste cleared the runners and motioned to the man behind him.

"Come with me! Golemar! You shall stay behind. You shall fall in the drift—" The old man was talking excitedly, almost childishly. "No? Then come—Eet is your own self that must be careful. Ba'teese, he cannot watch you. Come!"

At a run, he went forward, to thread his way through the pines, to flounder where the snow had not melted, to go waist-deep at times, but still to rush onward at a speed which taxed even Houston's younger strength to keep him in sight. The wolf-dog buried itself in the snow, Houston pulling it forth time after time, and lugging it at long intervals. Then at last came the little clearing,—and the cabin. Ba'tiste already was within.

Houston avoided the figure on the bed as he entered and dropped beside the older man, already dragging forth the drawers of the bureau and pawing excitedly among the trinkets there. He gasped and pulled forth a string of beads, holding them trembling to the light, and veering from his jumbled English to a stream of French. Then a watch, a ring, and a locket with a curly strand of baby hair. The giant sobbed.

"My Pierre—eet was my Pierre!"

"What's that?" Houston had raised suddenly, was staring in the direction of an old commode in the corner. At the door the wolf-dog sniffed and snarled. Ba'tiste, bending among the lost trinkets that once had been his wife's, did not hear. Houston grasped him by the shoulder and shook him excitedly.

"Ba'tiste! Ba'tiste! There's some one hiding—over there in the corner. I heard sounds—look at Golemar!"

"Hiding? No. There is no one here—no one but Ba'tiste and his memories. No one—"

"I tell you I heard some one. The commode moved. I know!"

He rose, only to suddenly veer and flatten himself against the wall. The yellow blaze of aimless revolver fire had spurted from the corner; then the plunging form of a gnarled, gangling, limping man, who rushed past Houston to the door, swerved there, and once more raised the revolver. But he did not fire.

A furry, snarling thing had leaped at him, knocking the revolver from his hand in its plunging ascent. Then a cry,—a gurgling growl. Teeth had clenched at the throat of the man; together they rolled through the door to the snow without, Golemar, his hold broken by the fall, striving again for the death clutch, the man screaming in sudden frantic fear.

"Take him off!" The voice of the thin-visaged Fred Thayer was shrill now. "Take him off—I'll tell you about it—she did it—she did it! Take him off!"

"Golemar!" Ba'tiste had appeared in the doorway. Below the dog whirled in obedience to his command and edged back, teeth still bared, eyes vigilant, waiting for the first movement of the man on the ground. Houston went forward and stood peering down at the frightened, huddled form of Thayer, wiping the blood from the fang wound in his neck.

"You'll tell about what?" came with sudden incisiveness.

The man stared, suddenly aware that he had spoken of a thing that had been mentioned by neither Ba'tiste nor Houston. His lips worked crookedly. He tried to smile, but it ended only in a misshapen snarl.

"I thought you fellows were looking for something. I—I— wanted to get the dog off."

"We were. We've found it. Ba'tiste," and Houston forced back the tigerish form of the big French-Canadian. "You walk in front of us. I'm—I'm afraid to trust you right now. And don't turn back. Do you promise?"

The big hands worked convulsively. The eyes took on a newer, fiercer glare.

"He is the man, eh? His conscience, eet speak when there is no one to ask the question. He—"

"Go on, Ba'tiste. Please." Houston's voice was that of a pleading son. Once more the big muscles knotted, the arms churned; the giant's teeth showed between furled lips in a sudden beast-like expression.

"Ba'tiste! Do you want to add murder to murder? This is out of our hands now; it's a matter of law. Now, go ahead—for me."

With an effort the Canadian obeyed, the wolf-dog trotting beside him, Houston following, one hand locked about the buckle of the thinner man's belt, the other half supporting him as he limped and reeled through the snow.

"It's my hip—" The man's mind had gone to trivial things. "I sprained it—about ten days ago. I'd been living over here with her up till the storm. Then I had to be at camp. I—"

"That was your child, then?"

Fred Thayer was silent. Barry Houston repeated the question commandingly. There could be no secrecy now; events had gone too far. For a third time the accusation came and the man beside him turned angrily.

"Whose would you think it was?"

Houston did not answer. They stumbled on through the snow-drifted woods, finally to reach the open space leading to the sleigh. Thayer drew back.

"What's the use of taking me into town?" he begged. "She's dead and gone; you can't harm her now."

"We're not inquiring about her."

"But she's the one that did it. She told me—when she first got sick. Those are her things in there. They're—"

"Have I asked you about anything?" Houston bit the words at him. Again the man was silent. They reached the sled, and Ba'tiste pointed to the seat.

"In there," he ordered. "Ba'teese will walk. Ba'teese afraid—too close." And then, in silence, the trip to town was made, at last to draw up in front of the boarding house. Houston called to a bystander.

"Is the 'phone working—to Montview?"

"Yeh. Think it is. Got it opened up yesterday."

"Then call up over there and tell the sheriff we want him. It has to do with the Renaud murder."

The loafer sprang to the street and veered across, shouting the news as he went, while Ba'tiste made hurried arrangements regarding the silent form of the lonely cabin. A few moments later, the makeshift boarding-house lobby was crowded, while Barry Houston, reverting to the bitter lessons he had learned during the days of his own cross-examinations, took his place in front of the accused man.

"In the first place, Thayer," he commanded. "You might as well know one thing. You're caught. The goods are on you. You're going up if for nothing else than an attempt to murder Ba'tiste Renaud and myself."

"I—I thought you were robbers."

"You know that's a lie. But that's a matter for the court room. There are greater things. In the first place—"

"About that other—" Still he clung to his one shred of a story, his only possibility of hope. Conscience had prompted the first outcry; now there was nothing to do but follow the lead. "I don't know anything. She told me—that's all. And she's dead now."

"Ah, *oui*!" Ba'tiste had edged forward. "She is dead. And because she is dead—because she have suffer and die, you would lay to her door murder! Eet is the lie! Where then is the ten thousand dollar she took—if she kill my Julienne? Eh? Where is the gun with which she shot her? Ah, you cringe! For why you do that—for why do you not look at Ba'teese when he talk about his Julienne! Eh? Is eet that you are afraid? Is eet that your teeth are on your tongue, to keep eet from the truth? *Oui*! You are the man—you are the man!"

"I don't know anything about it. She told me she did it—that those were Mrs. Renaud's things."

"Ah! Then you have nev' see that ring, which my Julienne, she wore on her finger. Ah, no? You have nev' see, in all the time that you come to Ba'teese house, the string of bead about her neck. *Oui*! Eet is the lie, you tell. You have see them—eet is the lie!"

And thus the battle progressed, the old man storming, the

frowning, sullen captive in the chair replying in mono-syllables, or refusing to answer at all. An hour passed, while Tabernacle crowded the little lobby and overflowed to the street. One by one Ba'tiste brought forth the trinkets and laid them before the thin-faced man. He forced them into his hands. He demanded that he explain why he had said nothing of their presence in the lonely cabin, when he had known them, every one, from having seen them time after time in the home of Renaud. The afternoon grew old. The sheriff arrived,—and still the contest went on. Then, with a sudden shifting of the head, a sudden break of reserve, Thayer leaned forward and rubbed his gnarled hands, one against the other.

"All right!" he snapped. "Have it your way. No use in trying to lay it on the woman—you could prove an alibi for her. You're right. I killed them both."

"Both?" They stared at him. Thayer nodded, still looking at the floor, his tongue licking suddenly dry lips.

"Yeh, both of 'em. One brought on the other. Mrs. Renaud and John Corbin—they called him Tom Langdon back East."

CHAPTER XXV

It was staggering in its unexpectedness. A gasp came from the lips of Barry Houston. He felt himself reeling,—only to suddenly straighten, as though a crushing weight had been lifted from his shoulders. He whirled excitedly and grasped the nearest onlooker.

"Go get Medaine Robinette. Hurry! Tell her that it is of the utmost importance—that I have found the proof. She'll understand."

Then, struggling to reassure himself, he turned again to the prisoner. Two hours later, in the last glint of day, the door opened, and a woman came to his side, where he was finishing the last of many closely written sheets of paper. He looked up at her, boyishly, happily. Without waiting for her permission, he grasped her hand, and then, as though eager for her to hear, he turned to the worn-faced man, now slumped dejectedly in his chair.

"You understand, Thayer, that this is your written confession?"

The man nodded.

"Given in the presence of the sheriff, of Ba'tiste Renaud, of myself, and the various citizens of Tabernacle that you see here?"

"Yes."

"Of your own free will, without threats or violence?"

"I guess so."

"And you are willing to sign it?"

The man hesitated. Then:

"I'd want to know what I was signing."

"Certainly. I intend to read it to you—so that all witnesses may hear it. It is then to be filed with the district attorney. You can signify its correctness or incorrectness after every paragraph. Is that agreeable?"

"I guess so."

A pause. At last:

"'My name is Fred Thayer. I am forty-four years of age. Prior to about a year ago, I was employed by the Empire Lake Mill and Lumber Company as superintendent. I had occupied this position for some fifteen or twenty years, beginning with it when it was first started by Mr. Houston of Boston.' Is that right?"

A nod from the accused. Houston went on:

"'I figured from the first that I was going to be taken in partnership with Mr. Houston, although nothing ever was said about it. I just took it for granted. However, when years passed and, nothing was done about it, I began to force matters, by letting the mill run down, knowing that Mr. Houston was getting old, and that he might be willing to sell out to me if things got bad enough. At that time, I didn't know where I was going to get the money, but hoped that Mr. Houston would let me have the mill and acreage on some sort of a payment basis. I went back to see him about it a couple of times, but he wouldn't listen to me. He said that he wanted to either close the thing out for cash or keep on running it in the hope of making something of it.' That's all right, isn't it, Thayer?"

"Yes."

"'I tried two or three times to get him to sell out to me, but we couldn't get together on the terms. He always wanted cash, and I couldn't furnish it—although I pretended that I had the money all right, but that I simply did not want to tie it all up at once. About this time—I think it was three or four years ago; I am not exactly clear on the dates—a nephew of his named Thomas Langdon came out here, under the name of John Corbin. He had been a black sheep and was now wandering about the country, doing anything that he could set his hand to for a living. I had known him since boyhood and gave him a job under his assumed name. He pretended that he was very close to Mr. Houston, and I thought maybe he could help me get the plant. But his word was not worth as much as mine.' Have I taken that down correctly, Thayer?"

"Yes. Except about Langdon. He told me when he came here that his uncle had sent him out to straighten him up. But I don't guess it makes much difference."

Houston, nevertheless, made the changes, glancing up once to assure himself that Medaine still was there. She had not left his side. He went on with the reading:

"By this time, the mill had gotten to be a sort of mania with me, and I almost had myself believing that Houston had promised me more than he had given me. Then, a woman came out here, an Agnes Jierdon, a stenographer, on her vacation. I met her and learned that she was from Boston." A slight pressure exerted itself on Houston's arm. He glanced down to see Medaine Robinette's hand, clasped tight. "She spent nearly the whole summer here, and I made love to her. I asked her to marry me, and she told me that she would. She was really very much in love with me. I didn't care about her —I was working for a purpose. I wanted to use her—to get her in Houston's office. I wanted to find out what was going on, so that I would know in advance, and so that I could prepare for it by having breakage at the mill, to stop contracts and run things farther down than ever, so the old man would get disgusted and sell out at my terms. I knew there would be a mint of money for me if I could get hold of that mill. At the end of her vacation, she went back to Boston and got a job with Houston, as an office clerk. Almost the first thing that she wrote me was that the old man was thinking about selling out to some concern back East."

Houston looked toward the accused man for his confirmation, then continued.

"'While she had been out here, I had told her that Houston had promised to take me into partnership and that he had gone back on his word. I put it up to her pretty strong about how I had been tricked into working for him for years, and she was sympathetic with me, of course, inasmuch as she was in love with me. Naturally, when she heard this, she wrote me right away. It made me desperate. Then I thought of Ba'tiste Renaud.'"

"Ah!" The word was accompanied by a sharp intake of breath as the big French-Canadian moved closer to hear again the story of a murder. But the sheriff motioned him back. The emotions of the old trapper were not to be trusted. The recital went on:

"'Everybody around this country had always talked about how rich he was. There was a saying that he didn't believe in banks and that he kept more than a hundred thousand dollars in his little cabin. At this time, both he and his son were away at war, and I thought I could steal this money, place it in other hands, and then work things so that if I did get hold of the mill, people around here would merely think I had borrowed the money and bought the mill with it. By this time, a cousin of Miss Jierdon's, a fellow named Jenkins, had gotten a job with Houston and was working with her, and of course, I was hearing everything that went on. It looked like the deal was going through, and it forced me to action. One night I watched Mrs. Renaud and saw her leave the house. I thought she was going to town. Instead, after I'd gotten into the cabin, she came back, surprising me. There wasn't anything else to do. I killed her, with a revolver.'"

"*Diable*!"

"Easy, Ba'tiste. That's the way you gave it to me, isn't it, Thayer?"

"Yes. I shot twice at her. The first bullet missed."

Again the door of the tiny lobby opened and closed, and a form edged forward,—Blackburn, summoned from his mill. Thayer glanced at him, then lowered his eyes. Houston made the additional notation on the confession and went back to his reading:

"'When I found the deed box, there was only ten thousand dollars in it instead of the fortune that I had supposed was there. I was about to take it out and stuff it into my pocket, when I heard a noise outside the window. Thinking it was Renaud's wolf-dog, and that he might give the alarm, I pushed the box under my coat and ran out the back door. The next day, Corbin—or Langdon—came to me and demanded his share of what I had stolen. He said that he had seen me at the deed box after I had killed the woman, that he had made the noise outside the window. I put him off—denying it all. But it wasn't any use. At first he threatened that he would go to the sheriff at Montview, and for several days he came to me, telling me that this was the last chance that he would give me if I didn't let him have his share. I played him for time. Then he began to beg small amounts of money from me, promising to keep still if I gave them to him. I guess this kept up for two or three months, the amounts getting larger all the time. At last, I wouldn't stand it any longer. He threatened me again,—and then, suddenly, one day disappeared. I hurried to Montview, thinking of course that he had gone there, hoping to catch him on the way. But no one had seen him. Then I went to Tabernacle and learned that he had bought a ticket for Boston, and that he had left on a morning train. I knew what was up then; he was going back to tell Old Man Houston and try to step into my shoes when I was arrested. But I beat him there by going over the range in an automobile, and taking an earlier train for Boston. I picked him up when he arrived and trailed him to young Houston's office. After that I saw them go to a cafe, and from there to a prize fight. I bought a ticket and watched them from the rear of the hall. I had my gun with me—I had made up my mind to kill them both. I thought Langdon had told. After the fight, they started out, myself in the rear. Young Houston had gotten a mallet from the timekeeper. On the way home, I could hear them talking, and heard Houston asking Langdon why he wanted to see the old man. By that I knew that it hadn't been told yet—and I felt safer. Then they got in a quarrel, and my chance came. It was over the mallet—Langdon took it away from his cousin and started to fight him. Houston ran. When he was well out of sight, I went forward. No one was near. Langdon still had the mallet in his hand. I crept up behind him and clubbed my revolver, hitting him on the head with it. He fell—dead—and I knew I was safe, that Houston would be accused.'"

Barry looked earnestly at the man before him.

"That's all true, isn't it, Thayer?"

"I haven't made any objection, have I?" came surlily.

"I merely wanted to be sure. But to go on: 'Then I thought of a way to get what I wanted from Miss Jierdon. This was several months afterward, just before the trial. I argued that I was sure young Houston hadn't committed the murder, and that if some woman could testify to the fact that Langdon had that mallet, it might free Houston, and make a hit with the old man and that maybe he would make good on his promises. I did it pretty skilfully and she listened to me, largely, I guess, because she was in love with me. Anyway, it ended with her testifying at the trial in a sort of negative way. I didn't care about that—it was something else I wanted. Later after the old man had died, I used it. I wanted her to switch some papers on young Mr. Houston for me, and she bucked against it. Then I told her that she had done worse things, that she had perjured herself, and that unless she stayed by me, she could be sent to the penitentiary. Of course, I didn't tell her in those exact words—I did it more in the way of making a criminal out of her already, so that the thing she was going to do wouldn't seem as bad to her. I wasn't foolish enough to threaten her. Besides, I told her that the mill should have been rightfully mine, that the old man had lied to me and gotten me to work for him for years at starvation wages, on promises that it would be mine some time, and that he had neither taken me in partnership, nor left it to me in the will. She got her cousin to help her in the transfer of the papers; it was a lease and stumpage contract. He affixed a notary seal to it. The thing was illegitimate, of course. Shortly after that, young Houston came out here again, and I got her to come too. I wanted to see what he was up to. He fired me, and while he was in Denver, and Renaud away from the mill, I got Miss Jierdon and took her for a walk, while one of the other men kept watch for the cook who was asleep. But she didn't wake up. On the way back, Miss Jierdon saw that the mill was burning, and I directed her suspicion toward Renaud. She accused him, and it brought about a little quarrel between Miss Jierdon and young Houston. I had forced her, by devious ways, to pretend that she was in love with him—keeping that perjury thing hanging over her all the time and constantly harping on how, even though he was a nice young fellow, he was robbing us both of something that was rightfully ours. All this time, I had dodged marrying her, promising that I would do it when the mill was mine. In the meantime, with the lease and contract in my hands, I had hooked up with this man here, Blackburn, and he had started a mill for me. I guess Miss Jierdon had gotten to thinking a little of Houston, after all, because when I forced her to the final thing of telling some lies about him to a young woman, she did it, but went away mad at me and threatening never to see me again. But a little while later, she came back. Our relations, while she had been at the Houston camp, hadn't been exactly what they should have been. Miss Jierdon is dead—she had stayed in a little cabin in the woods. I had lived with her there. About ten days ago, the baby died, while I was laid up at camp with a sprained hip. To-day I went there to find her dead, and while I was there, Renaud and young Houston caught me. This is all I know. I make this statement of my own free will, without coercion, and I swear it to be the truth, the whole truth, and nothing but the truth, so help me God.'"

The little lobby milled and buzzed, drowning the scratching of the pen as a trembling man signed the confession, page by page. Then came the clink of handcuffs. A moment later two figures had departed in the dusk,—the sheriff and Fred Thayer, bound for the jail at Montview. Houston straightened, to find a short, bulky form before him, Henry Blackburn.

"Well?" questioned that person. "I guess it's up to me. I—I haven't got much chance against that."

"What do you mean?"

"Simply this," and the bulky Blackburn drew a nervous, sweating hand across his brow. "I ain't above dealing with crooks, I'll admit that. I've done a few things in my life that haven't been any too straight, or any too noble, and when Thayer came to me with this contract and lease, I didn't ask any questions. My lawyer said it was O. K. That was enough for me. But somehow or other, I kind of draw the line at murder. I'm in your hands, Houston. I've got a mill up there that I've put a lot of money in. It ain't worth the powder to blow it up now—to me, anyway. But with you, it's different. If you want to make me a fair offer, say the word, and I'll go more than half-way. What say?"

"Is to-morrow time enough?"

"To-morrow—or the next day—or the next week. Suits me. I'm in your hands."

Then he went on, leaving only three figures in the lobby,— the bent, silent form of Ba'tiste Renaud, grave, but rewarded at last in his faithful search; the radiant-eyed Houston, free with a freedom that he hardly believed could exist; and a girl who walked to the window and stood looking out a moment before she turned to him. Then impetuously she faced him, her eyes searching his, her hands tight clasped, her whole being one of supplication.

"I'm sorry," she begged. "Can you—will you forgive me?"

Boyishly Barry Houston reached forward and drew away a strand of hair that had strayed from place, a spirit of venture in his manner, a buoyant tone in his voice.

"Say it again. I like it!"

"But I am—don't you believe me?"

"Of course. But then—I—I—" Then he caught her hands. "Will you go with me while I telegraph?" he asked in sudden earnestness. "I want to wire—to the papers back in Boston and tell them that I've been vindicated. Will you—?"

"I'd be glad to."

They went out the door together, Houston beaming happily downward, the girl close beside him, her arm in his. And it was then that the features of Ba'tiste Renaud lost their gravity and sorrow. He looked after them, his eyes soft and contented. Then his big hands parted slowly. His lips broke into a smile of radiant happiness.

And it was with the same glad light in his eyes that three months later Ba'tiste Renaud stood on the shores of Empire Lake, his wolf-dog beside him, looking out over the rippling sheen of the water. The snow was gone from the hills now; the colors were again radiant, the blues and purples and greens and reds vying, it seemed, with one another, in a constantly recurring contest of beauty. Afar off, logs were sliding in swift succession down the skidways, to lose themselves in the waters, then to bob along toward the current that would carry them to the flume. The jays cried and quarreled in the aspens; in a little bay, an old beaver made his first sally of the evening, and by angry slaps of his tail warned the rest of the colony that humans were near. Distantly, from down the bubbling stream which led from the lake, there sounded the snarl of giant saws and the hum of machinery, where, in two great mills, the logs traveled into a manufactured state through a smooth-working process that led from "jacker" to "kicker", thence to the platforms and the shotgun carriages; into the mad rush of the bank saws, while the rumbling rolls caught the offal to cart it away; then surging on, to the edgers and trimmers and kilns. Great trucks rumbled along the roadways. Faintly a locomotive whistled, as the switch engine from Tabernacle clanked to the mills for the make-up of its daily stub-train of lumber cars. But the attention of Ba'tiste Renaud was on none of these. Out in a safe portion of the lake was a boat, and within it sat two persons, a man and a woman, their rods flashing as they made their casts, now drawing slowly backward for another whip of the fly, now bending with the swift leap of a captive trout. And he watched them with the eyes of a father looking upon children who have fulfilled his every hope, children deeply, greatly beloved.

As for the man and the woman, they laughed and glanced at each other as they cast, or shouted and shrilled with the excitement of the leaping trout as the fly caught fair and the struggle of the rod and reel began, to end with another flopping form in the creel, another delicacy for the table at camp. But at last the girl leaned back, and her fly trailed disregarded in the water.

"Barry," she asked, "what day's to-morrow?"

"Wednesday," he said, and cast again in the direction of a dead, jutting tree, the home of more than one three-pounder. She pouted.

"Of course it's Wednesday. But what else?"

"I don't know. Let me see. Twentieth, isn't it?"

This time her rod flipped in mock anger.

"Barry," she commanded. "What day is tomorrow?"

He looked at her blankly.

"I give it up," came after deep thought. "What day is to-morrow?"

She pressed tight her lips, striving bravely for sternness. But in vain. An upward curve made its appearance at the corners. The blue eyes twinkled. She laughed.

"Foolish!" she chided. "I might have expected you to forget. It's our first monthiversary!"

Choose from Thousands of 1stWorldLibrary Classics By

A. M. Barnard	Booth Tarkington	Edward Everett Hale
Ada Leverson	Boyd Cable	Edward J. O'Biren
Adolphus William Ward	Bram Stoker	Edward S. Ellis
Aesop	C. Collodi	Edwin L. Arnold
Agatha Christie	C. E. Orr	Eleanor Atkins
Alexander Aaronsohn	C. M. Ingleby	Eleanor Hallowell Abbott
Alexander Kielland	Carolyn Wells	Eliot Gregory
Alexandre Dumas	Catherine Parr Traill	Elizabeth Gaskell
Alfred Gatty	Charles A. Eastman	Elizabeth McCracken
Alfred Ollivant	Charles Amory Beach	Elizabeth Von Arnim
Alice Duer Miller	Charles Dickens	Ellem Key
Alice Turner Curtis	Charles Dudley Warner	Emerson Hough
Alice Dunbar	Charles Farrar Browne	Emilie F. Carlen
Allen Chapman	Charles Ives	Emily Bronte
Alleyne Ireland	Charles Kingsley	Emily Dickinson
Ambrose Bierce	Charles Klein	Enid Bagnold
Amelia E. Barr	Charles Hanson Towne	Enilor Macartney Lane
Amory H. Bradford	Charles Lathrop Pack	Erasmus W. Jones
Andrew Lang	Charles Romyn Dake	Ernie Howard Pie
Andrew McFarland Davis	Charles Whibley	Ethel May Dell
Andy Adams	Charles Willing Beale	Ethel Turner
Angela Brazil	Charlotte M. Braeme	Ethel Watts Mumford
Anna Alice Chapin	Charlotte M. Yonge	Eugene Sue
Anna Sewell	Charlotte Perkins Stetson	Eugenie Foa
Annie Besant	Clair W. Hayes	Eugene Wood
Annie Hamilton Donnell	Clarence Day Jr.	Eustace Hale Ball
Annie Payson Call	Clarence E. Mulford	Evelyn Everett-green
Annie Roe Carr	Clemence Housman	Everard Cotes
Annonaymous	Confucius	F. H. Cheley
Anton Chekhov	Coningsby Dawson	F. J. Cross
Archibald Lee Fletcher	Cornelis DeWitt Wilcox	F. Marion Crawford
Arnold Bennett	Cyril Burleigh	Fannie E. Newberry
Arthur C. Benson	D. H. Lawrence	Federick Austin Ogg
Arthur Conan Doyle	Daniel Defoe	Ferdinand Ossendowski
Arthur M. Winfield	David Garnett	Fergus Hume
Arthur Ransome	Dinah Craik	Florence A. Kilpatrick
Arthur Schnitzler	Don Carlos Janes	Fremont B. Deering
Arthur Train	Donald Keyhoe	Francis Bacon
Atticus	Dorothy Kilner	Francis Darwin
B.H. Baden-Powell	Dougan Clark	Frances Hodgson Burnett
B. M. Bower	Douglas Fairbanks	Frances Parkinson Keyes
B. C. Chatterjee	E. Nesbit	Frank Gee Patchin
Baroness Emmuska Orczy	E. P. Roe	Frank Harris
Baroness Orczy	E. Phillips Oppenheim	Frank Jewett Mather
Basil King	E. S. Brooks	Frank L. Packard
Bayard Taylor	Earl Barnes	Frank V. Webster
Ben Macomber	Edgar Rice Burroughs	Frederic Stewart Isham
Bertha Muzzy Bower	Edith Van Dyne	Frederick Trevor Hill
Bjornstjerne Bjornson	Edith Wharton	Frederick Winslow Taylor

Friedrich Kerst
Friedrich Nietzsche
Fyodor Dostoyevsky
G.A. Henty
G.K. Chesterton
Gabrielle E. Jackson
Garrett P. Serviss
Gaston Leroux
George A. Warren
George Ade
Geroge Bernard Shaw
George Cary Eggleston
George Durston
George Ebers
George Eliot
George Gissing
George MacDonald
George Meredith
George Orwell
George Sylvester Viereck
George Tucker
George W. Cable
George Wharton James
Gertrude Atherton
Gordon Casserly
Grace E. King
Grace Gallatin
Grace Greenwood
Grant Allen
Guillermo A. Sherwell
Gulielma Zollinger
Gustav Flaubert
H. A. Cody
H. B. Irving
H. C. Bailey
H. G. Wells
H. H. Munro
H. Irving Hancock
H. R. Naylor
H. Rider Haggard
H. W. C. Davis
Haldeman Julius
Hall Caine
Hamilton Wright Mabie
Hans Christian Andersen
Harold Avery
Harold McGrath
Harriet Beecher Stowe
Harry Castlemon
Harry Coghill
Harry Houidini

Hayden Carruth
Helent Hunt Jackson
Helen Nicolay
Hendrik Conscience
Hendy David Thoreau
Henri Barbusse
Henrik Ibsen
Henry Adams
Henry Ford
Henry Frost
Henry James
Henry Jones Ford
Henry Seton Merriman
Henry W Longfellow
Herbert A. Giles
Herbert Carter
Herbert N. Casson
Herman Hesse
Hildegard G. Frey
Homer
Honore De Balzac
Horace B. Day
Horace Walpole
Horatio Alger Jr.
Howard Pyle
Howard R. Garis
Hugh Lofting
Hugh Walpole
Humphry Ward
Ian Maclaren
Inez Haynes Gillmore
Irving Bacheller
Isabel Cecilia Williams
Isabel Hornibrook
Israel Abrahams
Ivan Turgenev
J. G.Austin
J. Henri Fabre
J. M. Barrie
J. M. Walsh
J. Macdonald Oxley
J. R. Miller
J. S. Fletcher
J. S. Knowles
J. Storer Clouston
J. W. Duffield
Jack London
Jacob Abbott
James Allen
James Andrews
James Baldwin

James Branch Cabell
James DeMille
James Joyce
James Lane Allen
James Lane Allen
James Oliver Curwood
James Oppenheim
James Otis
James R. Driscoll
Jane Abbott
Jane Austen
Jane L. Stewart
Janet Aldridge
Jens Peter Jacobsen
Jerome K. Jerome
Jessie Graham Flower
John Buchan
John Burroughs
John Cournos
John F. Kennedy
John Gay
John Glasworthy
John Habberton
John Joy Bell
John Kendrick Bangs
John Milton
John Philip Sousa
John Taintor Foote
Jonas Lauritz Idemil Lie
Jonathan Swift
Joseph A. Altsheler
Joseph Carey
Joseph Conrad
Joseph E. Badger Jr
Joseph Hergesheimer
Joseph Jacobs
Jules Vernes
Julian Hawthrone
Julie A Lippmann
Justin Huntly McCarthy
Kakuzo Okakura
Karle Wilson Baker
Kate Chopin
Kenneth Grahame
Kenneth McGaffey
Kate Langley Bosher
Kate Langley Bosher
Katherine Cecil Thurston
Katherine Stokes
L. A. Abbot
L. T. Meade

L. Frank Baum
Latta Griswold
Laura Dent Crane
Laura Lee Hope
Laurence Housman
Lawrence Beasley
Leo Tolstoy
Leonid Andreyev
Lewis Carroll
Lewis Sperry Chafer
Lilian Bell
Lloyd Osbourne
Louis Hughes
Louis Joseph Vance
Louis Tracy
Louisa May Alcott
Lucy Fitch Perkins
Lucy Maud Montgomery
Luther Benson
Lydia Miller Middleton
Lyndon Orr
M. Corvus
M. H. Adams
Margaret E. Sangster
Margret Howth
Margaret Vandercook
Margaret W. Hungerford
Margret Penrose
Maria Edgeworth
Maria Thompson Daviess
Mariano Azuela
Marion Polk Angellotti
Mark Overton
Mark Twain
Mary Austin
Mary Catherine Crowley
Mary Cole
Mary Hastings Bradley
Mary Roberts Rinehart
Mary Rowlandson
M. Wollstonecraft Shelley
Maud Lindsay
Max Beerbohm
Myra Kelly
Nathaniel Hawthrone
Nicolo Machiavelli
O. F. Walton
Oscar Wilde

Owen Johnson
P.G. Wodehouse
Paul and Mabel Thorne
Paul G. Tomlinson
Paul Severing
Percy Brebner
Percy Keese Fitzhugh
Peter B. Kyne
Plato
Quincy Allen
R. Derby Holmes
R. L. Stevenson
R. S. Ball
Rabindranath Tagore
Rahul Alvares
Ralph Bonehill
Ralph Henry Barbour
Ralph Victor
Ralph Waldo Emmerson
Rene Descartes
Ray Cummings
Rex Beach
Rex E. Beach
Richard Harding Davis
Richard Jefferies
Richard Le Gallienne
Robert Barr
Robert Frost
Robert Gordon Anderson
Robert L. Drake
Robert Lansing
Robert Lynd
Robert Michael Ballantyne
Robert W. Chambers
Rosa Nouchette Carey
Rudyard Kipling
Saint Augustine
Samuel B. Allison
Samuel Hopkins Adams
Sarah Bernhardt
Sarah C. Hallowell
Selma Lagerlof
Sherwood Anderson
Sigmund Freud
Standish O'Grady
Stanley Weyman
Stella Benson
Stella M. Francis

Stephen Crane
Stewart Edward White
Stijn Streuvels
Swami Abhedananda
Swami Parmananda
T. S. Ackland
T. S. Arthur
The Princess Der Ling
Thomas A. Janvier
Thomas A Kempis
Thomas Anderton
Thomas Bailey Aldrich
Thomas Bulfinch
Thomas De Quincey
Thomas Dixon
Thomas H. Huxley
Thomas Hardy
Thomas More
Thornton W. Burgess
U. S. Grant
Upton Sinclair
Valentine Williams
Various Authors
Vaughan Kester
Victor Appleton
Victor G. Durham
Victoria Cross
Virginia Woolf
Wadsworth Camp
Walter Camp
Walter Scott
Washington Irving
Wilbur Lawton
Wilkie Collins
Willa Cather
Willard F. Baker
William Dean Howells
William le Queux
W. Makepeace Thackeray
William W. Walter
William Shakespeare
Winston Churchill
Yei Theodora Ozaki
Yogi Ramacharaka
Young E. Allison
Zane Grey